RIGHT WRONG SHIFTER

GOOD BAD MAGIC
BOOK 2

ISA MEDINA

THE PARANORMAL BUSINESS OWNERS ASSOCIATION meeting was in full swing. And by full swing, I mean Sonia had just balled up a piece of paper and thrown it at someone's head.

"Jacob, stop looking at your phone," she snapped. "Your failed date is not going to text you back."

A low rumble of laughter filled the big room. We sat in rows of plastic chairs facing a small stage at the front of the room, where Sonia, the PBOA's president, held court sitting behind a folding table.

"I don't see why Bosko should appear above my shop on the brochure," a woman complained loudly from the opposite aisle. "His shop's an eyesore."

A man snapped to his feet a couple of rows ahead of where I sat next to Ian. "Watch what you say, Belinda."

"Sit down," Sonia ordered.

Bosko did, grumbling to himself.

I had to agree with Belinda—Bosko's tourist trap of garish T-shirts and flip-flops and other cheap summer souvenirs was a little eye-watering. It'd make for an amazing Halloween display once he switched to that, though.

I brought out my phone, checked Sonia wasn't looking my way—although, surely, not even Sonia could reach this far back with her throws, could she?—and opened one of my to-do lists. October first was around the corner, and there was much to be done. I'd already gotten the witch hat and pumpkin cutouts for the walls and windows, but I still needed to order the cotton for the fake spiderwebs, and I was undecided on whether to get an old-fashioned broom. The Tea Cauldron aimed for a cozy, modern witchy vibe, and brooms made of branches and straw didn't exactly scream twenty-first century.

By my side, Ian asked in a low, deep murmur that made me want to squirm in all the good, fluttering ways, "What are you doing?"

"Shopping list for Halloween decorations."

"Hope Avery," Sonia boomed from the front of the room.

I winced and looked up guiltily. Her gaze was laser-focused on me with an accuracy few engineering tools could ever hope to achieve. I waved and smiled brightly. "Present!"

For a second, she looked ready to throw her cane at me. "Pay attention, Miss Avery."

"I am," I assured her before she also took a dig at my dating life. "I was just checking my Halloween to-do list to make sure I have no lingering questions."

Her suspicious stare stayed on me for a few more seconds before switching to the stack of folders in front of her. "Next."

"But Sonia!" someone complained with a whine.

Everyone's attention switched subjects, and I slumped back in my chair with a sigh of relief. I felt Ian's body shake with silent laughter, but when I glared at him, he was his usual granite self, his deep-green eyes cold like stones.

"Ha-ha, so funny," I grumbled. "Hope getting called out in the middle of class. Hilarious."

The corner of his mouth twitched. He was wearing his

usual armor of black—black T-shirt, black jeans, black boots. The watch around his wrist was black, as was the tie holding his shoulder-length brown hair back. I wondered if his Halloween decorations would be all black too. Black spiders, black spider-webs, black pumpkins. Probably his favorite season of the year.

Would he get a cute little black coat for Fluffy too?

The image of Ian's small, ecstatic white fluffball of a dog in a costume almost melted me on the spot.

"What now?" he asked.

"Nothing," I choked out, fanning myself with my hand. "Absolutely nothing."

He shifted in his seat, reminding me of the breadth of his shoulders and the muscles on display under the cover of macho goth as he crossed his arms over his chest. Being a semi-retired bounty hunter and running a repairs and remodeling company on the side kept Ian Cavalier in shape. That and walking the dogs, I supposed. And taking care of the old cemetery he owned.

We were a little weird here in Olmeda.

On his paranormal side, Ian was a shifter who refused to have anything to do with the local pack. The feeling was mutual, which was a shame because the local pack was led by his half brother.

Not for the first (or second, or tenth) time, I checked the thirty or so people present, but Ian's brother was nowhere to be seen.

About three weeks ago, after I'd survived the attempted murder and theft of my witch shop, Derek Hutton had appeared at my back door and dropped the following ominous words:

"I need more of my special potion."

As a Council-sanctioned witch shop owner, it was my duty to provide potions to the local paranormal community—

shifters, mages, demons, berserkers, and what have you. Unfortunately, as a Council-sanctioned witch shop owner, I was not a psychic and couldn't read Hutton's mind, therefore I had no clue what his special potion was. A potion that allowed one to know someone else's thoughts had yet to be invented.

However, a potion that would force someone to talk to you could be arranged, provided you were into illegal things like dark magic.

Alas, that was not the way of the Oakes-Avery witches. Grandma's and my way.

Besides, to use such a potion, you'd need to be near the person, and so far Hutton had proved beyond elusive. I didn't have his number, the official pack phone receptionist had told me they'd pass on the message more times than I was willing to admit, and Dru's friend of a friend of a friend who knew someone in the pack had netted zero results for other phone numbers.

I'd hoped to catch Hutton at the PBOA meeting, but he was apparently too busy to attend.

A glance at Ian told me he was focused ahead, his mouth a straight line, his body language one of *touch me and die by extreme negative temperatures*. Which was funny, considering how much body heat he could produce if you weren't careful.

I could ask him for Hutton's private number. Being a bounty hunter, it wouldn't be too difficult for him to procure the number from one of his many contacts. But if I asked him, he would want to know why I needed the number, and I wasn't sure I wanted to tell him about Hutton's cryptic request.

Here is the thing. My lovely, cozy modern witchy vibes tea shop with an occultism, tarot, and Wicca products bookshelf also happened to be a murder house used by a dark witch for decades to peddle highly illegal, morally bankrupt, bad-for-the-soul dark magic.

Said witch now haunted my shop.

But that wasn't the problem. The problem was I couldn't be sure if Hutton had meant a normal special potion or a special-*special* potion.

Until I was sure he wasn't asking for dark magic, I wasn't telling anything to anyone, family connections or not. What if he'd meant dark magic? If I told Ian, and it turned out Hutton was doing something illegal, how would he take it? I didn't want to make their relationship worse than it already was. Ian might proclaim he had no love for his little brother, but I'd noticed signs that told me otherwise. Besides, he'd chosen Olmeda to semi-retire and start his other business, hadn't he? Perhaps, deep inside, he was looking to close the breach their parents had created.

Sonia clapped her hands to gain everyone's attention, and I sat up straight, afraid I'd gotten caught not paying attention. Thankfully, her scowl was directed at the papers on the table.

"Next," she announced. "Shifters meeting. Is everything ready? Hollis and the Donovans are already settled into the B&B. Is the pack ready?"

"Yes, Sonia," a young woman answered from the first row.

It was the first time I'd seen her at a meeting, which wasn't saying much considering this was only my third one, but it told me Hutton liked to cycle his PBOA meeting envoys. In any case, she had eaten one of my lukewarm grilled ham-and-cheese sandwich offerings, unlike pretty much everyone else, so I was sure she was a smart girl with a bright future and Hutton was right to trust her with the responsibility of coming to the PBOA meeting.

"Are you sure?" Sonia insisted. Perhaps she'd seen her eat my sandwich, too, and had drawn her own conclusions.

"Yes, ma'am..." The young woman faltered under Sonia's glare.

The urge to reach over and console her was strong, but walking up to her would earn me Sonia's ire, and I, too, was unsure how Sonia liked to be addressed in these situations.

Instead, I leaned into Ian and whispered, "What shifter meeting?"

He pursed his lips, as if he was considering whether to answer. After a couple of seconds, he leaned in as well, and I almost lost my train of thought at the nearness of those green eyes. They matched the green streak in my blond hair and the hand-stitched cover of Grandma's spellbook.

"Packs have alliances and hold meetings. They rotate which pack gets to hold them."

"Like a shifter convention?" I hadn't noticed any increase in shifter presence. But then, with all the tourists, it might not be obvious unless you were looking for it. Shifters were the easiest creature to recognize due to the innate power that clung to them—how I could tell Ian was an alpha, too—but nature had gifted paranormals with the ability to remain undetected unless they chose to show their magical side. There were potions that could help with that, but it could prove expensive in the long run.

I still had no idea what kind of paranormal most people in this room were, and the only reason I knew Dru was a demon was because she'd shown her claws while mauling her ex-boss. But I already told that story, and you should read it—very thrilling!

The whole hidden talent thing was also the reason Vicky had lasted undetected for so long—the only way to tell a witch was a witch was if they chose to perform magic in front of you.

"More like an alpha convention," Ian murmured back.

Interesting. It made sense. Shifters were an old-fashioned faction and firm believers in tradition—marking their territory, face-to-face threats, that kind of thing. Online meetings didn't have the same charm.

"And it's Hutton's turn to host?" I asked.

Once again, the mention of his brother produced no reaction, not even a flicker in his eyes. And believe me—I was paying close attention.

As a witch, it was my responsibility to help the local community. Putting my nose where it didn't belong was all but a sacred duty, some might argue. So far, I'd chosen a more relaxed approach, but that didn't mean I didn't take my responsibilities seriously.

Very seriously, I agreed with myself, studying his face.

Ian answered my question about whose turn it was to host the alphas with a wry *what do you think* look, and I sat up straighter. I would not feel bad or blush. As Grandma liked to say, no question was too stupid.

Was this why Hutton hadn't gotten back to me yet? If he was too busy preparing for the meeting to follow up about the potion, that was excellent news. It meant whatever his *usual potion* was, he wasn't in a hurry. In my experience so far, those looking for dark magic potions wanted them done and wanted them now.

"I wonder if the alphas will visit the shop," I murmured to myself.

"Doubt it," Ian murmured back.

Maybe I should change the menu I'd planned for next week, make it something a little wolfy. Hair of the dog? No, too on the nose, and I didn't have an alcohol license.

A ball of paper bounced on the empty chair next to me, and I jerked my attention back to Sonia. Goodness, she should've joined a pro softball team—we were sitting all the way in the back.

"Pay attention, Avery," she admonished.

I cleared my throat. "Yes, Sonia."

Ian's mouth twitched again. The moment Sonia looked away, I grabbed the ball of paper and threw it at his head.

"*Avery,*" came Sonia's strident voice.

"Sorry!"

Laughter spread along the room, and my smile widened. Even Ian chuckled softly. If my sandwiches wouldn't win over these people's hearts, being the naughty kid in class would have to do.

"What about Garreth the Hound?" Sonia addressed the shifter again.

"We're taking care of it," the shifter assured her.

"I want names by next week," Sonia said. Her attention switched to the other aisle. "Xavier, where are we on the website? It's almost October. It needs to be done yesterday."

"Garreth the Hound?" I asked Ian while Xavier and Sonia got into a heated discussion about time and resources and *I'm doing this in my own free time, you know* and *do you think I'm getting paid to mother you all like you're five years old?*

"Local legend," Ian answered.

I nudged him with my elbow. "Don't make me tickle it out of you."

He harrumphed. Fair—hard to tickle granite.

"Garreth's owner was killed by a small mob for daring to pursue a gentleman's daughter."

My smile fell. "Oh."

"Next night, the dog sneaked into each of the killers' houses and tore out their throats in their sleep."

"Aww." My heart constricted. "How sweet." Fluffy would totally do that for me.

Ian rolled his eyes. "The dog supposedly got caught before he could finish the job, so every year, on the night of the massacre, he comes back, searching for the killers who got away."

"Let me guess—the anniversary happens to be Halloween."

"You must be clairvoyant."

"How considerate of the mob to choose that day." I mulled over the story for a few moments. Vicky had skipped that one on her gruesome-and-morbid tour before attempting to give me my own gruesome-and-morbid death. Too sweet for her tastes and not enough dark magic, probably. "So now Sonia gets one of the shifters to run around and howl at the moon during Halloween?"

"It's even on the printouts," Ian said somberly.

"There are printouts?"

"Printouts, brochures, posters, banners."

That wouldn't be a problem—I had plenty of space on the windows and counter. The thought of helping with the festivities filled me with excitement. "Is there a parade?"

"Yes."

Perfect!

"Cavalier," Sonia said.

She was scowling, so I leaned away, in case. No need to get caught in the crossfire.

Ian lifted his chin in acknowledgment.

"Can we use the cemetery for a special midnight haunted tour?"

"No."

Sonia's focus snapped to me. She glared like it was my job to change his mind and I better succeed or else.

A bead of sweat formed on my brow.

Once she had moved on to chewing out someone else, I asked, "Special midnight haunted tour?" Ian's family owned a very old private cemetery closed to the public, although at one point it had offered tours.

"No."

I frowned. "But it sounds like fu—"

"No."

"Ia—"

"No."

"Will you let me finish my sentences?" I asked with a laugh.

The corner of his mouth kicked up. "No."

I relented, but this would not be the end of it. And not just because I wanted to stay in Sonia's good graces. My shop was still in the six-month probation period, and while the initial saboteur had been dealt with, that didn't mean I was in the clear. A good grade from the PBOA's president would go a long way toward convincing the witches' Council to award me the shop for good.

Besides, a special haunted cemetery tour sounded fun. We could decorate the gravestones and his house, give everything a creepy atmosphere. We could even put him and his big dog Rufus in front of the gate and their scowls would assure everyone that scary times were ahead. Perfect advertisement.

"Whatever you're thinking—no," Ian said.

"Okay." I patted his arm reassuringly. Plenty of time to come up with a plan to convince him—two weeks, at least. Luckily, my sister was a genius with business strategies.

He glanced at me suspiciously, but I kept my smile bland. Before taking ownership of the Tea Cauldron, I had worked at a coffee shop back home for a few years. I knew how to keep people thinking they had won the round.

My witch magic might not be the greatest in the universe— or the meeting room, or the immediate vicinity, counting the chair under me—but I was a woman with skills.

After Sonia brought the meeting to an end, Ian asked me to dinner. Off-handedly, as if it wasn't a big deal.

I accepted, of course. It had become our own small ritual,

and rituals like this needed repeats to turn into traditions. I liked traditions. Traditions were a cornerstone of a true home.

Like on the previous two occasions, we walked over to a nearby mom-and-pop restaurant and ordered burgers, a beer, and a diet soda. Also like the previous two times, Ian rearranged my onion rings and gave me some of his fries.

Shifters could be weird.

A companionable silence filled the car as he drove me home from downtown Olmeda.

It was on the tip of my tongue to ask if he'd had any luck with deciphering Bagley's ledger—the one listing all her dark magic clients—when my phone chirped with an incoming call.

Unknown number.

Last time I'd gotten a call from an unknown number it had been Ian. Since Ian had both hands on the steering wheel, I used my keen intellect to deduce this was someone else. Curiosity, my greatest asset—unless you asked my mother—won over the need to maintain the easy silence between us.

"Hello?" I asked into the phone.

"Where's my goddamn potion, witch?"

2

NOT IAN, but the closest thing to him.

I sent Ian a wary glance. I didn't want to mention Hutton's name aloud. "Could you call me tomorrow?"

"No, I will not call you tomorrow. I've given you enough time. I want my potion now."

The irritation in the alpha's tone was contagious. "I've been calling you for three weeks," I ground out. "If you had bothered to return my calls, you could've had your potion days ago."

"Bagley knew what to do."

My eye twitched. "I'm not her."

"Apparently." The derision in his voice painted me a perfect mental picture of the sneer he must be wearing.

"If you want her—" I stopped myself before telling him to go dig up her corpse if he wanted her potions. If Ian heard that, he'd hound me until I made a full confession of who wanted Bagley's potions and why. It was our agreement—he'd help me deal with anyone who came searching for dark magic potions and my conscience would rest easy at night for not reporting her doings to the Council.

I took a deep breath and managed a cheery smile for Ian.

Who wasn't even looking my way. With a sigh, I dropped the effort and squared my shoulders. "I'm busy right now. We'll talk tomorrow."

"Witch…" Hutton warned.

"Tomorrow," I said firmly and ended the call.

The phone rang again. I ignored it and saved the number to my caller list. Under Ass 2.

"Who's ass one?"

I hid my phone from him. "Guess."

"The Council?"

"Yup."

Not my fault Ian had chosen to call me for the first time after we'd had a big fight.

The twinkling in his eyes told me he knew I was lying, but I didn't want to go down that road for the same reason I hadn't wanted to mention Hutton's name aloud. As Dru had once told me—he was a shifter, not stupid.

———

The next morning dawned sunny and lovely. Now that we were almost in October, the heat didn't feel as asphyxiating, and a delicious chill permeated the morning air.

By the time I got everything ready to open, Dru had arrived for her shift, box of muffins in hand. Fairy Circle's—my favorite.

I clucked my tongue at her plain T-shirt. I had given her one with the shop's logo on the same day I'd agreed to hire her part-time, but I had yet to see it make an appearance.

"That's not the Tea Cauldron-approved uniform. Where's the tee?"

She returned my words with a blank stare. "In the washer."

As it had been for the last week.

"One day," I remarked, "it might even see the dryer."

"I wouldn't hold my breath," she muttered as she snuck behind the counter.

I glanced down at my T-shirt. The shop's logo wasn't *that* bad—a bubbling cauldron, teabag tag included, with a witch hat and a spellbook on the side, and the shop's name arching overhead in the cutest spiraling font the internet could offer.

"You think I should take out the spellbook?" I asked. "Too busy?"

"Nah, it's perfect...for you."

The logo did make me grin like an idiot whenever I saw it. The fact that I could wear it in my own shop... There were no words to describe the tremendousness of the situation. In moments like these, my heart became so light I might start floating up like a balloon at any time. Bet that'd attract clients.

The shop wasn't exactly thriving, but it had begun to acquire a wider clientele than paranormals needing the occasional potion. It was the only reason I could afford to pay Dru.

Dru had worked at the shop next door until the owner's early retirement—under her claws. Unfortunately, Mr. Lewis's promise of leaving her the shop had turned out to be a scam.

Mr. Lewis had been a lying sack of many different things, none of them nice. Not only had he failed to mention Dru on any official papers or business records, but he had been riddled with debt and now the bank owned the shop.

Better to find out now than be surprised later after she'd put in more time, I'd told Dru. Dru had said something different. Louder and not quite as pragmatic.

Giving her a job while she figured out things was the least I could do after she'd saved my life. I also enjoyed the company. Vicky had been my first friend here, and part of me missed her. She might've had ulterior motives, been a murderous dark magic user, and tried to steal my shop, but it had been nice to have someone to talk to every day.

Now I had Dru.

"Why are you smiling at me like that?" Dru asked, full of suspicion. "You're not thinking of making us wear witches' hats for Halloween or anything, are you?"

My mouth dropped open. "Oh, my God."

"No!"

"But they'd look so cute…"

She glared at me like I'd just come crawling out of the gutter. "*No.*"

"A hairpin with tiny hats?"

"Piss off."

Fine, maybe not for *her*. I brought up my phone and added another item to the Halloween shopping list.

"Hope," she said in warning, her hand tightening around one of the muffins.

"No witch hats for you," I agreed before she could demonstrate her aim and waste a perfectly good piece of bakery. "Don't worry."

I took a photo of the muffins in the glass display for the shop's social media, which now boasted all of twenty followers, then ducked into the back of the shop and called Hutton.

As his phone rang, I walked up and down the hallway. The back half of the first floor had a kitchen, a supplies room, a tiny bathroom, the stairs going up to the living quarters upstairs, and the door into the backyard.

The Tea Cauldron was situated in the older area of Olmeda. Most buildings here were two- and three-stories high, some with small backyards like the ones in this row of houses, and some with front yards in the case of the older mansions. It was a quaint, cheerful area full of shops and restaurants that catered to the tourist trade.

The call went to voice mail, so I tried again.

After the third time, my irritation rose like the thirst of a vampire waking up after a four-hundred-year nap.

This was the second time Hutton had dropped a bomb on my lap, then proceeded to ignore me.

It would be the last.

I went back into the shop and grabbed one of the carton boxes for deliveries. Dru got out of the way as I crouched by the potion cabinet behind the counter and examined its contents. I'd recently made a bunch, so we were well stocked in all the popular ones—glamour, memory, focus, sleep.

"Delivery?" Dru asked.

Indeed. "For the pack." I settled on five memory potions, then added some scrunched brown paper to keep them in place inside the box. "I'll be back in an hour or so."

"Sure, boss," she drawled.

A shudder ran down my spine. "Don't say it like that. It makes me think you keep a dart board with my photo on it."

"Nah, not yours."

Mr. Lewis's, then. That, I could get on board with. "Bring it over. We can hang it out back and play during our breaks."

"You know, I might at that."

I went into the backyard, where I kept my newest treasure —an old, scuffed, gloriously yellow Vespa, courtesy of one of Alex's friends.

So far, only one person had made use of my new potion delivery business, but that number would grow. The news simply needed time to spread among the paranormal community. The days of finding time to go to the shop were over; witches-on-wheels were the future.

I stuffed the box in the seat compartment and put on my helmet, which had cost almost more than the Vespa. I wasn't sure what to make of that, but Alex had assured me his buddy was good for it and that the yellow deathtrap—Ian's words, not mine—wouldn't break down on me. Yet.

Dru was giving it until Christmas.

I patted the top of the headlight. "Don't worry, Bee-Bee," I murmured lovingly. "I got your back." With enough love and nurturing, it'd last at least until Easter.

The trip to the pack's compound was a breeze in the early morning traffic. I zigzagged among delivery trucks and squeezed between the cars stuck on the way downtown. If everything went according to plan, I'd upgrade to an electric motorcycle within two years.

I was a responsible witch, after all.

Olmeda's pack owned a patch of forested land, with one side rear-ending into the street by Ian's family's cemetery and the actual entrance on the opposite side. I imagined that was how Ian's parents had met—his father, the alpha, out on a stroll on the quiet streets near pack territory, his mother, the cemetery witch, out on a stroll before she had to open the graveyard for tours.

It was unfortunate that it hadn't worked out, because that meet-cute must've been movie-worthy.

The shifters lived in a series of buildings hidden by the trees and the brick wall running the edges of their territory. I had walked by once before, curious after Hutton's visit, but had never gone inside. As far as the paranormal-unaware humans went, it was an exclusive gated community, complete with a security guard booth at the gate.

I parked the Vespa and approached the booth with my box of potions. Shifters went through memory potions at an excellent rate, so it was a sure bet someone inside was running short on them. A memory potion wouldn't wipe someone's memory completely—not the legal kind anyway—but instead made recollecting anything magical-related difficult until the memory eventually faded into "must've imagined it." It was handy for occasions when normal humans witnessed a shifting.

I greeted the shifter in the booth with a bright *Hello!* He was wearing a dark-blue uniform and stood straight and alert. Last time I'd been here, the shifter on duty had looked bored out of her mind, and I'd been tempted to return with a muffin to cheer her up.

"'Sup," the shifter said, his attention focused on the other side of the gate, where two men were laughing and talking animatedly like a pair of good friends who hadn't seen each other in a long time.

"I need to deliver potions to the alpha," I said.

The shifter gestured at the floor. "Leave them here."

"To the alpha," I repeated firmly. "He's expecting me."

"Oh, really?" he drawled, unimpressed.

From his attitude, I wasn't the first person to arrive with an excuse demanding to meet the alpha.

"I'm Hope Avery from the Tea Cauldron. I took over for Bagley." Look at me, not even blinking at saying the name of the antitheses of everything I stood for. Dru would be so proud. If she knew about the whole dark magic, evil incarnate ghost in the shop. "Hutton asked me to deliver these personally." I jutted my chin toward the inside of his booth. "I'm sure he can confirm it."

"Let's find out," the shifter said, grabbing his phone.

He turned his back to talk quietly into the phone, and I shook my head in disappointment. If I'd lied about my identity, I could easily throw a freezing potion at his back now, then waltz right inside.

Sure, once inside I'd get caught in two minutes flat, but it was the principle of the thing.

Ian would never give anyone his back.

Wouldn't surprise me if he walked backward better than he did forward.

The shifter ended the call and pressed a button inside the booth. A small side door to the big gate opened. It reminded me of Ian's setup at the cemetery's fence. Yet another similarity that made me think Ian and his half brother were more alike than either of them wanted to admit.

"Stay," he said when I went to walk forward. "Someone's coming to get you."

A minute later, another shifter came into view, and I grinned in recognition—the man had come into the shop a couple of times and seemed like an amiable fellow.

"Good morning." He smiled back and gestured for me to follow. "Welcome to Clawstone Park. Let me show you around."

"Thanks."

The thick trees protecting the compound from view ended abruptly not far in, allowing for a big open area. The road made a wide circle in front of a square brick building, with other narrower paths leading forward among more trees. An expanse of grass filled the middle of the circle and several vehicles occupied a parking area on the side—UTVs, a couple of pickup trucks, and some cars.

Fluffy would absolutely love it here.

So would I, if I weren't here under duress.

Where is my potion, I mimicked in my head. Did Hutton think I could read minds?

A man hurried across the road. Two shifters nearly collided with each other trying to enter the building.

"This is the main office," my shifter guide—Keith—explained. "Visitors aren't allowed beyond, but for you," he added with a wink, "we'll make an exception."

I fanned my face with my hand. "Oh, you flatterer."

He laughed and led the way across the grass toward one of the paths. "The housing is mostly over there." He pointed to another path. "But the alpha's private quarters are this way."

We stopped to let a woman run past us. She slowed down when she noticed the box in my hand. I also recognized her from the shop.

"Hey, Hope. Got any focus potions in there?"

"Just memory. Come later by the shop?"

"Sure thing." She continued on her way.

"Is it always this busy?" I asked, watching another shifter yell at someone from a window.

"Not usually."

Ah. The alpha convention, of course.

"I guess the shifter meeting is keeping everyone on their paws?" I asked. He sent me a withering look, and I cleared my throat. Probably not the first time he'd heard that one. "Toes. Everyone on their toes."

"You could say that."

"What exactly do they do in these meetings?"

"This and that."

Since I didn't want to get kicked out for being too nosy, I kept silent and followed him down the path. Contrary to my expectations of individual rustic cottages planted in the middle of a thick forest, the compound looked like any normal gated community. Trees grew here and there, but it was easy to see the houses all standing together in a pretty row.

We passed a trio of shifters in their late teens playing rock-paper-scissors. One of them pulled a scissor against two rocks and groaned with melodramatic despair. The other two laughed.

"Seven out of twelve," the loser demanded.

Snickers met his request.

Odd, but endearing. Was this how young shifters entertained themselves? My theories had run more toward video games, howling competitions, and shedding on each other's beds.

One of them elbowed the other. "Look. It's the new witch lady."

My ear fought against its fleshy confines to try to catch the answer.

"Shane said she's cool."

"Shane's a loser."

"Like your face," said the other shifter. He howled in laughter when the first one gave him the finger.

"Don't mind them," Keith said. His steps hastened, and I had to trot to keep up. "They're trying to decide who gets to play Garreth for Halloween."

"You don't assign the role?"

"We like for the younger ones to take on responsibilities from early on. It's up to them to figure out who gets which shifts." He cackled malevolently. "Without drawing blood or breaking anything."

I suppressed a shiver. Good to know. I thought of Alex and Shane, Ian's stray shifters, and wondered how they settled things—I'd never seen them bruised or scratched.

"They like playing the hound for Halloween?"

"Highlight of the year."

That, it was promising to be. My thoughts wandered to Ian and his cemetery. Surely there must be some way to convince him to open the place for a couple of nights for Halloween. I could sell tickets at the shop, and it would be so much fun. The strays could make their own Garreth the Hound appearance among the headstones and one-up these young shifters. Loser? Hah. Shane would show them.

"Here we are," Keith said.

We stopped at a bigger house than the ones I'd seen through

the trees. It had its own attached garage and a smaller building on the other side—perhaps a guest house. The front yard was small and unadorned by flowerbeds or bushes, and the whole picture made for an impersonal, no-nonsense atmosphere.

Keith went up the front steps and opened the door. I followed and found myself inside an average house. Living room on one side, dining room on the other, entrance hallway and stairs in front. It had none of the lived-in charm of Ian's place, no decorations or signs of use, as if Hutton was simply renting the place for the time being and didn't want to get charged a cleaning fee.

But then, if this was where he conducted official alpha business, it made sense he'd keep the space sparse. One didn't come here to knock back some beers and talk about the good old days; one came here to get orders or be censured for some wrongdoing.

Keith led me to a room down the hallway and rapped on the thick wooden door.

"Come in," came Hutton's voice.

Keith opened the door and waved me in. He closed it as soon as I stepped inside. It didn't quite slam, but there was a finality to it that made goosebumps erupt along my arms.

"Hello—"

Hutton lifted an imperious hand. I snapped my mouth shut and waited. After a few seconds, the sound of another door closing made it into the room.

I looked at him expectantly.

"What the hell are you doing here?" he asked with deadly calm.

3

UNLIKE IAN, whose deadly calm tone made me want to turn into a quivering blob and escape through the drain, Hutton's voice barely provoked the merest of shivers between my shoulder blades. He was tall and lean instead of broad like his brother, and his features, while similar, ran toward the pretty rather than the harsh.

Also unlike Ian, he took no care to keep his alpha power contained but let it roam free and saturate the air. It wasn't as intense as the first time I'd met him, but there was no doubt I was in the presence of an alpha.

"Answer," he hissed.

Ah, yes. The reason for my trip. My irritation, so far overshadowed by my curiosity at being inside pack territory, made a triumphant return like a phoenix rising—exploding!—from the ashes.

My mouth stretched and fixed into the kind of smile that left customers everywhere debating whether it was sincere or utterly patronizing.

"I'm here to talk about..." I walked up to his desk, opened

my hands, and let the box fall on top of his desk. It landed with a small thump and a clinking of the bottles inside. "Potions."

"You brought my potion here?" he asked in outrage, taking a step back and colliding with his chair. The room was obviously an office, decorated in dark mahogany with a wide window that did crap-all to infuse the insides with any kind of light. Or maybe that was his dark mood, sucking the sunlight right out of existence.

"No, I didn't."

He relaxed slightly. "Good. The last thing I need is someone getting curious and sniffing around."

"I haven't brought it," I said sweetly, "because I haven't made it."

"*What?*"

"But, say it was ready," I said, because he raised an excellent point. "How exactly am I supposed to give it to you if you don't want me to come to your office?"

"The usual way," he answered in a harsh whisper.

I crossed my arms, refusing to be cowered. "I have no idea what 'the usual way' is."

"Bagley—"

"Is dead and left no instructions."

Not exactly true, as I was sure she'd give me all the instructions in the world if only I did her the tiny favor of giving her mobile corporeal form so she could keep terrorizing the world.

Hutton rubbed his face with his hands. "Are you kidding me right now?"

"Nope."

"You should've called."

I pointed at his chest with a snap of my arm. The temerity of the man. "I've called! You never return my messages."

"Call my personal number, for God's sake."

"I didn't have it until yesterday! I called this morning, and you didn't pick up."

"I was busy," he said defensively.

"Not my problem." I gave him a flat stare. "If you don't want the witch to come knocking, you should answer the witch when she comes calling."

"Whatever," he muttered ungraciously, running a hand through his short, dark brown hair. Another difference compared to Ian's shoulder-length, wavy locks. Intentional? Perhaps. "Where's the damn potion?"

"About that. You're going to have to be more specific."

"What do you mean?"

"I've no clue what kind of potion you want."

If he were a fire mage instead of a shifter, I'd have been ashes in that moment. I was pretty sure his arms got a bit hairier, and some fang showed when he spoke next, low and growling, and leaning over the desk as if he wanted to wrap his hands around my neck and squeeze till his precious potion poured out of my body.

"I want my alpha potion."

I blinked in confusion. "What alpha potion?"

"My. Alpha. Potion."

"Your alpha potion?"

"Yes." A literal growl this time.

"What alpha potion?"

In four strides, he rounded the desk and was looming over me. For the first time since I'd entered the room, a thread of real fear entered my chest, vining around my heart and squeezing in warning.

"Are you playing with me, witch?" he asked in a sleek, soft voice.

The thread tightened.

"No," I said with all honesty. "I don't know what you mean by alpha potion."

The only thing that remained from Bagley's possessions was her client ledger, and while that might've given me an inkling of what Hutton meant, it was in code and currently in Ian's possession for deciphering.

Hutton walked a circle around me, and I followed his progression through the corners of my eyes.

"Bagley left nothing behind, but you have taken over her business?"

"That's right."

"The *other* business."

"Yes." I wasn't about to tell him that my plans for Bagley's dark magic dealings included a lot of placebo potions and zero actual dark magic. "You saw the shop's listing." The one in the dark web marketplace Brimstone and Destruction, the fire mage, had done for me after I'd made him a fake dark magic potion.

Hutton completed the circle and propped a hip on the edge of his desk. After a few more seconds of scrutinizing my face, he leaned in and spoke again:

"I need a potion to enhance my alpha powers."

I almost blurted out that it was impossible, but I stopped myself in time. Dark magic could do a lot more than good magic could. All it took was a lot of unwilling blood, running afoul of Council law, and a permanent scorch mark on your soul.

"Enhance your alpha powers?" I asked cautiously.

His lips firmed into a tight line. "Produce."

It took me a few moments to get his meaning. "A potion that gives you alpha powers?"

"Yes."

My neurons were still getting lost on the way to work.

"Because...?"

His features contorted into a ferocious scowl. "What do you think?"

Nothing, apparently.

"I don't have alpha magic," he gritted out.

My mouth fell open in shock. "But your father...?"

"Was an alpha, yes."

I studied his face closely. Even with the snarl twisting his mouth, there was no denying his likeness to Ian. Too much to be coincidental, too much for him to be illegitimate. Ian had alpha powers, therefore Hutton should have them too. I had felt them the first time he'd come to the shop. Heck, I was feeling them right now, trying to choke me as his irritation increased.

"I don't get it," I said.

"That makes two of us, lady."

"When did the powers start to disappear?"

"They were never there."

"Never?" I parroted like the smart witch I was.

His nostrils flared. "Would you like me to shout it so everyone at Clawstone Park hears it?"

"Sorry, I'm just shocked." I rubbed my chin, trying to get my thoughts into a resemblance of order. "You've been taking the potion since your shifting powers appeared?"

"Yes."

Shifters, like all paranormals, grew into their powers in their late teens. Hutton was in his late twenties—that was a long time to have been faking being an alpha.

"Why?" The answer came as soon as the question left my mouth. "Never mind. Don't answer that." To have a kid who hadn't inherited the father's alpha powers would've been seen as weak. One of his parents—or together—must've started him on the potion to safeguard his future, and once started, once he'd taken over the pack, how could he explain he'd been lying to everyone all these years?

Oh, Mother.

Alpha powers were almost a tangible thing once unleashed —they saturated the atmosphere, made you aware of the predator in the midst, and enhanced a shifter's physical prowess. You couldn't fake them through will and determination.

No placebo potion was going to help with this one.

"Your powers—"

"Are fading," he snapped. He looked at his hands in disgust, as if he could see the alpha aura seep out from his fingers.

And perhaps he could. What did I know about how dark magic potions worked other than that their main ingredient was unwilling blood? Zilch.

"You've been a member of the pack for decades," I said. "They will accept you as alpha without alpha magic. It's not unheard of."

While shifters could be very traditional, simply having alpha powers wouldn't make someone their alpha automatically. A pack had to agree on their leader, otherwise they'd reject them. Alpha magic denoted a powerful shifter, and it helped with fights against other alphas, but it couldn't force other shifters to do anything. It didn't affect the pack's will.

"No, they won't," Hutton said derisively. "They will reject me, then invite another alpha to take over."

"You underestimate their loyalty and love," I said earnestly. "Give them a chance. They will surprise you. You don't need the potion to keep your pack."

Also, whatever spell Bagley had used was long gone, turned into ashes in my backyard's fire pit. Not that I was going to tell him that.

"Witch," he said, "you have no idea of how packs work."

He had me there. "I know they all seem to genuinely like you."

"Oh?" he asked sarcastically. "Do your powers extend to reading minds?"

"You can learn a lot from interactions. You should be proud their appreciation of you is so obvious, you know."

Like most paranormals, I believed in some sort of afterlife. I liked to think that Grandma was in a safe place, enjoying her best un-life, maybe traveling the stars as a cloud of sentient ghostly energy. Which was a long way of saying that I hoped there was no Hell because lies like the ones I was spouting would take me straight to it.

I'd no clue what his pack thought of him other than since he was still alpha, he must be doing a decent job. The shifters who had saved me from the hitman had been happy enough to obey his orders, and Dru hadn't mentioned any gossip about them hating their boss, so that had to mean something, didn't it?

Hutton went to the window and stared at his backyard. It was another expanse of grass lacking anything to obstruct the view from the trees. These were thicker than the ones by the other houses, and it wouldn't have surprised me if we were next to the forest part of the pack's territory, the one that reached all the way to the cemetery side.

"I can't risk letting anyone know right now," he said.

"Why not?"

"None of your business."

I snapped my fingers. "The alpha convention."

"The what?"

"You don't want to appear weak in front of your allies. But not being alpha isn't being weak." Irritation sparked to life. As a witch dwelling on the lower end of the power spectrum, I took offense at his stance. Lacking power did not mean lacking greatness. I was nowhere near being a great witch, but I could be. I *would* be, given enough time with the shop.

If the Council didn't take it away from me before my probation time was over.

I shoved the unwelcome reminder to the side. "Aren't these people supposed to be your friends anyway? With their support, you can cement your role as leader without needing any kind of alpha power."

He snorted like he couldn't believe his ears. "That's not how things work."

"You gotta think more positive." I encouraged him with a smile. "My grandma was a firm believer of—"

"Your grandma isn't here, is she?"

"You never know. She might be. In spirit."

"I. Don't. Care."

If he expected me to help him, he'd better start caring.

Something in my expression must've translated my feelings because a muscle jumped in his jaw. "Let me explain pack politics to you: loyalty is a myth. There is always someone looking to take advantage and claim power."

"You think someone in your pack is trying to get you ousted?" I asked in surprise.

"No. Yes. It's complicated." He sighed deeply and went back to staring outside. "Some of the alpha visitors have good friends in the pack. The twins, especially. If they sense any weakness, they'll try to take over. I can't risk it."

"And the pack will let that happen?"

"Like I said, they have friends among my shifters. If they prove I'm not worth following, the pack will switch loyalties in the blink of an eye."

And discovering Hutton and his parents had been lying to them for years would be the perfect justification to make them switch.

"I see your problem."

"Good. When can I expect the potion?"

I eyed the door behind me. Shifters were fast; I wouldn't make it.

"I'm not sure I can make the potion for you," I confessed in my most customer-soothing tone. The one that said, *You are wrong, I did put four espresso shots in your drink as you asked, but I'm going to act like I'm the dumb one here so please stop screaming and spitting in my face.*

His body went taut like a violin string. "What do you mean?"

"I'm trying to create my own brand. I don't want to reuse Bagley's potions."

"Then find your own way to make it."

"That's not going to be possible."

In a heartbeat, he was standing in front of me, so close our bodies were nearly touching. He loomed, and I felt none of the warmth and excitement that coursed through my veins whenever Ian pulled this move on me. I felt small and insignificant and filled with the urge to scurry and make my escape through any crack available.

But the Oakes-Avery witches did not scurry. They made an informed decision to retreat. And I wasn't retreating.

If I wanted to be a permanent part of this community, I needed to learn how to deal with the local alpha.

"Either make the potion, or I'm getting you fired," the local alpha informed me.

"Fired?" I let him see my obvious doubt. Shifters were powerful, but they held little sway over the Council, and—

I gasped and took a step back. "No!"

"Oh, yes. You have two choices, witch: make the potion, or I'm telling the Council that you're a dark witch."

The Oakes-Avery witches also did not go down without a

fight. "If you do that, I'll tell everyone about your alpha powers. They'll sense they're gone and you'll be going down with me."

A humorless smile twisted his mouth. "And I'll tell them you poisoned me when you learned I was about to turn you in and that's why my powers are gone. Who do you think they'll believe?"

"You have no proof..." My words died as I remembered the dark web listing for my shop and Brimstone and Destruction's glowing review about my dark magic potion. Son of a b—

No. I inhaled deeply, felt the air fill my lungs and fortify my insides. I would not insult Fluffy by acknowledging she might birth such a horrible mess.

"Yes, witch," Hutton said with relish. "I have all the proof I need. So, what's it going to be? Potion or Council jail?"

The dark web marketplace listing I could explain away as someone trying to set me up—the same person who had tried to sabotage me during the first couple of weeks of opening the shop—but Hutton's accusations would carry a lot of weight. He'd been a member of Olmeda's paranormal community since birth. I was a newcomer who had recently taken over a dearly beloved witch's shop. The Council might not fully believe Hutton, but the damage would be done. My probation period would get cut short, and I'd get replaced in the blink of an eye. Plenty of witches out there eager to own shops who wouldn't cause the Council so much headache.

If they replaced me, there went Dru's temporary job.

There went my dreams. Because nobody who had been accused of being a dark witch once would ever get permission to open another witch shop.

Without a shop, how would I propagate Grandma's message of goodness over power? What would I even do with my life? Go back to living with my parents, selling trinkets online and working at the local coffee shop?

It had only been a month, but this was my home now.

The shop, Dru, Ian, Fluffy and Rufus, the strays, the couple of repeat customers I'd gained, the goldfish ghost in my pipes.

I didn't want to lose any of it. Not without a fight.

"Fine," I gritted out. "I'll make your potion."

He didn't gloat or laugh with triumph. His nod was curt and businesslike. "Good. I expect to hear from you soon."

"Then you better pick up the phone." I spun on my heel to face the door.

"And don't tell the bounty hunter about any of this," he warned as I opened the door. "Or I'll hunt you down and the Council will be the least of your worries."

Slamming doors wasn't my thing, but I had to admit there was some satisfaction in doing it.

4

By the time I returned to the shop, my natural optimism was cautiously back in control.

"Problems," I told my Vespa as I pushed it inside the backyard, "are not the enemy but lessons in life."

That didn't make them any more appealing, I had to admit, but it beat them being indestructible walls. If I went about this like the adult, professional businesswoman I was, there was no reason I couldn't find a solution that would make everyone happy. Hadn't I found a one-hundred percent dark-magic-free answer for the love-potion girl and the power-hungry mage? This would be no different.

Dru was dealing with a customer at one of the two tables, so I slipped behind the counter and began washing the small pile of used glasses.

"Ah, Hope, you're here," the customer at the table said. She was a professional photographer in her late forties who had recently moved to Olmeda. More importantly, she had never met Bagley and had no fondness for the old bat or a need to compare us, which meant she was my favorite repeat customer.

"Good morning, Hannah," I answered brightly. "Got any clients today?"

She lifted her compact photographer's bag. "Not today. Going to take some photos of the city for my portfolio."

"That's great."

Hannah went back to browsing on her phone, Dru went back to sitting bored behind the counter, and I went back to brainstorming a plan of action.

And don't tell the bounty hunter, Hutton had said. Unfortunately, the bounty hunter was in possession of Bagley's encoded ledger of dark magic clients, which meant Hutton's name was buried somewhere in there. I had to get the ledger from Ian before he cracked the code, but it was going to take some subtlety. Calling him and demanding he return it would only make him curious.

In all honesty, I had no idea what would happen if Ian discovered the truth. Would he tell the pack about his half brother's deception? Would he stand back and let another alpha take over the territory? Would he tell the Council and watch the bounty hunters get involved?

Or would he ask me to make the potion because this was his little brother, after all?

Everyone insisted there was no love lost between them, but I disagreed. Presumptuous, I know, but I had a stepsister, and I'd do anything for her. So I'd do this for Ian without putting him in a position of having to make a choice that might hurt his soul.

At its base, this was a problem between me—the local witch—and the pack. No need to involve anyone else. Dark magic aside, this was the reason witches were a pillar of the paranormal community—they were dependable, a haven for people's problems. That had been Grandma's aim, and that was what I would be.

To have another alpha take over the pack would bring discord to the shifters. Some might welcome a new leader, but I couldn't imagine all would. Fights might ensue, the pack might end up dispersing. Nobody would come out as the winner.

Also, I didn't want to lose the shop, not to mention the possibility of ending up in Council jail if Hutton didn't get his potion, lost his pack, and sold me out in retribution.

The chime tinkled as a couple entered the shop. Dru plastered a fake smile on her face and waited for their order. I couldn't blame her for her less-than-enthusiastic attitude. Going from manager of a prestigious antiques shop to serving tea and coffee was a big change.

At least now she was putting on a smile instead of the perennial scowl she'd sported last week.

"Tea," she barked under her breath.

I dutifully turned to the water urn.

Using dark magic for Hutton's potion was out of the question, but maybe if I figured out the original ingredients Bagley had used, I could modify them in a way that didn't require the blood of an unwilling victim.

Bagley remained blissfully quiet during business hours and when Dru was around, probably biding her time like the evil spawn that she was, but I still heard her laughing loud and clear in my head: *Shouldn't have destroyed my spellbook, dumbass!*

I had zero regrets. That thing had been evil and deserved to go up in flames.

So, since I didn't have the spellbook, and asking the dead witch would give her power over me, I'd have to improvise.

What did I know about spells and potions regarding power infusions?

Not much.

The urge to run upstairs and check every page in Grandma's spellbook tore at me. Even though I had read the book so many times I knew it by memory, the longing for that physical contact almost hurt in its intensity. Grandma might've died when I was eight, but all her teachings lived in those pages—in the painstakingly drawn illustrations, in the neat handwriting. In the goodness pouring out of every fiber of paper.

As her successor, it was my duty to fill the empty pages with my own spells.

It was my duty to find new ways to help. And this would be a new way.

Tearing my thoughts away from the spellbook upstairs, I considered my options.

The obvious solution would be to use another alpha's blood.

And oh, hey, I happened to know one.

But I wasn't ready to abandon my pledge of protecting Ian's brotherly sensitivities yet. If Hutton was truthful about using the potion since his teens, no way Bagley had used an alpha's blood to make the potion every time. Alphas were the kind of paranormal who would be noticed if they went missing. They made a mark in the world, even loner ones like Ian.

For magical purposes, blood could only survive for so long, spelled or au naturel. If Bagley had produced this potion for a decade, she'd have needed access to an alpha's blood often enough to be noticed. Even if she didn't do the bleeding herself —and she was definitely the kind of witch to prefer a hands-on approach—and ordered it from a supplier, the cost would've been prohibitive for more than a onetime potion.

No way alpha blood didn't cost a house's down payment. If you were going to risk kidnapping, mauling, and possibly murdering an alpha to gain access to their unwilling blood, you'd damn well make sure the rewards were worth the effort.

Bagley hadn't survived so long by taking unnecessary risks, so...

Actually, it was a miracle Bagley had survived so long with all the murdering and dark magic scheming, but she'd obviously been smart about her business and hadn't called attention to herself.

Which meant there had to be a way to make this potion with your average unwilling cursed blood.

And where average was involved in the magic world, there was hope.

Now, I just had to figure out what ingredients aside from the blood were needed, and perhaps there would be an option to do this potion with someone's willing blood. Mine, for example.

Once the new customers had their drinks and were chatting animatedly at the free table, I stepped closer to Dru.

"What do you know about this alpha convention shifter meeting thing happening with the pack?" I asked in a whisper barely audible over the soft music running in the background.

Magic was only one side of this problem. If I could untangle the mess from the other, there might not be a need for a potion. If Hutton's fears of the other alphas sniffing around his territory were unfounded, that would make my life a lot easier.

Wishes were their own kind of magic. "If you put it out in the universe, the universe might gift it back."

"Oh, Lord, is it time for affirmations again?" Dru murmured. "I thought you did those at breakfast."

"Anytime is a good time for affirmations, my friend," I answered sagely. "What do you know about the visiting alphas?"

"The same thing I told you when you texted me last night."

"You told me to Google it."

Her evil smile showed me two rows of perfectly white teeth. "Exactly."

"I tried, but there are too many paranormal romances." It

was the magical community's perfect disguise, but it also made it hard to find anything.

Dru shook her head with a roll of her eyes, then brought the shop's laptop closer and opened a private browser window. "You're like a baby. How have you lasted this long?"

"I know several good witch forums." Unfortunately, they all focused on potions and spells. "We can trade log-in info if you want."

"Do I look like a witch to you?"

"You look like you can be anything you want."

She blinked, her mouth opening and closing but no words coming out. She really did look like a winner, with her pretty dark curls and smooth light brown skin and long drop earrings and cauldron-less vibrant blue T-shirt.

Her mouth finally stopped gaping and stretched into a reluctant grin. "Okay, that wins you a freebie."

"You were going to charge me?" I asked with a bit of a pout.

She typed a website address. "I'm not a library."

"Fair." I checked our customers were still busy doing their thing and huddled closer to Dru. The website—an address which I was fully committing to memory—was a loose copy of other popular message boards. Once Dru logged in, one-line topics filled the screen from *What town should I move to?* to *M(22) had a fight with BF(25) over his wolf running buddy M(30), AITA?*

"Sorry," one of the new customers said. "Could I have a coffee refill?"

"Of course." I grabbed the pot and went around the counter to fill her mug.

She thanked me warmly and continued talking with her companion. By the time I made it back to Dru and the laptop, she had navigated to a section filled with headers related to shifters. The posts here had a definite stalkerish vibe to them.

My cousin's alpha and his two beta at the pack's pool—FMK? or *alpha Liu at a restaurant today + photos!!!*

"Is this some sort of shifter fan board?"

"Don't you have one for witches?"

"Is there one for demons?" I countered, not wanting to admit I'd voted on *Best witch of the year, shirtless only* three years in a row.

"Duh."

"Yeah, okay, there's one for witches too. But not quite this..." I pointed at the screen. "Obsessive." An idea popped into my mind. "Is there one for bounty hunters?"

"Not that I know of. Those guys would shut that shit down fast. No point in being a bounty hunter if your face and details are all over the internet, is there?"

I licked my lips. "So, you don't think there are photos of Ian in here?"

Dru snorted. "Hell, no."

"Good." Then another thought came to mind. "Hey, has anyone mentioned us in here?"

"Are you a shifter?"

"No?"

"Am I a shifter?"

"No."

"Then why would they mention us?"

I tsked, then returned my attention to the list of topics on the screen. "One day," I murmured.

"One day you'll be a big shifter celebrity that melts people's pants?"

"One day our shop will be so well known that people will recommend it when others ask if they should move to Olmeda," I told her proudly. A sly smile curved my lips. "And then you'll have to wear the official T-shirt."

"Please kill me if I'm still working here when that happens."

An affirmative grunt filled the space. It hadn't come from me, it hadn't come from the customers, and Dru didn't seem to have heard it. I scowled at the organic candies bowl—Bagley's current haunted object of choice.

Actually, I wasn't sure she had any choice in the matter, and I didn't want to ask. All I knew was that her soul attached itself to an object in the shop, and if I took it out of the room or the object broke, her soul disappeared for a time until it snapped back to haunt something else. It was tempting to think about what would happen if I took everything out, but then she might get stuck to a wall or the ceiling fan, and I appreciated having the choice of taking her out of the room if the need for private conversations or blissful silence arose.

"Here." Dru poked the screen.

"Hot alpha shifter meeting in Olmeda next week," I murmured, reading the title. "Is Hutton on the best-of list?"

"What do you think?"

I honestly didn't know. Most shifters ran on the hot and handsome side of the beauty scale, so it was hard picking favorites. "Too surly to make it in."

"Nah." Dru clicked on the link. "Too many paranormals in Olmeda to stand out."

The post had a list of names and the question, "Any sightings?"

We scrolled down. A photo of an older man and a woman talking outside one of the clubs in Guiles and Romary followed with the caption *Caught them yesterday afternoon*. Someone had replied asking for a photo of the twins.

"The twins?" It rang a bell.

"One of the pack's allies is led by twins." She typed something into the search bar and only a handful of results popped up. It was normal for sites like this to scrub older content for security reasons.

The first link took us to a photograph of two identical tall, blond men standing on the street in jeans and flannel shirts. One held two cups of coffee, the other was talking on the phone. They were wearing sunglasses, but I recognized them immediately.

"I saw one of them earlier." I peeked closer at the screen to make double sure. "Talking with someone outside Clawstone Park." Leaning back, I drummed my fingers on the counter. "Do alphas take over other packs often?"

Dru shrugged. "Often enough. Usually when the pack's alpha wants to retire or dies and there's nobody around to take charge."

"What if the alpha is alive and doesn't want to retire? Wouldn't the pack reject anyone else if they just come and try to impose themselves?"

"Not if they have strong ties inside the pack. They might convince the rest that the new alpha is better for all, especially if they do some macho shit like an official challenge."

Shifters did love their traditions. "Why risk that?" I had no doubt an official challenge would be harsh and bloody and take no prisoners, just like shifter justice.

"Who knows? Merge of assets? Real estate?"

The thought of someone taking over a pack just to sell their land shocked me. Paranormals should be better than that. I thought back on the twin joking around with the other shifter outside Clawstone Park. Surely, if one of the visiting alphas wanted to do a hostile takeover, they'd be a little more covert than that.

"You ever heard of the pack being dissatisfied with Hutton?" I asked.

Dru's eyebrows raised to the ceiling. "You think someone's trying to take over Hutton's pack? Did you hear anything when you went over there?"

Her doubtful tone was reassuring. I gestured toward the laptop. "Just curious with the whole alpha convention going on."

She thought for a moment, then shook her head. "Doubt it. The pack has a very strong history with Hutton and his father."

Wonderful news. Too bad Hutton probably wouldn't take her word on it and still insist on his potion.

"Are we done here?" Dru asked.

"Yep."

Instead of closing the browser right away, she backpedaled to the main page and went to find out the general consensus on the guy mad about his boyfriend's running buddy. She seemed to have accepted my excuse for asking about alpha hostile takeovers. Or didn't want to be involved, which was the smart choice.

I took out my phone and pretended to busy myself with it while I organized my thoughts.

From Dru's words, it seemed unlikely someone could waltz in and take over Hutton's territory without his pack being opposed to it, but I understood him wanting to keep up appearances in front of the other alphas.

As Dru had said, shifters and their macho shit.

Which meant that, paranoia about a takeover or not, Hutton would sink my ship to the bottom of the Mariana Trench if I didn't provide an alpha-power potion to him.

The couple stood to pay and leave, taking one of the candies with them. Hannah also used the opportunity to pay for her drinks and move on with her day.

"Thank you, and come back again," I exclaimed after them.

A cold breeze moved through the shop as the door closed, and I rubbed my arms with a shiver. It was getting colder, which was good news for a cozy tea shop, but bad news for my budget. I'd have to get long-sleeved tees printed with the logo and eventually bust out the heater. No central heating for this jewel of old architecture. If you wanted warmth, you'd have to fight for it, like in the old days.

I'd have to do my research like in the old days, too. The kind of spell I needed for Hutton's potion was not something you found online. For this kind of spell, I'd need some serious research.

Even if I used the willing blood of an alpha, Hutton couldn't simply up and drink someone's blood and be done with it—he was a shifter, not a vampire.

But first, I had to get the ledger from Ian so he didn't accidentally decode it and find his brother's name on the list of Bagley's clients. If he used the information against Hutton, I was a dead shop owner walking.

I checked the wall clock. Midday on a Thursday. At this time of day, Ian was likely still busy repairing someone's faucet with the help of the strays.

Which meant his house would be empty and open for someone to casually break in and take the ledger.

But no, that would raise questions. I'd ask for it like an adult, and he'd give it back because it wasn't his to keep. All I had to do was come up with a reasonable explanation to satisfy his curiosity, and I was nothing if not a well of excellent ideas.

I was in the process of diving deep into said well when thunder cracked the air. The sunshine-filled air.

Oh, Mother.

5

Dru looked up, surprised. "Huh?"

I slid toward the archway into the back. There was only one person who announced his presence with so much melodrama.

Brimstone and Destruction, fire mage and dark magic user, entered through the front door in all his tall, lean, elegantly dressed blond glory. He brought a young woman to stand in front of him.

"This is my niece," he intoned in his favorite truculent voice. "She needs a job."

Then he spun on his heel and left the shop.

Thunder reverberated outside, rattling the windowpanes.

We stood frozen like three deer who had barely missed being rolled over by a semi.

The young woman bit her lip and glanced down, then seemed to come to a sudden decision and looked back up, mouth firming with resolution. She appeared to be in her late teens—twenty at the most—dressed in a sweatshirt, jacket, and jeans. Her brown hair was gathered in a tail over one shoulder and fell in slight waves to her chest.

"Who was that?" Dru blurted out, breaking the awkward silence.

"Ah, uh, client." Clearing my head with a slight shake, I went around the counter to offer a smile and my hand to the young woman. "Hi," I said warmly. "I'm Hope."

She shook it hesitantly. "Hi. I'm Key."

How peculiar. "Key to what?"

Dru coughed a loud snort. The young woman's mouth drooped into a sad arc.

My brain blanked for a moment. *Oh.* A flush warmed my cheeks. "Welcome to the Tea Cauldron, Key."

Awkward.

Dru turned away from us, her shoulders shaking with barely restrained laughter.

The heat in my cheeks spread to my ears. "So you, uh, need a job?"

Key nodded, her gaze dropping again. "Uncle Jeremy said you could help me out."

"So you're a..." Witch or mage was my guess. Jeremy the fire mage wouldn't have dumped her here if she weren't part of the magical world.

"Earth mage," she muttered unhappily.

"Earth mage?" Hmm. What kind of job fit an earth mage? Sudden inspiration hit me. "Come with me."

I went into the back of the shop, down the hallway, and into the backyard. Once Key caught up, I pointed at the unruly grass, flagstone path, and wild weeds growing at the edges.

"Can you tell if there are any corpses buried there?" It paid to know when you lived in a murder house.

To her credit, Key didn't run and scream for the police. She studied the sad state of my backyard and wrung her hands nervously. "I'm not sure..."

"I'll pay you fifty bucks."

She rolled up her sleeves, went to the far corner of the yard, and knelt on the ground.

Dru walked up to me and whispered, "What the heck, Hope? You pay me a lot less."

"Independent contractors cost more."

Her eyes narrowed, and for a second, I thought she might strangle me and bury my body for Key to find.

Instead, she demanded in a harsh whisper, "What's going on? Who was that guy?"

It had been a naïve dream to expect I could keep the dark magic part of the business a secret from her now that she was working here. Fear of divulging my secret identity as a fake dark magic witch and getting the shop taken away had kept me from telling her the truth, even if I should've for her safety. But with Jeremy the mage putting my shop on the dark web for anyone to find, me being an actual good witch was a far better kept secret than Bagley's dark magic side business.

"So," I said, "it turns out Ms. Bagley sold dark magic."

Dru was unfazed. "Never liked the woman. Too perfect. And her cookies were too sugary."

I didn't have the heart to tell her Bagley's cookies had been chock full of dark magic, and she'd basically eaten blood pastry. "You know, people keep saying that, but when I first arrived here, everyone acted like she was goodness incarnate."

She shrugged. "Eh."

Over in the yard, Key dug her hands into the soil and bit her tongue, clearly concentrating on something. Not a whisper of magic clouded the air, but if we were to touch the ground with our bare skin, I was sure we would feel it coursing underneath us.

"What's the deal with her and the dude?" Dru tilted her head toward the young woman.

"The dude is a fire mage who used to be a client of

Bagley's." I told her about my idea of making placebo potions for the mage and how I'd ended up being listed as the new dark magic supplier in town.

"Show me," she urged all gleeful eagerness.

I opened the dark web marketplace listing on my phone, and she whistled.

"Damn. If only you had those reviews on the real shop."

If only. My public ratings and reviews were getting better, but they were a slow drip. I liked to think that, like coffee, the slower the drip, the greater the final product.

"And her uncle or whatever is a fire mage who uses your fake potions?" Dru asked.

"Yep." I made a face. "Crap."

"What?"

"If I don't help her out, he might take offense and make things difficult for me." What if he sold me out to the Council? Bye-bye shop. A familiar pang of anxiety stabbed my heart at the idea. How did people survive shop openings with so much stress involved? "I can't afford a third hire."

"Do you think she knows about the dark magic stuff? Does he expect you to teach the girl how to do dark magic or something?"

Good Mother Earth, I hoped not. "She probably knows, given who her uncle is, but better not to assume."

Dru watched Key move onto another patch of backyard with a thoughtful expression on her face. "You know, earth mages are supposed to be good with animals."

I'd read that too. Unlike my knowledge of shifters, my research on witches—spirit mages at their base—and other mages was up to date. "You don't think...?"

"Why not? Wilburn gave us until next week before he sells Dora and the carriage off. Hey, Key," she added in a louder voice. "You like horses?"

Key sat back on her heels and looked at us in surprise. "Sure."

"You're good with them?"

"Yeah, sure."

"Can you drive a carriage?"

"I... I guess?"

Dru gave me a look of triumph. "There's your third hire."

The idea was so genius I could've kissed her. Vicky, my former best friend and nightmare enemy, had operated a one-woman tour business in Olmeda that raked in the cash in tips. After her disappearance, the owner of the stables who rented her the carriage and mule had offered us the same deal. Unfortunately, neither of us was good at driving horses or giving tours. In fact, we were so awful, Wilburn had banned us from trying again and given us a one-week ultimatum before he gave Dora to the other tour business in town.

But if we could hire Key to do it for us... She would have a job, we would share some of the profits, and Jeremy the mage would be satisfied and not call the Council on me. Happiness all around! My favorite kind of ending.

"Do it," I told her.

Dru was already talking on the phone. When she was done, she told us, "Test drive tomorrow evening. Eight o'clock."

"I'll be here at seven thirty," Key promised. She stood and dusted off her jeans. "A few small bones—animals, I think—but no human corpses."

If I'd wanted a sign that good things were ahead, I didn't have to look any further.

———

Key left after getting paid, and Dru followed a little later—she had another part-time job lined up for the evening—but not before reminding me to watch my back with the whole dark magic thing.

"You told your assistant," a disembodied grandmotherly voice said with clear disapproval. "Always a mistake."

"Why?" I noticed a mug ring on the counter and grabbed the bottle of cleaner. "You told Vicky."

"And look where I ended up."

Dead at the bottom of her own stairs and now haunting the shop.

"Point taken." I sprayed the candy bowl with the cleaner in warning. "Don't even think of talking to her."

An outraged squeak filled the air, so I sprayed the bowl again.

"Child, I am not a cat!"

"More's the pity." I wiped the bowl, then got to work on the counter. If I had to be haunted by a talking evil entity, the least it could do was come in a cute, fluffy package.

"You better watch yourself," Bagley said darkly. "You never know when someone's going to stab you in the back."

"I don't think Dru's going to resort to shoving me down the stairs, Ms. Bagley."

"We all have our secrets. When it comes down to it, you can't count on anyone's loyalty."

"Speaking of loyalty, how many local clients did you have?"

"You tell me. You stole my ledger." Her voice sweetened. "Would you like to know how to decode it?"

I sure would. Unfortunately, Bagley would want my soul in exchange for the answer. "No need. All codes fall to someone smarter than the encoder."

"Ah, it burns!"

I glanced at the bowl. It stood in all its clean, proud woodenhood.

"My pride, child. My pride. I take your words to mean you're not trying to decode it yourself?"

Grabbing the bowl, I went into the back.

"Don't dish it if you can't ta—"

Bagley's voice disappeared the moment I stepped through the bead curtain.

"Blessed silence," I muttered, bringing the bowl into the kitchen.

A series of strange gurgling pipe noises greeted my entrance. Ian had promised to check my pipes at some point, but by now I was reasonably sure my goldfish ghost theory was correct.

The idea of having my own pet, ghost or not, made a sudden yearning constrict my chest.

I missed Fluffy something fierce. Ian's dog was always so happy, being around her was a true cleansing of the soul. Whatever haunted my pipes appeared friendly enough, don't get me wrong, but its options for petting were limited to the kitchen faucet and the upstairs bathroom.

Taking out my phone, I dialed Ian.

"Hope," he answered, curt as usual.

"Are you going to be home for dinner?" I asked. I'd get to pet Fluffy and get the ledger back before Ian had a chance to decode it and find out his brother had been one of Bagley's clients—a two-for-one special. The best kind of deal.

A pause ensued. Then, "Yes."

"Great. I'll be there. Nine thirty?"

"No, it's two twenty-three."

"Ha-ha. Don't stand me up or Fluffy will be mad," I warned.

"We wouldn't want that," he said dryly.

"Indeed."

I hung up and returned to the shop. Weekdays' early afternoons were always a bit of a lull, so I used the free time to search for local car rental places. Serious research of magic spells meant a library specialized in magic, which meant I was going to have to go to Montel and pay the Council offices a visit. Dru could open in the morning, so it wasn't as much of a loss as the last time I'd had to go to the Council on a weekday.

The last time I'd made the trip to Montel I had nearly gotten murdered on the way back, so, hopefully, the day would also end very differently.

By the time I arrived at Ian's on my Vespa, Cavalier Repairs & Renovations's white van was pulling in through the private gate of the cemetery. I drove behind it and parked by the main house. The van came to a stop by the garage on the side, and Ian's strays jumped out. They greeted me with a wave as they walked to the back to start unloading.

Both about twenty years old, the taller one, Shane, had short, dark hair and olive skin and sported an eye patch while Alex looked like your stereotypical surfer dude—all grins and bleached shoulder-length hair—although I had an inkling the hair thing was more him trying to emulate Ian than anything beach-related.

Young shifters who hadn't found a place with a pack were considered strays. Usually, strays moved around quite a bit, but Shane and Alex had chosen to stay in Olmeda, and Ian had chosen to give them jobs.

For someone who wanted nothing to do with shifter packs, Ian was doing a poor job of not surrounding himself with his own tiny pack.

The front door of the two-story brick-and-gables house opened, and a white blur of fluff and happy barks hurried my way.

"Fluffy," I exclaimed and crouched to give her a well-deserved greeting. "You got a haircut!" Her coat had been cropped and shone in bright shades of white.

Ian watched from the threshold, arms crossed and one shoulder leaning against the door frame, dressed in his usual all-black. He looked big and solid and dangerous and warm and he almost made me forget why I was here or how my shop-owning, pillar-of-the-community dream was, once more, in danger of being destroyed. Rufus stood by his side, deigning to greet me with a single woof.

"Good evening." I lifted a bag. "I brought takeout." At Ian's unimpressed look, I added, "Don't worry. There's some homemade stuff in there too."

He eyed the bag. "That's not going to be enough."

With a flourish, I opened the seat compartment of the Vespa and produced a second bag. "Ta-da!"

Ian huffed but couldn't stop a smile. "Get in before that gets any colder."

Grinning, I went up the steps and into the house. A real, lived-in house, not the cold shell of Hutton's residence. For a loner, Ian's home looked like a full family lived inside. An outsider might blame the strays, but they lived elsewhere in town.

"You like my living room?" Ian asked from the entrance into the kitchen.

With a start, I realized I'd stopped in the middle of the room, studying everything with a satisfied smile on my face— the comfy sofa, the low glass table covered with coasters and old architecture magazines, the big fireplace, the dog toys strewn around. The fact that Bagley's ledger wasn't in plain sight didn't deter me one bit. What kind of bounty hunter would he be if he left that kind of stuff lying around?

Getting him to return the ledger wouldn't be hard. Doing it without him getting curious was the tricky part.

"It's very cozy," I said. "What's not to like?" By my side, Fluffy yipped and wagged her tail in agreement.

"As you keep reminding me..." Ian pointed toward the fireplace and what lay beyond—the actual cemetery.

"Oh, yeah, that." I gave the room one last longing glance before walking up to him. "I suppose one could learn to compartmentalize living in a cemetery. Out of sight, out of mind?"

He gave me an odd look. "If you say so."

I, too, wasn't sure why I was trying to talk myself into living right next to a bunch of graves. It wasn't like I was buying his house or looking to rent a room.

We stepped into the kitchen, which was as spacious and cozy as the living room. The main centerpiece was a huge wooden table, and I put the bags of food on top. A big bag with a local Mexican food place logo was already there.

"Aw, you brought extras?" I shook my head in mock disappointment. "No faith."

"I don't know what you're talking about. That's breakfast."

"Breakfast for dinner?" I clapped my hands. "My favorite!"

A boyish grin took over his face, instantly transforming his expression from harsh and forbidding into charming and playful. It lasted for about two heartbeats before the shields slammed down again.

If I were to be honest with myself, I lived for those two heartbeats.

I busied myself unpacking the bags as I silently reminded myself of another of my favorite affirmations: accept your weaknesses, forgive yourself, and move on.

Well, maybe not the "move on" part. I was quite happy where I stood.

The strays burst in through the back door, their faces alighting at the sight of all the food covering the table. Even Shane's usually stern features took an edge of wonder.

"Awesome," Alex said. He grabbed plates from a cupboard

while Shane got a bunch of cutlery from one of the drawers. They made loud clinking noises as he dropped them on the table before picking up a plate.

Ian glared at them.

"Right." Shane put the plate down. "Sorry, boss."

They moved to the sink and washed their hands. I covered my mouth to hide my amusement.

Ian sent me a withering glare.

"Yes, boss," I said obediently and joined the strays at the sink. They smelled of sweat and dust, and I didn't mind one bit. It was hard to be put off by so much energy and enthusiasm.

I felt right at home.

We sat at the table and distributed the food, Alex sitting by my side and Shane and Ian on the opposite side, Shane's good eye facing us. Fluffy whined and pawed at my leg until I allowed her to sit on my lap.

"Gross," Shane commented. "Gonna get dog hair everywhere on your food."

I buried my face in Fluffy's soft warmth. "Worth it. Oh," I suddenly remembered, "I saw one of your shifter friends at Clawstone Park this morning."

Alex bit into a garlic knot from my favorite Italian place. "Impossible. Shane has no friends."

Shane could do some amazing single-eyed glares, but he didn't bother this time. "Not in the pack." He took a piece of cooked chicken and fed it to Rufus.

"You visited the pack?" Ian asked in a bland voice. His green gaze was fixed on me as he lifted a forkful of lasagna to his mouth with unerring aim. I couldn't help but be impressed—now, *that* was skill.

"Had to deliver some potions. Looks like they're busy with alphacon."

Shane and Alex stared at me blankly for a second, then laughed.

"Alphacon," Alex repeated. "They should put that on T-shirts."

Not a bad idea. I worried my lip, working out the logistics in my head. The shifters could carry them in their sport equipment stores and I'd get a cut of the profits. Not a lot, because there was no way they'd give me a favorable deal, but if we got them done fast, it might sell enough to the paranormal community to get us a tidy sum.

"No." Ian shoved another forkful of lasagna into his mouth.

"No?" I asked sweetly.

"Forget about T-shirts. The shifters won't go for it."

"Boss's right," Shane said. "They don't like other people nosing into their business."

I arched my eyebrows and focused on my plate, choosing not to say anything. If the shifters wanted their potions, they'd better be open to any future cooperation ventures, Hutton's pending potion or not.

"They're assholes," Alex agreed.

"They seemed nice," I said. Except for their alpha, but that wasn't the other shifters' fault. I glanced at Ian and found him studying me. Oh, no. I didn't trust the speculation in his eyes. "It's a nice place they got there."

"Oh?" he said.

"Don't worry, I like yours much better."

He snorted and reached for his beer. Alex let out a *duh*. Shane fed Rufus more food.

I took some of Shane's chicken and fed it to Fluffy. She lapped at my fingers happily, and I melted into the chair. Goodness, but she was cute and the room cheerful and the company excellent and I never wanted to leave.

Unfortunately, I was here to do a job.

The future of my dreams might just depend on it.

"In fact," I said, "I'm sure your place would look even better covered in Halloween decorations."

Alex studied the kitchen thoughtfully. "She's right, boss. We should put up stuff this year."

"No," said the boss.

"What's more," I continued, "it'd be the best-looking place in town if you also decorated the graves."

"No."

"It's the perfect mood, really. Imagine all those tilting headstones and the weeping trees illuminated at just the right angle with just the right color."

"No."

I opened my arms, as if the gift of my idea was all but bursting out of my chest to make its way across the table. "Heck, you might as well open the gates and lead the townspeople on tours so they can appreciate all the grandness of this place."

6

SHANE CHOKED on his food and sputtered. Alex began laughing loudly. Fluffy jumped off my lap and began doing laps.

Ian leveled me with a flat stare. "Nice try. No."

My mouth drooped at the corners. "Aw. I'm sure Shane and Alex would love the opportunity to play Garreth the Hound."

The two strays fell abruptly silent; their heads snapped toward Ian.

"That might be cool, boss," Alex said in a hopeful voice.

"We still have time to work something out," Shane agreed. "Order in some lights and stuff."

Ian's glare promised retribution. I chuckled silently, malevolently, letting him see my evil glee in all its glory.

"I'll think about it," he muttered.

I hid my grin and ate some more food. "Do these alphacons last long?"

"Dunno," Alex said. "I wasn't here for the last one."

Shane shrugged when I glanced his way. "I don't remember. Couple of weeks?"

That wasn't too bad. Surely, I could come up with something to tide Hutton over for that long. Maybe not a potion to infuse him with alpha power, but one to extend and augment what was already there. In fact, that had probably been Bagley's trick—direct alpha power for the first few times, then a steady dose of maintenance potions. Would've been cheaper for her that way while still charging full price.

As if Hutton had been reading my mind, my phone dinged with a text from him. I gave it a fast glance and frowned in irritation.

Is my order ready yet?

How fast did he think magic potions of this caliber took to make? They weren't fast food. I answered with a curt *No*. Then rethought my approach—wouldn't be good to make a man capable of sinking my shop too mad—and made it a *Not yet*.

"Why are you so interested in the shifters?" Ian asked.

I returned my attention to the table and tried to appear nonchalant. "Just curious. There wasn't a paranormal community where I used to live. This is all new to me."

"No shifters?" Shane asked.

"None that I knew of."

"Sucks," Alex put in.

Now that I'd lived in Olmeda for over a month, I had to agree. Things were a lot more interesting here than back home, where I only had myself and the witch forums to entertain me, magically speaking.

"Do you think one of the visiting alphas will try to recruit you?" I asked the two young men. The possibility hadn't occurred to me until now. Opposite from me, Ian tensed.

Alex waved that aside, unconcerned. "No way."

Shane snorted. "Who would want us?"

I threw a gnocchi at his face, making him jump.

"You define your own worth," I said sternly. "Nobody else's opinion matters. Choose a path befitting who you know your-self to be, not who others say you are."

And that, as my bathroom mirror could attest, worked like a charm.

They both grinned. "Sure, boss."

I didn't relent. "And...?"

Shane made a face but answered dutifully, "We're worth a pile of gold, and it's their loss."

"Yeah, screw them," Alex agreed. "We don't want them, anyway."

I nodded with approval. Not that they needed it or my advice—they weren't my children—but it was good to remind them of this lesson. Many a breakdown had been avoided with this line of thinking.

For once, Ian wasn't looking at me, but the half smile curving his lips warmed my insides all the same.

Shane stood, wiping his mouth with one of the paper napkins. "Thanks for the food. We're off."

Alex followed suit. "Yeah, thanks."

"Are you sure?" I asked, sad to see them go in spite of my mission. The dinner had been fun. "There's tiramisu in the fridge."

"Ooh." Alex made to sit again, but Shane planted a heavy hand on his shoulder.

"We're *leaving*." He jutted his chin at me and Ian.

Alex stared at us for a moment, then comprehension dawned. "*Ooh*." He shrugged off Shane's hand and pushed him playfully toward the back door. "You owe me dessert."

"Whatever."

Once the back door closed behind them, I dared a glance at Ian. He appeared unfazed by the strays' inference that we wanted time alone. If he wasn't going to feel awkward about it, then I wouldn't either. But my heartbeat sped up at the thought of being alone with him nonetheless. Being in his kitchen felt a lot different from being out in some random small restaurant or the confines of his car.

This felt homey, like we'd done this a dozen times already. Like it was dessert time, then we'd catch up on some show, then we'd go upstairs to sleep in the same bed. In each other's arms.

I couldn't decide if the idea was ridiculous, or not outlandish at all.

To cover my internal debate, I retrieved the tiramisu container from the fridge and distributed two generous servings.

"How come the strays don't live here?" I asked, searching for something to focus on other than sleeping in the same bed, in each other's arms. Camp *why not?* was gaining an edge, and I didn't want to get distracted. The dinner had been wonderful, but my respite was over—I'd come here for the ledger without making Ian suspicious, and I needed all my wits to succeed.

"This is their workplace, not a shifter dormitory," he said wryly.

Ah, the last vestiges of resistance at admitting he had his own pack. How adorable. "Whatever helps you sleep at night."

He scowled. "What does that mean?"

"Nothing. But..."

"But?"

"Maybe you should attend alphacon. Get some tips for the future."

He used his spoon to flick some tiramisu at me.

"Hey," I exclaimed. "Food goes in, not out." I scooped the glob of mousse with my finger and licked it clean because I have no shame.

Ian harrumphed but kept the rest of his dessert to himself. "Had any run-ins with any of Bagley's clients lately?"

Did he know about Brimstone and Destruction's visit this morning? Until I got the situation with Key figured out, I probably shouldn't tell him. Besides, the mage hadn't asked for dark magic, only some nepotism.

"I got a message through the dark web listing a few days ago," I said. "But it was spam."

Ian's spoon paused halfway to his mouth. "Spam?"

"Ten high quality, verified reviews for under two hundred dollars." Which was a complete robbery. I could buy twenty thousand social media followers for that much.

"What's the world coming to?" Dry amusement filled his tone.

I pointed my spoon at him. "Exactly."

"Nothing else aside from that?"

Just Hutton dumping the future of his alphaness along with the future of my shop in my lap.

"Not a peep," I said with as much indifference as I could summon. My lower back began to feel unusually sweaty.

"Are you sure?"

I met his gaze steadily, praying that my eyes were not windows into my thoughts. "Very sure. I'd know if someone had come asking around for dark magic, wouldn't I?"

He sent me a knowing look. "Would you?"

"Low blow." My cheeks warmed. "How was I to know people were asking for dark magic?" It had taken me a couple of clients to figure out Bagley had been a dark magic dealer. "Everyone kept saying Bagley was a saint."

"I knew she wasn't," he said matter-of-factly.

"Too bad you didn't tell me." The reminder made some lingering resentment rise inside my chest and erase the trepidation about not revealing Hutton's problems nesting there. I still hadn't completely forgiven Ian for suspecting me of being a dark magic witch. The duality of man meant I could both enjoy spending time with him in his kitchen and be unreasonably angry at him for not magically knowing I was a good egg. And since I wasn't a man, I could also throw keeping stuff from him into the mix. The triality of witchhood.

As if sensing the slight souring of my mood, he changed topics. "Did you find out anything interesting at Clawstone?"

Talk about a loaded question. "They play rock, paper, scissors to figure out who gets to play Garreth during Halloween."

"No."

"I wasn't even thinking about it," I exclaimed with a laugh. "*And* you told Shane and Alex you'd consider it."

His gaze strayed to the wide windows of the kitchen. They faced the garage and back lawn, now covered in darkness. "I don't want strangers roaming everywhere."

"It wouldn't be everywhere." I imagined the cemetery as it could be in all its Halloween splendor. "There would be marked paths and a guide. We could research some of the oldest graves, find out if anyone interred here did something creepy. Or make stories up."

"I'm sure the dead would love that."

"They might. You never know. They could be hanging around waiting for something to entertain them." I leaned in and added in a conspiratorial whisper, "If you want, I could do some spells, see if any spirit has stuck around."

"And have them haunt me like your ghosts? No, thank you."

I thought of Bagley and the goldfish and any other haunting that had yet to make themselves known. "You make a good point. Have you decoded the ledger yet?"

A fast blink of his eyes betrayed his whiplash at the change of topic, and I ate the last bit of tiramisu with unconcealed relish. Getting a reaction out of Ian had fast turned into a favorite pastime.

"Not yet." Finished with his dessert as well, he leaned back in his chair and scratched behind Rufus's ears, who had come to lean his head on his lap. Fluffy had taken over the big dog's bed, resting from a very exciting day of zooming around.

"I want to give the code a shot," I said. After much brainstorming, I'd decided this would be the most realistic excuse for getting the ledger back.

"Oh?"

"I found some hints about it. In the shop."

"I thought you burned everything from the witch."

"There was a hidden compartment at the bottom of the counter." I'd briefly considered going for the good old "compartment under the floorboards" but that might've been a tad too cliche. Bound to arouse instant suspicion. "It held a few papers. I think one was a reminder of the code."

"Why would she need a reminder?"

"Too many evil deeds to keep track of in her head? She was getting old."

"Are you lying to me?"

"I would never." And if my face didn't reflect the absolute deer-in-the-headlights feeling in my head at his sudden slam of a question, it would be an utter miracle. "Okay," I amended, because, *Really, Hope? I would never?* "I would totally lie to you, but I really think I found something that might help decode the ledger."

Not a full lie, I told myself. If I figured out which line or lines in the ledger belonged to Hutton, that'd go a long way to deciphering the rest of the names and transactions.

"You didn't make some kind of deal with the witch, did you, Hope?"

There was a dark, sly edge to his tone that made my skin prickle with awareness. Thankfully, this question I could answer with all honesty. "No."

"Are you sure she's not offering you something for the

code? We don't need the names on that ledger. They're just a bonus."

"I'm not stupid, Ian," I told him seriously. "I know you're worried I might fall into her evil clutches, but I'm good. You don't need to mother me."

He muttered something under his breath, then said, "I don't think you're stupid, but I know how much you want the shop to succeed."

"It'll succeed without Bagley."

"Of course it will."

The assurance in his tone took me by surprise. A slow smile spread across my lips. "Aww. You care."

He rolled his eyes. "I'll come around tomorrow with the ledger. I'll bring Fluffy."

Fluffy emitted a soft, sleepy yip at the mention of her name.

"I should get it now. I'm driving to Montel tomorrow."

"On the deathtrap?" His tone was a mix of incredulity and bone-deep resignation that made me want to laugh as much as filled me with outrage for my poor Vespa.

"Don't insult Bee-Bee. She's a good girl."

"Bee-Bee? Christ."

"What? Says the man who called his dogs Fluffy and Rufus. Plus, Bumblebee was taken."

Rufus woofed.

I pointed at the giant, shaggy black dog. "See? He agrees. Anyway, I'm not taking Bee-Bee. I'm renting a car."

"Take the SUV."

I shivered at the memory of what had happened the last time I'd borrowed someone's car to go to Montel. "I'm good."

"If you take the SUV, you could take Fluffy. I have a dog seat."

Fluffy again, and I almost gave in. She'd make the trip a lot more fun, and I bet everyone at the Council building would absolutely adore her. Unfortunately, in this, I needed to stay strong.

Ian was turning into a great ally—was turning into my favorite person to have around—but I needed to stay independent.

"I'll rent a car," I said with finality.

He acknowledged my decision with a curt nod and didn't try to change my mind. A few minutes later, he left the kitchen and returned with the ledger. I eyed it with distaste but took a hold of it gladly, enjoying the sudden release of tension. I had it. No chance of him accidentally learning about his brother.

"You'll let me know if you decipher it?" he asked.

"Of course."

He sent me an amused glance that told me he was aware I was keeping things from him, and I answered with an arch of my eyebrows that dared him to doubt me.

"You know," he said as he and Rufus and Fluffy accompanied me and the Vespa to the gate. "I'm running low on memory potions."

The question of why a man who never shifted needed memory potions faded into the surge of pleasure that rose at his words. By his own admission, he'd never used Bagley for his potions—for good reason.

That he was trusting me with them...well, he might as well have gone down on his knees and pledged his devotion.

"I'll get some to you ASAP," I told him happily. So happily I almost lifted onto my tiptoes to kiss his cheek.

Maybe he expected that, too, because he leaned down the merest bit.

Instead, I patted his arm. "I'll text you."

His hand found its way to mine, and he squeezed lightly.

"Come back for dinner anytime," he said.

A growing lump in my throat made me unable to speak, so I

simply returned the squeeze of his warm, warm, so very nice hand and got ready to leave. He watched me put on the helmet, start the Vespa, and drive away.

I was going to make him the best memory potions ever.

After I figured out how to make Hutton's before he decided to blame me for his lack of power and destroyed my shop-owning dreams.

7

CLOUDS DIMMED the exuberance of the early morning sunlight, but they didn't sour my enthusiasm as I sang along to the radio on my way to Montel. Sure, seeing Ian again to borrow his SUV would've been great, but I bet the inside of his car didn't smell nearly as wonderful as my independence.

I really needed to stop relying on the man so much.

Montel wasn't the tourist trap Olmeda was, but that didn't mean it didn't have its charms. The Council had taken over an old square brick building in the business area, looking more like a library than the offices of a secret paranormal group.

I showed my Council ID to the guard at the entrance, and she allowed me into one of the elevators. It felt good to be here on my own accord rather than because my shop was doing so badly I'd been called in. Things truly did improve if given enough time and nurturing—me and the shop, me and the magical community, me and...Bagley's dark magic business.

Win some, lose some.

The man in charge of the Council's archives smiled in recognition at the sight of me.

"Miss Avery, back again," he said warmly.

"Hello there," I answered happily, undeterred by the fact that I didn't remember his name.

"How can I help you today?"

As an official witch shop owner, I had access to the special bookshelf, where the higher-end research was kept under lock and key. Shop-owning witches like me had the justification of needing access to potentially dangerous spells and potions to satisfy the needs of our clients. Spells and potions that would otherwise be unavailable other than for pre-approved research purposes—a whole other level in the witch hierarchy.

Fleetingly, I wondered if there was a dark magic library somewhere where dark magic shop owners and scholars had access to the evil counterpart of this bookshelf, or if the whole dark magic business was more of an underground spellbook trade. But I couldn't see witches like Bagley willingly sharing their evil discoveries. What if another witch used them to steal their business?

The librarian—Dave, as it turned out—loaded me up with books pertinent to blood magic, power variants, and shifter magic. I brought them to one of the tables and settled in for my research.

All the hours spent in careful online research had left me wholly unprepared for the realities of physical tomes. I ran out of things to use as bookmarks fast, and all the referencing back and forth gave me a slight headache. I hadn't brought a notebook for my notes, as that would be too easy to discover and read accidentally, and inputting things into my phone was a lot more tedious than expected.

I gave up after a while and simply read on, going for information absorption rather than trying to remember everything.

There were no spells or potion recipes listed, but the book on shifter magic had some interesting research about alphas' power origins. Someone had tried to trace different alpha family ancestries to see if they had a common ancestor—they didn't—then had theorized there might be an intelligent design component to it, and shifter magic created new alphas if it sensed there weren't enough to account for all shifters in the world. A sort of linked system, not quite as strict as a beehive, but strong enough to sense the shifter community's needs.

An interesting read, but sadly useless for me.

The tome on blood magic was a little more useful. I had a feeling whoever had written it had been a low-key dark magic user. There were *don't try it at home* warnings all over the pages, but also a strange kind of gleefulness to the way the blood experiments were described that turned my stomach and made me want to wash my hands with bleach.

Definitely no licking of my fingertips to help flip the pages.

The book had an entire section for non-mages' blood experiments, and I reluctantly browsed through the pages, peeping through my fingers as if it were a scary movie. The author had found no real difference in using blood from different paranormal creatures, which was good for me, as it meant I might be able to do the potion with my blood if blood was needed. The book then went into a long-winded vent about how other creatures' blood could help *you*, the witch reader.

I would bet the shop this had been one of Bagley's favorite research tomes.

The book on power variants was focused on the differences among mages—spirit, air, earth, water, and fire—and didn't mention shifters at all. Still, I skimmed some parts, hoping for some inspiration about maintaining a fading power.

After a couple of hours, however, it became clear that researching this potion on my own was going to take a lot more time than I had if Hutton's fears about his leadership's fate were correct. And even if I read every book on the special shelf, I might still need extra help. The kind of potion Hutton needed required an expertise beyond my knowledge. Sure, I could test different things—and the books *had* given me some ideas—but I doubted Hutton would spend a week sitting in my kitchen patiently waiting for the next batch of *maybe this time* potions.

More likely he'd burn my world down and use me as an excuse to try to save his.

I closed the books and brought them back to Dave.

And, like every good shop manager, I delegated.

"Experts on power magic?" Dave repeated.

"They don't have to be local," I said. "Anyone you can think of?"

"I might have some names. Give me a moment."

He sat behind the counter and began typing on his computer. My attention drifted off to the shelves and the half-filled cart by the side. Most of the information kept here was on the document files and journals' side rather than books, and it made for a rather monochromatic view.

"Got a name for you," Dave said excitedly.

"Great." I brought out my phone.

"Valenti. She's one of the top researchers in the field. I'm sure she can help you with whatever you need." He grew thoughtful. "I think we've lent her books by mail in the past."

A twitch developed in my cheek. Lilian Valenti. A name I was familiar with from my disastrous witch internship days. She was a friend of *oh-call-me-Tammy* (and what are you waiting for, go fetch my coffee), my ex-boss. A boss who had taught me zero about being a witch, zero about doing magic, and negative numbers about the paranormal world at large.

She had, however, taught me a lot about the wonders of caffeinated beverages and the insides of a coffee shop, so perhaps I wasn't giving her enough credit. The knowledge had come in handy after all.

"Do you want her number?" Dave asked.

With an internal shake of my head, I refocused on the present. "Yes, please."

Valenti might not remember me, but perhaps I could use my internship under her dearest friend Tammy as a way to get her attention. Surely not all witches would be as bad as Tammy where sharing information was concerned.

Dave got me her contact number from the Council's directory and I saved it on my phone.

"Anything else?" he asked, a note of hope in his voice.

A note I recognized—working alone could get lonely. Online chats could only do so much.

"How much do you know about the local packs?"

"Olmeda's?"

"No packs in Montel?"

"None officially registered."

Once this whole alpha problem was solved, I would do my local paranormals' research, I swore to myself. If I was to be the community witch, I needed to be better informed of the entire area, not just Olmeda. "So there's only Hutton's pack?"

"Close by? Yeah. Good people. We never get complaints about them."

But then, why would they? The pack were shifters, not witches. If anyone were to get complaints about them, it'd be...

"What about the local bounty hunter guild? I know there's a bounty hunter in Olmeda."

"Cavalier." Dave nodded solemnly, and I was surprised Ian's fame had reached this far. Surprised, and exceedingly curious.

"You know him?"

Dave leaned in, and I automatically bent down to hear what he wanted to whisper.

"I should warn you about him."

"Warn me?"

"There are rumors about him. We haven't received any complaints about him yet, but he's got a *history*."

I leaned both elbows on the counter, fascinated. "A history?"

Dave licked his lips as if Ian's history was so awful a time-dimension hole might open up and swallow him whole if he spoke about it. I couldn't wait to hear this.

"He's a loner."

I wanted to snort. That went to show how little people knew about him.

"Not by choice." Dave's gaze grew intense. "He's apparently so dangerous even other bounty hunters leave him alone. The pack wants nothing to do with him either."

My reaction must've been less shocked than expected, because he rushed to add, "That's not all."

"It's not?" I widened my eyes in invitation for him to elaborate.

"He killed his partner, so now nobody wants to work with him."

Ian had built himself quite the reputation around these parts. I was impressed. Maybe he would give me pointers if I asked nicely. "He was charged with the murder?"

Dave frowned. "They're bounty hunters."

And bounty hunters, like shifters, took care of their own problems. I didn't want to point out that if Ian actually had been guilty of killing his partner, he wouldn't be around frolicking in the streets of Olmeda but would be either dead or deader—from what I understood, bounty hunters weren't big on long jail sentences.

"Thank you, Dave. I'll make sure to keep an eye on him."

An unnatural urge to giggle rose within me. Dave wouldn't understand, though. He thought Ian was a walking warning sign. He didn't know about Fluffy and Rufus and the strays and

Ian's harsh face and green eyes and how keeping an eye on him was really no trouble at all. It was, in fact, something I looked forward to.

"Be safe," he said, all seriousness.

I wondered if he'd given Bagley the same warning. "I will."

The elevator doors dinged open, and Emily Doyle stepped out, slightly winded.

"Ah, you're still here, Miss Avery. Good, good."

A shiver of unease ran down my spine. Doyle was in charge of overseeing the Tea Cauldron's progress during my six-month probation period. The fact that she was glad to see I was "still here" didn't bode well.

"Did you need something, Ms. Doyle?" I asked cautiously.

"Just wanted to catch up." She waved my concerns aside and walked up to the counter. "Since you're here and all."

Dave stood and disappeared into the shelves. Doyle looked me up and down, a smile of satisfaction curving her lips.

I relaxed. Things couldn't be too bad if she was smiling like that.

"I was quite happy to see some of those nasty reviews were deleted," she said with approval.

"Me too." It had taken several emails back and forth with the site administrators, but it had been a battle worth fighting. Vicky might've met an early end, but her campaign of sabotaging the shop had lingered behind.

No longer.

"I noticed a few new good reviews coming in," she added.

"We've gained some repeat customers," I told her proudly. "With the weather turning colder, I think we'll do brisk business."

"Excellent." She paused, as if collecting her thoughts. "How's Mr. Lewis's assistant working out?"

While I didn't have to report on the day-to-day business of

the shop, I'd erred on the side of caution and told her about hiring Dru. After the shop's rough start, I wanted nothing else to blemish my reputation with the Council.

Vicky's incident had hit home how much I wanted to keep my shop, and how badly others might want to take it from me. As far as official Council witch shops went, witches might as well be piranhas circling for a bite, myself included. And now that I had my chunk of meat, I was loath to let it go.

As Grandma liked to say, you can only do your best with what you have. The rest is out of your tiny fishy teeth.

Paraphrasing.

"Dru is working out great," I said. Doyle had had her doubts about the wisdom of spending the extra money, but I'd convinced her that having a part-time hire would help a lot as the shop got busier, especially someone already established in the local paranormal community. It'd make everyone feel more welcome.

"So sad to hear about Mr. Lewis's passing," Doyle said. "Such an upstanding man."

"Yes. So sad." As sad as me winning the lottery. "Such a nice man. What a pity about his shop. From all I've heard, it was such a staple in the community."

Doyle nodded. "It had an excellent reputation."

"It's too bad it's going to the bank." I gave her a hopeful look. "Can't the Council do anything about it?" The bank might not think much of Dru and her attempts at buying it from them, but she might have a better chance if the Council was involved and a witch backed her. Even if the witch was me.

Doyle scoffed. "Are you thinking of annexing it to the shop?" She shook her head. "No. It's too soon to consider an expansion. Even if the Council could afford the money, which I doubt, setting up a shop is not cheap, and adding the construction expense if you want to merge the two buildings? We're talking about a considerable budget. If that's even possible in Olmeda. They are very stringent with construction permits in the old neighborhoods. We would have to get approval from different associations, the city hall, and possibly an expert in the area's buildings before we could even begin to think about consulting architects for the project. No, no. First, you need to concentrate on passing your probation. Things might be going better right now, but it hasn't been two months. Focus on your shop as it is now, Miss Avery. Any other plans can wait."

I felt like a train had just run me over and I wasn't even on the tracks. "No, no. I don't want to expand." And that was the honest truth. I was happy with my little witch shop. I didn't need to run a big cafe or entertain a hundred customers at a time; I only needed to be a dependable nook for paranormals and normal humans alike. A small haven from the world outside and the depressing realities of life.

"I was only thinking that it would be nice if the shop could stay within the paranormal community," I continued. "I know Druscilla would love to take over, and she has the experience. She was working for Mr. Lewis for years." A fact Dru liked to bring up whenever she got worked up about his betrayal. "She'd be perfect to keep the Corner Rose alive."

Doyle pursed her lips, then shook her head again. "There is nothing we can do, unfortunately. It's not a Council building and nobody would approve spending the money when there are so many other Council matters that require our support."

"What if they bought the building, then sold it to Druscilla?"

"We're not a real estate firm."

For an important, influential witch, they might be, but not for me or my demon friend. They weren't to blame—that was the way organizations ran.

"Thank you for considering it, Ms. Doyle."

Her expression softened, and in her flowing floral dress, knit cardigan, and loose whitening hair, I could see in her an image of Grandma, the blurred lines of her smiling face in my memories, that is. The ones fading more and more with each year. "You have a good heart, Hope. But that's only a small part of running a shop. Don't let it stand in the way of smart business decisions."

Sound advice, more up my sister's alley than Grandma's, but appreciated all the same.

I thanked her and was about to say my goodbyes when she stopped me.

"One more thing."

"Yes?"

"We received a call earlier this morning from Olmeda's pack."

My smile froze. As did the rest of me. "I see."

"The pack leader has requested a meeting next Tuesday as part of their ongoing leader meetings. Your shop was brought up."

Truly, it was a miracle I could hear her with all the alarms blaring inside my head. "In a good way, I'm sure. The shifters love my memory potions."

"I was thinking it'd be a good idea if I dropped by for a visit since I will be in town," she continued, ignoring my words.

"That'd be wonderful." Wonderfully annoying. I kept the shop in order, and I had no question Bagley would stay silent, since the Council would burn the building down if they knew about the whole dark magic thing, but who knew what Hutton might insinuate to her? And if she talked to Sonia, it might get even worse. "I will see you next week, then."

Once outside, I brought out my phone and dialed Hutton.

"You called the Council?" I demanded the moment the call opened.

He chuckled. A dark, evil sound that made me want to stab him with a butter knife. "Just a little incentive, since you're dragging your feet."

"It's only been a day!"

"It should've been done weeks ago. You have until next week or you're done."

He ended the call, and I seethed all the way to where I'd parked the rental car. Oh, Hutton would get his potion, and I hoped it choked him on the way down.

Before getting started on the way back, I gave Lilian Valenti, the blood magic expert, a call. It went to voice mail, so I left a message identifying myself and my business.

If the witch was anything like Tammy, the chances of her returning my call were minimal, no matter how urgent I labeled the situation.

But one could always hope.

8

I MADE it back to Olmeda right in time for Key's carriage test. The drive went smoothly, with no major traffic jams and nobody trying to run me off the road or otherwise maul my lovely flesh.

It really improved my mood.

Key and I made our way to Wilburn's. I loved this about the old neighborhoods of Olmeda, how you could have a block of narrow houses fighting for space followed by a park or a chunk of forest. The stables were conveniently located near two parks, but they mostly did their business from the tours, as Wilburn reminded me the moment we arrived.

Wilburn didn't care who used the animals as long as they were used and he got paid for it, and for the last couple of weeks nobody had.

A lot less asinine than it sounds, I promise.

The man had Dora ready to go. Key cooed over her, introducing herself and offering a piece of apple, then running her hands down the mule's neck.

"She's beautiful," she told Wilburn with a shy smile.

"That, she is." The man checked Key's driving license and snapped, "Let's hop to it."

Key and I exchanged glances. Wilburn wasn't exactly warmth incarnate, but maybe—

He slapped the side of the red carriage. "C'mon people. I don't have all night."

"All right, all right," I muttered, getting on the second-row bench. Key climbed onto the first—the driver's bench—and Wilburn sat heavily on the last row.

"For the test drive, you don't need to fake giving the tour since you don't have a permit yet," Wilburn said. "Keep your eyes on the road until you get used to it. Don't twist to talk to us. Have you driven a carriage alongside cars before?"

Key shook her head. "Not in the city, sir."

Wilburn made a sound of displeasure. "It's not hard. Pretend it's a really slow car and ignore any assholes who honk at you. Dora's used to it, so don't worry about her."

"Yes, sir."

They looked at each other for a few more silent moments until Wilburn arched his brows and barked, "Let's go, let's go."

Key whirled to face the opening of the stables and the short road leading to the gate into the street. She whipped the reins and made an encouraging *tch* sound that sounded very authentic to my ears.

Dora began moving forward, easing into the same gait I remembered from my fateful tour weeks ago. The sound of the mule's clopping on the pavement and the noise of the wheels grinding brought on a shiver of unpleasantness and a flash of Vicky sitting where Key was, turning to look at me with a twinkle in her eyes.

The tour had been fun, until it hadn't. Like Vicky. Melancholia threatened to sweep me under for a few seconds. Vicky hadn't faked a thing in our friendship—we *had* clicked.

It was just that Vicky wanted the shop a lot more than she'd wanted a friend. Sometimes, late at night, I wondered if that was where I was headed. If given the choice, I'd side with the shop over anything else too. In moments like those, I grabbed Grandma's spellbook and slipped it under my pillow and prayed that the goodness imbued in its pages would cleanse my soul during my sleep.

A loud honk brought me back to the present. The carriage was slowly making a turn, taking both lanes and causing a line of cars to form.

"What are you doing?" Wilburn demanded from behind me.

"I'm turning," Key exclaimed, a note of panic in her voice. She pulled at one side of the reins, and I was pretty sure the words *Oh, my God, turn, please, turn, oh, my god* escaped her lips.

Dora completed the turn and trotted happily down the crowded street. Cars on the opposite lane passed us by, honking to let us know we had let them down and shame on us and our families.

Key relaxed slightly, then snapped the reins back as a couple darted in front of the mule.

Dora stopped obediently.

And refused to move again.

"Go on, Dora," Key said with growing alarm. "*Tch, tch.*" She whipped the reins to no avail. "Be a good girl. Move?"

Honks rose behind us. A few people stopped to take out their phones. Loud, distorted music from a store's speakers mingled with the other street noises.

"Dora?" I called loudly from over Key's shoulder. "Move for us, pretty mule."

Key snapped the reins again, and Dora finally began moving forward.

"Oh, thank God," Key murmured. She looked so tense, the next snapping of the rains might snap her arms right off.

"Turn left next intersection," Wilburn commanded.

Key swallowed audibly and nodded, her attention focused on Dora and the road. A group of people crossed in front of us, cutting it close, but this time Key didn't try to stop Dora. Smart move—the mule hoofing over someone would teach them a lesson while trying to get her to move again would teach us none.

"You're waiting too long to start the turn," Wilburn said. "What are you doing? Make the turn now."

Key pulled on the left side of the reins, and Dora changed directions, going left and left until she was in the wrong lane.

More honking ensued. A man rolled down his car's window and told us what to do with our lovely mule and quaint carriage. Nothing physically possible, but the man did seem to relish the imagery.

Key hurried to straighten the carriage and get it into the correct side of the street. A little girl pointed at us and loudly told her mother that she wanted on the princess pumpkin. I waved at them and shouted the shop's website address.

"Never leave an opportunity unexplored."

"What?" Key asked in a shrill.

"Nothing. Don't worry about it." I patted her shoulder. "You're doing great!"

"I'm doing great," she repeated under her breath. "I can do this."

"You sure can," I said encouragingly.

Like the good girl she was, Dora barely needed any guidance. In fact, she went right ahead and started a turn all on her own with no prompting needed.

"Don't go that way," Wilburn warned. "That's the tour's route. Take the left. Circle back to the stables."

"Okay." Key pulled the reins with more confidence.

Dora stopped and scraped one hoof on the asphalt, as if showing her displeasure, then moved right again.

Key reined her in. "No, Dora. Left. Go left."

Dora shook her head, then tried to go right.

"Left," I said loudly. "Go left, Dora."

"Get the damn horse out of the way," someone shouted.

Key retook her panicked rein whipping. "Left, please. Left!"

Dora attempted to move right.

"Oh, for the love of everything holy," Wilburn exclaimed, disgusted. He jumped off the carriage and went up to Dora. Grabbing her bridle, he pointed her toward the left, then came back to the carriage and crowded Key out of the driver's bench. She awkwardly moved over the seat to sit by my side.

Wilburn told Dora to move, and the mule complied, clapping happily down the correct street.

"You," Wilburn said above the Friday late evening noises, "are not touching this carriage again. I don't wanna hear it," he added without looking at us. I closed my mouth and allowed him to continue. "This was your last chance. I'm sorry, but I've waited long enough. Tell Dru I'm giving Dora and the carriage to Olmeda Tours."

"I understand," I said, properly chastised. "Thank you for giving us the opportunity."

He stopped the carriage. "You're welcome. Get off."

We hurried off the carriage and watched him drive away.

"You don't actually have any experience with horses or carriages, do you?" I asked conversationally.

Key shriveled under my question. Wordlessly, she shook her head.

"C'mon, let's get a bite." I pointed at a brightly lit restaurant with its wide doors open into the street advertising the best fried chicken in town.

Key followed, her shoulders slumped in defeat. This was good news. It meant she probably wasn't going to run back to Uncle Jeremy the fire mage and cuss me out for not giving her a job.

I felt no guilt at the heartlessness of the statement. She had been the one to lie, and now it was her time to reap.

We sat at a two-person table and ordered the day's special. I attacked the free bread the moment the small basket was set between us. Between the long drive and the adrenaline of the Dora experience, I was ravenous.

Key inhaled deeply, straightened, and looked me straight in the eye.

"I'm sorry."

I nodded, finishing chewing the piece of bread. "Why did you lie?"

Her expression was earnest when she answered, "I really need a job."

"I'm sure there are other jobs in Olmeda. You didn't have to fake knowing how to work with animals."

"But Uncle Jeremy trusts you."

Trusts me to give him his dark magic potions. "I don't know that he trusts me that much."

"When I told him I wanted a job in the paranormal community, he brought me straight to you."

"Hah. I think that has more to do with me being the only person he knows."

"Oh, no, he knows a lot of people."

Probably not the kind of people he'd want his niece hanging around. One decency point for the dark magic user. "I'm happy he trusts me, but I still don't understand why you're so desperate to work with me."

Our dinner arrived, and I got started on mine. Key played

with hers, obviously putting all her chicken thighs in a row before offering an explanation.

"I love it here. I tried working at one of the fast-food places, but it didn't work out."

"Oh?"

"I want to work for people"—she scanned our surroundings—"in the know."

"I worked with unaware people for a while. It's not that bad."

"But you opened a witch shop. You must've wanted it a lot."

She had me there. "It took a few years, though. You're young; you can take your time finding a job you really want."

"I like the shop."

"You were in it for two minutes."

She poked her chicken bits some more. "I like being useful. Nobody ever wants earth mages." She inhaled deeply. "You made me feel useful."

"Unfortunately, the only other person I know with a backyard is already aware of the bodies buried there," I said wryly.

Key made a face. "That *was* weird."

"Useful, though. You could talk with Officer Brooks."

She tensed and scraped her chair back, ready to bolt. "Officer Brooks?"

"Don't worry, I don't have her on speed dial or anything." Key relaxed, and I continued, "She's the local police contact for the community. What if you offered your services as some sort of cadaver dog?"

"Cadaver dog?" she parroted.

"Human corpse detector? Imagine all the time you'd save in investigations."

Now she looked ready to bolt for entirely different reasons.

Valiantly, she squared her shoulders and said, "I don't want to work for the police. And that would be *really* weird."

"Hard to explain the girl patting around on the ground, you're right," I conceded. "The thing is, though, that your magic can be plenty useful. You just have to think out of the box." And, oh, Mother, did that give me an excellent idea for her employment. "You don't have to stick to working in the food industry." I indicated her chicken. "Eat some. It's on me."

Key immediately snatched up a thigh and bit into it.

I murmured in contentment and finished my own meal. I wasn't sure if it was the best chicken in the city, but it had to be up there. "You grew up in Olmeda?"

"No, I moved here six months ago."

"Where are you from?"

She glanced away. "West."

"Me too!" I understood her need to be cagey. There was a good chance her whole family was involved in some way with the dark magic business, and if not, definitely in cautious territory with the legal arm of the system. "I used to live with my parents before taking over the shop. What about you?"

"I've moved around a lot." Her gaze strayed to her food. "My mom left when I was little."

A gasp of delight escaped me. "My father did too."

She frowned. "But you said you lived with your parents."

"Ah, I meant my stepfather. Mom remarried when I was six. My father was gone long before that, although I stayed at my grandma's a lot as a kid. I have a stepsister too. What about you? Any siblings?"

Her expression turned wistful. "A brother. But we don't talk. We lost contact long ago."

"That's too bad," I said with sympathy. If she had moved around a lot and was searching for a place to settle down, chances were her relationship with her father wasn't the best either. "All your family is in the magic business?"

"Some."

"Mages like you and your uncle?"

She nodded and finished eating her chicken.

"What are your plans?" I prodded when she said nothing else.

"I want to stay here." She looked at me with imploring eyes. Eyes that reminded me of Fluffy when she was in dire need of affection. "I really love the city, but rent is expensive, and I don't have much..."

Life had to be hard for an earth mage. They weren't showy like the fire or water or air mages, couldn't make spells like witches, didn't have a pack to join, nor did they have the physical prowess of berserkers that made them so excellent as security experts or bouncers. As far as their usefulness in the magical community went, they were down there with demons and other lesser common paranormal beings—dangerous when cornered, but with nothing much to offer otherwise. People like Key or Dru had to eke their way.

As underpowered as I was as a witch, at least I had the Council—a sense of community, an opportunity to belong. Mages had their own circles, but as with everything, there was a clear hierarchy, and Key would find it hard to enter it. Otherwise, her uncle would be showing her the ropes rather than dumping her in my shop.

"I'm sorry I lied," Key said in a somber, despondent tone, "but I don't want to move again. Isn't there anything you can do? I can work for half the salary until you can afford to pay me in full. Or I can do only a couple of shifts a week."

I studied her contrite expression, the way she kept her hands clasped on top of the table, the yearning on her face. That could've been me six years ago upon rediscovering the world of magic. It could've been me five years ago upon learning I'd landed a witch internship, upon realizing that I would finally *belong*.

I'd been lucky—I'd been able to land on my feet after the internship had gone so sideways there were no names for the maneuver. But Key didn't have that luxury. If this didn't pan out, Brimstone and Destruction might decide to start her in the dark magic side of the family business to earn some cash.

Key wasn't my intern, but she was part of Olmeda's community now. I owed it to her and to Grandma's memory to give her a hand. And while my budget couldn't take another hire yet, I knew someone who might.

"Come to the shop at eight o'clock," I said.

The hope on her face was a ray of sunshine on an otherwise dark and gloomy day.

9

AT EIGHT AND a half sharp the next morning, I rang Ian's cemetery doorbell. Key stood nervously next to me.

"Isn't this the bounty hunter's place?" she asked in a whisper.

"Don't worry, he's all gooey inside. Hard outside, gooey inside. Like an egg. You like eggs, don't you?"

"I... Yes?"

"See? Perfect." I leaned on the button. Distant barking reached my ears, and the side door snicked open.

Key followed me inside the cemetery and up the gravel path to the house and the garage. The white van was parked in its usual spot, and movement behind it told me Shane and Alex were getting ready for the day.

"Those are Shane and Alex," I said, waving at them.

They froze in their tracks, their attention snapping to Key. I sensed her stumble by my side.

"Hey," I exclaimed, clapping my hands. Their attention flicked to me. "Shoo. Keep moving."

They did so, if at a much slower speed than before.

"Don't mind them. They're harmless." I remembered

Shane's huge wolf form. "Mostly. They won't bother you, anyhow."

"Sure," she murmured, glancing at them, then immediately back to the house. "Why are we here?"

"I told you—trust me, it's a surprise."

"I'm not into surprises."

I chuckled. "That's good because the surprise is not for you."

The front door opened, and Fluffy flew outside, all kinetic energy.

"Fluffy!" I crouched to hug her and get slobbered all over. "Come meet Key."

Key eyed the dog like it was an alien from planet Drool. "Hi, Fluffy."

Fluffy sniffed her jeans, then pawed at her leg.

"She wants pets," I informed Key.

Key reached down hesitantly and scratched the back of Fluffy's head like she was a cat. It'd do.

"Good morning," Ian said from the door. He was in his usual black attire, wearing a Henley shirt to conform to the colder morning air. The sleeves were rolled halfway up his forearms. Strong, manly forearms. The kind of forearms sonnets and fan fiction were written about.

I cleared my throat, feeling extraordinarily heated. "Good morning." I hooked my hand around Key's elbow and brought her forward with me. We stopped in front of the steps leading up to the porch, Fluffy still doing circles around us. Rufus ambled out from behind Ian, making Key stiffen.

"Don't worry about the big, scary dog," I told her. "Rufus is an egg too."

"Excuse me?" Ian asked.

"Never mind. This"—I touched her arm lightly—"is Key. She needs a job."

Ian looked her up and down. The cynical kind of look that could freeze its object's veins. Key shivered and burrowed into her sweatshirt.

"Hi," she murmured, then looked at me with woeful eyes. "I thought I was going to work at the shop."

"In time. For now, I think you'll be a better fit here."

"Is that so?" Ian asked in an amused voice. He regarded Key again. "Where are you from?"

"I moved to Olmeda a few months ago," she murmured.

Ian's shifter-enhanced hearing had no trouble picking up the words. "And you want to work at the Tea Cauldron?"

"I was told it's very dependable."

The fact she wasn't mentioning her family connection told me she must be aware bounty hunters might have a problem with her uncle.

"Ah." Ian considered me for a few moments. "Congratulations on your new stray."

I blinked in shock. "What? No. I'm just helping out. It's what I do, you know."

Ian ignored me and whistled to the two strays. They snapped to attention. To Key, he told, "Go give them a hand while I talk to Hope, will you?"

Key gave me one last imploring look. At my smile of encouragement, she exhaled heavily and made her way over to the strays. Alex was all grins while Shane kept a narrowed eye on her.

I turned my attention to Ian. "Hear me out before you say no."

He folded his arms over his chest and rested his shoulder on the door frame. "Go ahead."

"Key is an earth mage."

"Okay."

"An earth mage would be invaluable in your line of business."

"Would she?"

"Imagine all the leaks she could find using her magic. It'd save you so much time."

"We get paid by the hour."

"Fast jobs will improve your reputation and allow you to book more clients." I stepped up onto the porch and gave him a knowing smile. The one baristas worldwide used to convince their customers that their coffee was one of a kind, and not one in a long line of people who thought their common combination of flavors was the best-kept secret in the world. "You restore a lot of old buildings, don't you?" I poked his chest. "Her powers could come in handy with all that old metal and stone."

For a moment he leaned in, his eyes fixed on my mouth, as if he was going to give me a fast peck on the lips. "You make a strong point."

"I am... Ah..." With a jolt of surprise, I realized I was rubbing his shirt, right in the center of his chest. I snapped my hand back.

His mouth curved into a slow smile. "Yes?"

I dropped my gaze to his chest, to the slight wrinkle on the Henley that marked the warm, firm spot I'd rubbed. "I am known for my business acumen."

He straightened and scratched the top of Rufus's head absentmindedly. What a couple they made. "If I agree to this..."

"If you agree to this?" I repeated, licking my dry, dry lips.

He smiled again at that, a short, blink-and-you-miss-it grin. "It'll be on a temporary basis."

"How temporary?"

"Does it matter?"

I sensed a trap, but I wasn't sure exactly where it was. "If it's going to be for only a week, I'd rather help her find something more stable." Dru might be willing to help, even if the Dora catastrophe had left her bemoaning the lack of trustworthy youth these days. I could convince her to see the good in the situation.

"I commend your interest in a complete stranger's well-being," Ian said.

"She's young and part of the community. Someone's gotta help her out."

"But she's not your stray."

It was my time to cross my arms. "Of course not. I'm simply being a good member of the community. If every person I helped was my stray—and by the way, witches don't have strays, they have interns—then I'd have to change the Tea Cauldron to the Tea Rescue."

"All right."

"All right?"

"I will give her a one-month part-time contract."

I brightened. "Excellent." A month was long enough for Key to get her bearings and find another job if necessary.

"And you owe me dinner."

"Sure thing."

Fluffy and I trotted to Key to tell her the good news, while Ian and Rufus followed at a more sedate pace.

Alex was pointing at different tools inside the garage and explaining what they did to Key, who watched with a mix of interest and wariness. Shane was muttering to himself as he loaded planks of wood into the back of the van.

"Key," I said excitedly. "Mr. Cavalier has agreed to hire you part-time for a month on a test basis."

Key's mouth pursed with disappointment for a second, but then she regained control of herself and squared her shoulders. "Thank you, Mr. Cavalier."

Alex elbowed her side and winked. "Call him 'boss.'"

"Thank you…boss."

Ian studied her again, from the tips of her scuffed sneakers up her faded jeans and sweatshirt, to the top of her brown hair. "You can start today. Help Shane and Alex get ready for the day, then ride with them." He turned to Shane, which told me he was the de facto leader of the pair, and added, "She observes today. We'll figure out the schedule tonight."

Ian didn't mention Key's earth magic, but I had no doubt he'd bring it up later when they made plans. He wasn't one to let something useful go to waste.

They ran over the plans for the day, then Ian accompanied me to the gate.

"Thank you." I turned to face him.

"Next time, warn me first."

Fluffy zoomed out of the gate and sniffed the outside of the fence. I grabbed her, squeezed her close, then dumped her into Ian's arms. Something else I wanted to squeeze.

"Let me know how she does, will you?" I said.

"Sure."

We stood there as I racked my brain for another way to prolong the conversation. Realization of what I was doing finally kicked in, and with a last pet of Fluffy's head, I said my goodbyes and walked away.

Not far. The moment I was around the corner, I took out my phone and looked up the address for their first job of the day. The name had sounded familiar, and luckily, it was the name for the house, not the family—much easier to find and a lot less creepy.

Twenty minutes and a share-ride later, I hid behind a tree near the property. Ian and the strays took their sweet time to drive over, but Ian's SUV and the white van eventually arrived. They parked in front of the house—a lovely three-story family home built by some rich guy at the turn of the century—and

Ian went to talk to the owner while Alex and Shane opened the back of the van and put their gloves on. Key stood awkwardly by the side, but I could tell her attention was riveted on what they were doing and whatever they were saying.

After a couple of minutes of talking, Ian gave them the go-ahead, and the strays began carrying blue plastic sheets and tools inside the house. Key picked up a bucket Shane pointed to and followed them.

They were including her in the job rather than simply humoring me and telling her to stay in the van.

Good.

A busy Key was a Key too busy to complain to her uncle, and an uncle who received no complaints was an uncle who wouldn't call the Council.

Satisfied, I called another ride and returned to the shop. I was late opening, but Saturday mornings were usually a bust. Business didn't pick up until later in the day when people got tired of visiting shops and popular sightseeing spots and needed a respite for their feet.

Bagley hadn't made a peep, but that didn't mean she wasn't back and waiting for the perfect moment to announce her presence, so I went into the downstairs kitchen and called Dru.

"How did it go?" she asked.

"Good so far." I'd already updated her on the Dora debacle the night before. "Ian's hiring her part-time for a month."

"You think that'll keep the mage happy?"

"I think so."

"Did you tell Ian about him?"

A drop fell from the faucet, and for a moment, a shadow followed it. It snapped back with a gurgle, and it all happened so fast my brain insisted I was seeing and hearing things. Just another day with a pipe goldfish ghost.

"Hope? Did you tell him?" Dru repeated.

"I should, shouldn't I?"

"Don't until it's been a few days. That way when he fires her, at least he'll owe her a week's paycheck."

"He won't fire her just because her uncle is an evil mage." Ian's predilection for collecting strays could be seen from space.

"Wanna bet?"

"Loser has to wear a witch hat for Halloween."

A brief pause ensued. "I changed my mind."

What a novice mistake—I'd asked for too much. I should've kept it vague. Ian's fault. His directness was rubbing off. "Chicken."

"That's a good one. Winner buys lunch."

"Sure." I made chicken noises.

A longer pause filled the call. "Hope, you need help."

"It's the adrenaline. It's making me do weird things."

"You can blame it on that if it makes you feel better, but I've seen you do weirder things with zero excuses."

"Getting into Ian's cemetery made perfect sense at the time."

"I was thinking more of the time you grabbed a complete stranger and asked her to check for buried bodies in your backyard. Do you really trust the girl?"

"I do, yeah." Otherwise, I'd have never taken her to Ian.

"Even after she lied about the horses?"

"My gut says she's a good person."

"Your gut trusted Vicky."

"My gut's gotta be right at some point," I told her enthusiastically.

Dru snorted and hung up. I went into the shop and sat on my stool behind the counter. It was time to work on Hutton's problem.

The moment my butt touched the seat, my phone rang.

Speak of the devil.

"Good morning." I forced some cheer into my voice. With my free hand, I angled the laptop my way and opened my email. I'd emailed myself the notes from my research trip.

"Good morning, my ass. I've been trying to call for ten minutes."

He'd likely called once, while I was busy with Dru, but I'd forgive the exaggeration because the man sounded quite stressed. "Well, I'm here now."

"Where's my goddamn potion?"

I scanned the notes in the email. "I'm working on it. These kinds of potions take time and preparation."

His voice lowered to a harsh, urgent whisper. "I need it *now*. My powers are fading fast. They're almost gone."

"What?" Alarm made me sit straighter.

"I'm afraid to leave the house. Someone's going to notice."

"Won't they think you're reining them in out of respect for the other alphas? So you don't end up in a power level pissing contest?"

He let out a laugh of incredulity. "That's not how things work. Just get me the damn thing or else I'm calling the Council ahead of time."

"You don't need to remind me," I muttered. "I might be able to do something temporary with Ian's blood."

"*No.*"

"But—"

"Find another way. Bagley never used his, I made sure of it."

"Bagley would have no trouble lying to you." Although he had the right of it—no way in hell Ian would've let Bagley anywhere near his blood. "Also, I'm not Bagley."

"Find. Another. Way." He ended the call.

I took a few deep breaths to calm myself and checked my voice mails. Nothing from Valenti. She might not have gotten to her calls yet, or she might be ignoring me. I left her another message, doubling down on the urgency of the situation.

For a fleeting moment, I toyed with the idea of calling my ex-boss and asking her to make the introductions, but… No. I wouldn't sink that low. Yet.

My notes were of no help. A lot of history but not many pointers.

"Ah, yes," came the familiar grandmotherly voice, "I remember Hutton's potion well. One of my best creations, I'm not ashamed to say."

Ignoring Bagley, I crouched by the cabinet containing my spell and potion supplies, hoping the sight of the ingredients would spark a genius idea. Also hoping it would hide my grimace. Having the phone conversation with Hutton in front of Bagley had been an awful idea.

"If you're nice," she said sweetly, "I might even give you the recipe."

"No, thanks."

"It's only a little dark magic. What can it hurt?"

Oh, nothing much. Only my soul, Grandma's trust, and, "Whoever I have to bleed dry to perform it?"

"Nonsense! It won't take more than a wine glass worth."

"Yuck."

A low chuckle filled the air. "Now, child, you don't need to kill someone to get that much blood. Perfectly survivable."

"Sure, but then I'll need another glass to make an evil memory potion potent enough to wipe all their memories."

"Eh, still survivable. Although, since you're at it, you might as well get some extra blood in case of emergencies."

I stood and glared at the dish towel her voice was drifting from. "You're a horrible human being."

"No, child," Bagley said with sudden seriousness. "I serve my clients exactly as you do yours."

"Doesn't make you any less of a murderer."

"Everyone's life has to end at some point," she said philosophically.

"If only you'd heed your own advice," I muttered.

She laughed at that, an evil cackle that made me think fairy tales were based on real events.

My phone dinged, and I resigned myself to reading an angry text from Hutton or a call for help from Key, or maybe Dru, finally sick of my antics and handing in her resignation.

It was from Brimstone and Destruction:

They're in your area, right? You're welcome.

A link followed. I clicked on it, then tried to backpedal in horror—I'd forgotten to turn on the VPN. Unfortunately, the site loaded immediately. It showed a highlighted post on some sort of message board.

Posted by: Borden1337
Potion. Power reduction. Time sensitive.

I scrolled past some of the other posts. They all followed a similar pattern—type of magic needed, what it needed to do, and whether it could wait or not. Was this some sort of wish list? My heartbeats increased as I checked more posts. Yes, it was —no question about it.

Who is "they"? I texted the mage.

The twins.

As in the alpha twins? The ones here for the alpha convention? The ones who were part of the group of alphas Hutton was convinced were sniffing around to take over his territory?

Oh, boy.

10

"DO YOU KNOW THE ALPHA TWINS?" I asked loudly.

"The alpha twins?" Bagley answered. "No, my dear. Although I used to correspond with a witch living near their pack. Back in the day when we had real pen pals, and things took forever to arrive by post. I can't say I miss those days."

If the twins had a dark magic witch living nearby, why did they need to put in a request for a potion?

Bagley caught on fast. "Oh, my. Do they need a potion? Perhaps he died!" No sadness to be heard, only evil glee. "I'm sure if you tell me what they need, we can create the perfect potion. These days it's so easy to ship everywhere in the country... You can add a service fee, too—they'll never know shipping is half of what you charge. I was actually planning on expanding my business like that before my untimely death," she finished in sorrowful tones.

Untimely only because someone should've offed her decades ago and not earlier this summer.

"Think about it," Bagley said. "We'd make such a wonderful team."

Oh, I was thinking about it. I was thinking about the fact

that two alphas who had come to visit Hutton needed an urgent potion that reduced someone's power. About the fact that Hutton might not be paranoid at all.

Alphas using dark magic to steal a pack was a hundred times worse than an alpha who used dark magic to stay alpha. Hutton might be a jerk, but he was acting out of necessity. The twins were acting out of greed—they had their own pack, they didn't need this one. They especially didn't need to cheat unless there was something big in it for them.

Clawstone Park occupied a nice piece of prime real estate in Olmeda. The possibility of the pack's new leaders intending to sell it made me shudder. To lose your home and all that was yours? To have your family history end up in only a single spellbook?

The Olmeda pack had been good to me. They'd saved me from the hitman, they'd gotten rid of Vicky, and they hadn't reported a thing to the Council.

In retrospect, that must've been Hutton covering his ass, but several shifters had made the effort to come to the shop and be friendly. They'd been welcoming at Clawstone.

They didn't deserve this.

I called Ian.

"Yes?" Sounds of hammering rose in the background. He hushed someone and silence fell.

"I need to talk to you. It's urgent. Meet me at your place." Mess up once, shame on you, mess up twice, learn from your mistakes and leave the evil witch lair behind and conduct highly private business a few city blocks away.

I ended the call and hurried to lock the shop's door and flip the sign to closed.

Things were getting out of control. The potion by itself, I could deal with on my own. But this latest development called for the big guns. Hutton could kill me later, once things had settled down and his pack was secure.

I drove Bee-Bee and was there in no time, which meant I had to wait for Ian's huge SUV to appear. It did, eventually, crawling along so below the speed limit that if he wasn't careful, he'd start moving backward.

The big gate opened with the slightest of motor whirls, and he took his sweet time going in. I pushed the Vespa after him, leaving it by the gate and running up the rest of the way.

Ian parked the SUV halfway up the slope, then got out. His granite face exuded displeasure.

"Is this about Key?" The worry on my face made no chink in his severe expression. "Just because she's your stray, you can't mother her, Hope."

I lifted a finger, then a second. "One, not my stray, and two, no, it's much worse."

Rufus barked from inside the house, a thunder-like sound that almost made me jump out of my skin.

"Rufus, quiet. It's all good," Ian shouted toward the house. A wry smile curved his lips. "He's checking everything is all right. Come."

I followed him to the house, and he opened the front door. Fluffy immediately shot out to paw at his leg. He reassured her in a soft murmur, then the fluff ball approached me to get her pets. Rufus sat on the floor mat like some ancient shaggy statue, his attention fixed on Ian. After he got his reassurance, the huge dog came up to me and leaned his head against my hip the way he did when he wanted attention from Ian.

Had he sensed my panic and come to reassure me? Oh, my goodness. I ran my hand over his furry head and scratched him behind the ears the same way I'd seen Ian do. Rufus let out a soft woof of approval that scattered my thoughts all over the lawn.

"What's 'much worse'?" Ian asked.

Did dogs like their necks scratched like cats did? Fluffy hadn't minded, but Fluffy didn't mind anything.

"Hope."

"Hmm?"

"What's so urgent that you needed to see me? Rufus, guard."

Rufus immediately left my side to sit by his owner, eyes scanning our surroundings.

Fluffy whined but went to sit right by Rufus. They looked absolutely adorable side by side.

"Hope."

"Sorry, sorry." I focused on the reason I was here, and all my worries returned like a slam to the chest. My hands shook as I showed him my text conversation with the mage. "It's the mage who put me in the dark web marketplace. He sent me this link."

"And you clicked on it?"

Heat crept up into my cheeks. "Anyway, it leads to some sort of message board where people make magic requests. Look."

"You just clicked on it again."

"It's not a lottery, Ian. The anonymity ship sailed the first time I clicked."

He smiled faintly at the slight censure in my tone and held my hand to angle the phone. His fingers were warm and his skin a little rough, and it sent tingles up my arm.

When he didn't react to the message, I added, "It's from the twin alphas."

"I see."

Did he? Because his reaction was less than stellar. "I think they want a potion to weaken Hutton and take over the pack."

"Hutton can take care of himself."

"There's more to that," I admitted. "He's already aware some of the alphas are sniffing around his pack."

"Shifters take care of their own business. Don't worry about it. If Hutton has the support of his pack, potions won't help the other alphas. If he doesn't, then it wasn't meant to be."

"You'd be happy with an alpha who cheats taking over the pack?"

He shrugged one shoulder. "It's not my business." He gave me a pointed look. "And it's not yours."

"Actually, it kind of is."

"Having a witch shop doesn't make you responsible for everyone in town, only your clients."

I toed the wooden board of the porch's floor. "Actually..."

Ian tensed. Rufus growled low.

Despite my best intentions, I took an involuntary step back. I didn't think Rufus would bite me, but it *was* an enormous dog.

Sensing my hesitance, Ian told the dogs to get back inside, then closed the front door. "Explain."

"Hutton is kind of my client."

"Selling them memory potions doesn't make their problems yours. You're taking this whole 'pillar of the community' thing too far."

That stung, but I'd suffered worse wounds. "It's not that. Although you're wrong—there is no way to take being a pillar of the community far enough. Hutton was a..." I swallowed, then forced myself to spit it out. "He was Bagley's client."

I winced internally at the huge crash marking the break of my promises to Hutton. The unspoken one dealing with client-witch confidentiality, and the more specific one about not telling Ian.

"Was he, now," Ian drawled.

I studied his features closely. I'd gotten better at reading his face, but right now he was giving me nothing. No surprise, no shock, no smugness, only stony blandness for miles and kilometers. It made me feel like I was no longer standing on the sturdy floor of his porch but a bog filled with quicksand.

No backing out now—the Oakes-Avery witches always ended what they started.

"He needs a potion to keep his alpha powers as they are." I couldn't make myself fill in the details—Ian was a smart man; he could connect the dots by himself. "The current one is fading, and he needs a refill."

"Does he, now."

"As you know—" One of his brows arched with amusement, but I refused to stop. He was going to get the rest of the lecture, cliché or not. "*As you know* I don't do dark magic, but I've conducted some research, and I think with your blood, I can make a potion that will keep him going at least until alphacon is over."

"No."

"If he can keep the alpha power running at max, it'll help a lot if the twins try to make a move. He'll be screwed if they sense he has no power—they won't even need a potion."

"No."

"You don't think they'll make a move the moment they sense he's weak?" I bit my lip. "I don't know, Ian. The fact that they asked for this dark magic potion—it's obvious they're planning a move. I think they didn't at first, but they must've sensed something once they arrived, or their contacts inside the pack are a lot more open to them taking over than they initially thought." The memory of the one shifter talking with the twin outside the gates like they were best friends returned. Turned out, maybe they didn't need to be secretive at all. "And that's why they're in a hurry now. What if they've somehow learned about Hutton's weakening powers and are ready to pounce?"

"No."

"Why else would they be in a hurry, then? I guess they might've checked me out but didn't want to ask the local dark witch for the potion, in case I had some loyalty to the pack."

Ian put his hands on my shoulders and turned me around until I was facing the lawn and the path to the gate.

"I'm not giving you my blood. You can leave now."

I spun to face him again. "What?"

He pushed me gently, and I was forced down the steps off the porch.

"I don't involve myself in pack politics."

"But it's your brother."

"I don't see him here, so it must not matter too much."

I tried to struggle, but the gates were inexorably coming closer and closer. It was the gentleness of it all, the unbreaking pressure of his push against my shoulders and the amusement in his eyes.

"What if he asks you? Will you help then?"

"He won't." We moved around his SUV until we stood by the Vespa. He unhooked the helmet and plopped it on my head.

"But what if he does?" I insisted. "Will you help then?"

"He will never ask." His voice was bland but full of conviction. "Why do you care who controls the pack anyway?"

"Hutton helped me before."

"They helped themselves, not you. The hitman was inside their territory. The witch was a danger to everyone."

I swatted his hands again as he tried to secure the helmet straps under my chin. The fact that he was treating me like a child made something snap inside of me. Things began to truly register—his immediate negative response, the lack of shock or reaction as I'd confessed something that should've been a complete revelation. "You're very calm about all this."

He stood there, patiently waiting for me to connect the dots with what could've been pity shining in his expression, but surely not, because no way he wanted to wake up one day looking like a green Smurf.

Then outrage filled me as I figured it out. "You knew he's been using a potion! You've known all along."

The urge to stand on my tiptoes, wrap my fingers around his neck, and squeeze the life out of him was almost overpowering. My hands itched so badly that I had to clasp them together.

"Let it be, Hope," he said, neither confirming nor denying the accusation. But that in itself was answer enough, wasn't it? "Let Hutton deal with his own shit."

"I can't," I ground out. "I have to help."

"No, you don't."

"Yes, I do. If I don't help him, he'll tell the Council about the shop's dark magic business."

He rubbed his chin, his expression a mixture of intensity and consideration. That last part reignited my hope—where there was consideration, there might be a crack I could use to pry his defenses open.

"Make a fake one like you did with the others," he said.

"There is no faking this potion." I gave him my most beseeching look. "I have a sister. I'd do anything for her. Whatever happened between your parents—it's not Hutton's fault. He doesn't need to know you helped out."

He opened the door of his SUV, and I barely restrained myself from clapping my hands in delight. He was doing it. He was going to drive with me to the shop.

Then he clicked something, and the gate whirled open. He glanced over his shoulder, unreadable once again.

"I need to get back to work," he said. "You should get going too unless you want to get stuck here and have to jump over the fence again."

11

I TOLD Ian what he could do with his fence and drove back to the shop. What an insufferable jerk. Insufferable, selfish, hard-headed ass.

Grandma would not have approved of this particular way of dealing with stress.

But then, what did I know? Maybe behind her soft eyes and kind smile, she'd been howling insults at the unfairness of life. Who knew what actually went on inside people's heads?

No, stop that. Going down that road would not help anyone. I flipped the sign to open and let the coolness of the glass seep through my hands all the way into my soul. Calming, soothing.

"Did you get the blood?" Bagley asked eagerly. "Oh, oh, please say you got the blood! This is going to be so much *fun.*"

I grabbed the dish towel and threw it into the hallway. It crashed against the bead curtain hiding the archway and flopped to the floor, so I gave it a swift kick.

Not my best moment, but it helped. And right now, I could use all the help that came my way.

I replayed the conversation with Ian inside my head. It was

hard to process. That he had known about Hutton's problem made sense—he'd known about Bagley's dark magic side business, so he was probably suspicious of anyone who came to the shop. Or maybe it was a family bond thing. Maybe it had allowed him to sense Hutton's alpha powers were out of whack.

The part where he wouldn't help?

That made zero sense.

Could I simply tell the other alphas about the twins' dark magic request? Surely, they'd be outraged. They might even put a bounty on the twins. Nobody wanted that kind of bad publicity associated with them.

Unfortunately, that would raise questions about how I'd found the dark web listing, which might end up with me being the one with a target on my back.

An anonymous report? Would anyone listen to it? They must get a hundred troll reports a month—why listen to mine without a real name to give it some weight?

I sat heavily on one of the counter stools. Desolation filled my chest, a hole of emptiness slowly expanding as it gnawed on my insides.

For some unfathomable reason, I'd been counting on Ian's cooperation. In the back of my mind, I'd been sure that when push came to shove, he'd be there, ready to help. What would Hutton think of Ian's no-nonsense refusal? Did he also, at some unconscious level, count on his big brother's help?

It was shocking Ian had shut down my plans so easily, with no show of regret or doubt, no sign that he'd thought about it beyond the time it took for his brain to process my words. If he'd answered any faster, I'd have thought he could read minds.

Perhaps he'd expected this day to come. Perhaps he'd been waiting to see what happened with Hutton and his potion since the moment I'd proved myself to be on the legal, fully blooded consent side of things. Was this revenge for their father's breakup with his mother? Ian's demeanor usually gave icebergs a run for their money, and, as they say, revenge is best served cold. What better way to get revenge on the couple who broke his mother's heart than by watching their kid crash and burn?

I retreated behind the counter and called Hutton. He didn't pick up, so I left a voice mail warning him about the twins and their request. I didn't want to text and have someone else read it by mistake.

A couple of women entered the shop, giving the room appreciative glances. Any other time, I'd have basked in them, recorded them in my memory to replay on loop next time I got a *place kind of bland, service lacking, what's with all the witch stuff* two-star review, but today I couldn't muster the effort. My brain was too busy looping Ian's denial, the twins' request, and my rapidly dwindling stack of options if I wanted to save Hutton, his pack, and by extension, my shop.

The women asked for the day's special, and I busied myself preparing the tea, then serving it at a table along with a chocolate chip muffin cut in half.

Hannah came in a few minutes later, ordered a coffee, and sat at the second table. She and the women nodded at each other in greeting, and I wondered if she'd recommended the shop somewhere. If so, she was getting a free drink—you couldn't buy word of mouth. It was priceless. Just look at the mage and my shop and the dark web. Worked wonders.

My phone rang, and I answered quickly, breathlessly, thinking it was Ian and not bothering to read the screen. "Yes?"

"Did you take the job?" Hutton demanded.

The man was more efficient at drowning moods than the iciest of showers. "What job?"

"The twins'," he said in whispered outrage.

"Of course not." Who did he think I was?

A dark witch, that was who. And witches who dabbed in dark magic weren't known for their loyalty or principles.

"I would never betray our community," I added. If I couldn't be known for my wholesomeness, at least I'd build my trustworthiness.

"Good, because if I learn you've talked to them, you're going down so fast you won't even know it happened until you're rotting in Council jail."

"Threats, like antibiotics, lose their strength the more you use them."

"*What?*"

"Nothing. I won't give the twins the time of day, I swear."

"You better, witch."

I was starting to get the impression that whenever he said that word, he was imagining a very different first letter.

"And make my goddamn potion," he shot as a last salvo before ending the call.

That reminded me to check my messages. Still no word from Lilian Valenti.

Did it even matter? I'd mulled this over and over, and the only option with a chance of success was using Ian's blood. Alpha and sibling—a better match you couldn't ask for.

Unless I figured out where they had interred their father, dug up his bones, and scooped out the marrow?

No. *Nooo.* "Too much, Hope. Too much."

"Everything okay?" Hannah asked, concerned.

I gave her my best smile. "Yeah, everything's good."

Cavalier Repair & Renovations' van came to a stop in front of the shop. Key and the two strays stepped out and came inside.

Key stopped by the counter, playing with the hem of her sweatshirt and looking uncertain. "They offered to drop me off."

Alex was reading the blackboard with the day's special while Shane's eye bored into the back of Key's head. The intensity there reminded me of Ian.

"Hey, these sound good." Alex pointed at the specials.

I grinned. "I'd like to think so."

"Can I have a muffin to go?"

"Sure thing." I opened the glass display and hovered a hand between both plates. "Chocolate or banana?"

Alex huffed. "Banana."

Shane made gagging noises but shut his mouth the moment Key turned to watch them.

I swallowed a laugh. "Banana it is." I gave him the muffin but shook my head when he went to take out his wallet. "On the house." I glanced at Shane. "Chocolate?"

"I'm good," he said a bit gruffly. Trying to show off in front of Key? Possibly.

"You want anything, Key?"

"She can have part of mine," Alex said. He broke off a bit of his muffin and offered it to Key.

Key took it hesitantly. "Thanks."

Shane stiffened and watched closely as she took her sweet time to eat the mouthful. Oh, boy. I should warn Ian about this love drama in the making.

But then, why should I? Let him deal with this windfall. He was a smart guy, he'd figure out what to do.

And if the idea of Ian having to deal with a couple of lovesick shifters howling at the moon gave me a bit of an evil thrill, well, Grandma wasn't around to judge, and Dru would bring the popcorn.

"I love the shop," Key said, wide eyes scanning the room. "It's so cozy and neat."

"First time in a witch shop?" I asked, because I think we could all agree her first visit didn't count.

She shook her head. "I've been in others before, back home, but this one is different." She scrunched her nose. "The others were old and musty and smelled weird. Creepy stuff."

"I bet," Alex said.

"I like that you offer occult stuff," Key added shyly.

"You like tarot?" I asked.

Her expression softened with memories. "My grandma was a card reader. She was great at it."

"And you've taken after her?"

"I do sometimes, but I'm not as good as her."

"It just takes practice." Witches and tarot card readers hadn't gotten along in the past, but times were changing, and if we couldn't take over Vicky's guided tours business, maybe Dru and I could go into the tarot reading one. All we needed was a room, a table, and a webcam.

I studied Key. The thought of feeding her to the internet wolves didn't sit well. Maybe in a couple of years, when she was a little older than her current nineteen or twenty.

"All right, we're out," Shane said.

Alex grinned at Key. "See you tomorrow?"

"Tomorrow's Sunday," I reminded him.

Shane shook his head and pushed the door open. "Dumbass."

"Shut up." Alex shoved Shane into the street. They bickered as they got into the van, then drove away.

Key made a face. "It's my fault, isn't it?"

"Nah. They're grown up, nobody to blame but themselves. Want some tea?"

She studied the different jars and merchandise piled on the shelves behind the counter but ultimately shook her head. "No, thank you. I should get going."

"What's your number?" I noted it into my phone as her face shone bright like a star. "In case I'm in need of extra help."

"Thank you," she said again, a lot more effusively, then left the shop.

I watched her walk out of sight and sighed. She reminded me of myself, all shy eagerness as I took my first steps into the world of magic. Although, unlike me, Key had been around paranormals all her life. Perhaps it was the change of scenery and being new in these parts. Moving cross-country made one feel like a total newbie all over again.

Hannah left shortly after, and I served the two women a drink refill and another muffin to share. No judgment—I'd played the "a half twice doesn't count as one" game plenty of times.

They returned to their animated conversation, and I refocused on my problem:

Ian.

Yes, not the alpha, or the twins, or dark magic, or Valenti refusing to return my call, or Bagley's bag of soul-rotting tricks, but Ian.

There had to be something more to Ian's full rejection of his brother and the pack. He could've stayed away, but he'd chosen to semi-retire here. Had he thought about reconnecting with his little brother once their dad died, then, in typical bounty hunter fashion, dug into Hutton's life and discovered his lack of natural alpha power and his use of dark magic? Like cheating father, like cheating son.

But he hadn't done anything or said a thing about it to anyone. Deep inside, Ian might still be struggling between the need to reconnect and the hurt of the past.

If I could find something that nudged him on the side of reconnecting, he might see that Hutton was acting out of desperation to keep the pack together.

The key had to be buried in what'd happened with their parents—I needed to find out exactly how that had gone down.

12

ALL I KNEW about Ian's parents' breakup was what Dru had told me—Ian's father and mother had been blissfully happy and thinking about marriage and making his mother an official mate when his father's actual mate had waltzed into the scene. Shifter mates were a title, but on rare occasions, they were also an instinctual, deep connection between one shifter and another. Hutton's mother had been this for Ian's father. Ian's mother had stuck around to try to make things work as friends for the sake of Ian, but the new mate had grown territorial, and Ian and his mom had eventually moved away.

A tale as old as time.

But maybe not quite correct. After all, it had been three decades since all this had happened, and rumors tended to be embellished and refined for the sake of shock and clickbait. It was entirely possible that Ian's parents had been on the verge of a breakup, or already separated when the new woman had entered the picture, but that wouldn't make as good a tale. The way things had gone down might not be as black and white as Ian thought. He had been a little kid when they moved away—

his mother might've told a different story for the sake of appearing like the better person in her son's eyes.

If I showed Ian that there were two sides to the story, and he'd only heard one, it might be enough to convince him to help this one time, get this threat out of the way, and then figure out where to go from there.

It was all highly patronizing, and if I were Ian or his mother, I'd give me a few choice words before erasing me from my life, but desperation opened up paths you could have sworn were too low to walk.

Time to put on the rain boots and trudge through the metaphorical mud.

Who did I know that could remember the full, real story?

I considered the strays, but they were new to the area, and anything they'd heard would be from a similar source as Dru. Besides, their loyalty was to Ian. One of them might say something to him, and then my plan to ambush him with the harsh reality of his parents' separation would die a fast, agonizing death.

Bagley might know, but, as usual, I'd rather ask a rattlesnake.

It was too bad Mr. Lewis had turned out to be a murdering jerk because he must've known every sordid detail.

However...

I thought back to my first PBOA meeting. Mr. Lewis had been there, had even introduced me to a couple of his cronies. Those people were the old guard. They would've been around for the breakup and all the drama. They might be eager to share the story for old times' sake. With the internet these days, it was a good bet nobody ever came to them for gossip anymore. They might want to show off how much they knew about stuff.

The women in the shop seemed to have settled in for the long haul, and it broke something in my heart to have to tell them the shop was closing, but this mess with Ian and Hutton was more important than my brisk Saturday evening business. Oh, Mother, did it hurt to think that. Dollar bills fluttered in front of my eyes, flying, flying... Gone.

The women were very sorry about my emergency and reassured me they'd return next week. I let the blinds drop and flipped the open sign. Maybe I did need to hire Key for times like this. Dru had her other part-time job, and you never knew when a witch emergency could pop up.

I left the Vespa behind and made my way on foot. Saturday traffic was already turning into a nightmare, and the walk would do me good. The shop I wanted to hit first was a few blocks away, smack between Guiles and Romary and Balton Square, right in the path of thousands of tourists every day.

Bosko ran one of the souvenir shops specializing in cheap T-shirts printed with Olmeda logos and dumb jokes, baseball caps, and other paraphernalia tourists ate right up. Personally, I thought his T-shirts were on the garish side, but then, someone had yet to buy one of my lovely tea cauldron and spellbooks tees, so maybe I stood to learn something from the master.

The sidewalks of this part of old Olmeda were on the narrow side, and tourists spilled onto the road, halting the traffic. Loud music reverberated from some of the bars, and scouts for the restaurants were out in full force, menus in hand and hunting for their next prey. Best chicken wings in town, best gumbo, best seafood, and even best paella, which wouldn't be much of a stretch. I exchanged greetings with a couple of them, my stomach reminding me we hadn't eaten yet.

There was a cozy, festive quality to the whole area that always brought a smile to my lips. The bright lights, the constant murmurs of conversations, the shouts advertising something, the mix of music from a dozen different sources, and the faces of visitors, lit up and hopeful and ready for a night full of fun. The ambiance reminded me of Vicky's tour of doom. It had been such a great experience until it hadn't. I should rip off the Band-Aid and take another tour, go back to enjoying my new hometown in every way.

Strange as it sounded, going on another guided tour felt like a betrayal to her memory.

But not as big as the sense of betrayal I'd felt when I'd tried to get into the secret witch relics room at the Modern Cabinet of Curiosities Museum, and the guy at the entrance had looked at me funny. How unfair was that? The least Vicky could've done was tell the truth during her tour.

I banished my memories of Vicky as I approached Bosko's shop. It was narrow—a long hallway full to the brim with rows of hanging T-shirts and other pieces of apparel. Already several customers ambled inside, browsing through the T-shirts and giggling at the jokes printed on them.

Maybe the trick was to make my T-shirts more obvious. Not hidden away in one of the shelf cubicles, but hung on display right next to the daily specials. No, I decided regretfully after a moment. It'd dilute the message of the shop. I studied the interior of this shop again. Would Bosko take some of my T-shirts on consignment?

I squeezed past the visitors and reached the glass counter at the end. It displayed more expensive items like earrings and necklaces and replica figurines of famous spots in the city. Bosko himself was manning the counter—tall, thin, with graying blond hair and sharp eyes fixed on the people behind me. He probably got a lot of grab-and-runs.

"Good evening, Mr. Bosko," I said jovially.

He grunted and indicated for me to move to the side. I complied happily—anything to endear myself to the man.

"Do you ever sell on consignment?" Might as well break the ice with a useful topic.

"No."

"Not even as a favor?"

He snorted. "No."

"Was that for any favor, or just me?"

He sneered down at me, and I got my answer. Awkward.

Undeterred, I showed him my most winning smile. "I'm sure I'll grow on you. We're neighbors now." I studied the top of the counter, which sported an old-fashioned register, a couple of notepads, and a few piles of colorful leaflets offering discounts for the nearby bars. "What about leaflets? Maybe I can leave some for the shop here?" I served beverages, therefore I fit the clubbing theme.

"Sure." Then he spat out a price that almost gave me a heart attack.

"A little expensive, isn't it?" I choked out through my shock.

"This is prime real estate, lady."

As if to underscore his pronouncement, one of the visitors approached the counter with a couple of T-shirts and a pair of socks with leering cartoon jars of sangria. Her eyes lit up at the stacks of colorful papers and she grabbed a few.

Bosko rang up her purchase, then gave me a *See? Worth its space in gold* look.

"What if you only have them out in the mornings?" I asked.

"You think I have time to go around replacing shit on my counter all day?"

"Of course not," I said, going for contrite. "Your shop really is something."

"I do all right." He shrugged modestly. "Did Sonia send you? I told her I'd email her the stuff on Monday."

"Nah, just browsing on my own." I played with the hem of a nearby tee that read *When in doubt, boobs*. Ugh. I dropped my hand and rubbed it surreptitiously on my jeans. "Your shop's been here a long time, right?"

A satisfied smile of pride curved his lips. "Here since the seventies. It was a shoe store, then. Pops ran it."

I eyed the neon green flip-flops peeking beneath a pile of cheap hand towels patterned in cocktail glasses with winking anime eyes inside. Oh, how the mighty had fallen. "You must know everyone in the community, then."

"Duh."

"What about the shifters?" I pointed at a T-shirt with a howling wolf's head and the words *Get your woof on* arching above. "You knew Hutton Sr.?"

"Derek's pa? Sure. Man was solid."

"You were friends?"

"We weren't tight or anything, but he always came to inquire about the family."

I snapped my finger and pointed at him. "That's right. You're married, right? Have one kid?"

The possibility hadn't even occurred to me until now.

"Two. Sarah helps me run the shop," he said proudly.

"That's nice. Keeping it in the family and everything."

A speculative gleam shone in his eyes. "You related to Bagley?"

"No. Council gave me the shop. I heard she was great, though."

"She was all right." He glanced behind me and shouted, "Take that and I'm breaking your arms."

I whirled in surprise. A young teen grinned and dashed out of the shop. The other customers laughed nervously.

"What was I saying?" Bosko said. "Oh, yeah, Bagley. Too saccharine for my tastes, if you know what I mean."

"Old ladies can be like that," I agreed, to the instant

condemnation of every older woman in existence. "I'm taking the shop in a new direction, though."

"I saw. All that witchy stuff." He gave me a considering look. "Smart business move."

"Thanks." I stood straighter and my smile became more genuine. "I have plans."

"You should talk to Sonia about advertising at her store."

Sonia would rather eat her cane than let me touch her store. "Not a bad idea. I'll float the notion, see what she says." My gaze strayed back to the wolf T-shirt, and I pointed at it. "What about the pack's stores? Are they a new thing?"

"Derek's father opened them some years ago. The pack used to have a restaurant. Served the best damn fried chicken in town."

"Used to?"

"Sold it after his folks died. Without his ma, the place wasn't the same."

"That's sad."

"Place is a fast-food joint now." He shook his head. "Disgusting."

"Gross," I agreed, although a cheap, fake burger sounded like absolute heaven right about now. "Who knows what they'll end up doing with Mr. Lewis's old shop?" I scrunched my forehead into a deeply thoughtful expression. "Say, weren't you and Mr. Lewis friends?"

"Sort of. He had good ideas for the neighborhood." Bosko shook his head. "What a waste. Now they'll go and open one of those fancy coffee places with ten kinds of seasonal flavors."

My mouth went dry, and a needle of anxiety poked at my insides. Would that be a good contrast to the Tea Cauldron or a complete disaster? I crossed my fingers and tapped them together at the lack of nearby wooden surfaces. Let us hope it didn't come to pass. "I bet you two knew all the gossip about everyone around."

He huffed a laugh. "I know some stories. Move over."

I stepped aside and let another customer pay for their purchases.

"You do brisk business," I said with true admiration.

"Weekends are good. Winters kill me, though. Need to do most of my business between May and November. After that…" He made a downward gesture with his hand and added a low whistle. "Every purchase counts."

It didn't take a genius IQ to see where this was going. I opened my mouth in undisguised shock. "Oh, look." Carefully, I pried the neon green flip-flops from under the pile of hand towels. With any luck, it'd remind him of his father and put him in a reminiscent mood. "I was looking for something to use in the backyard." I checked the tag and made a happy noise. "My size. Perfect." If my shoe size were a man's large.

"The color suits you." He nodded at the green streak in my hair.

"That's right." He made an excellent point. Maybe I'd use them, after all. Or give them to Ian as a sign of goodwill. I waved toward the rows of T-shirts. "Which one do you think is good as a joke for Cavalier?"

Bosko made a sound of disgust. "None, if you're smart, lady."

I leaned my elbows on the counter, all wide ears. "I bet you knew him when he was a little kid. Before he and his mother moved away."

"He was a cute kid, I'll give you that. For a while there, we all thought Marcus and Charlotte were going to get married."

"But then his mother came into the picture, right? Derek's, I mean."

"Ian's ma used to run one of those tours through the cemetery. See that shirt over there?"

I followed the direction of his pointing finger and found a T-shirt printed with a design of cartoon tombstones, each containing one of the following words and number: *I am dead 4 you*. "Uh-uh."

"Got my inspiration for that one from her." He considered me for a moment. "It sort of fits your shop, doesn't it?"

"It sure does," I said cheerfully. I picked the topmost tee with the design and added it to the flip-flops. All I needed now was a pair of leggings and a bandanna and I'd be set. "Cavalier's mom sounds like a nice person."

"Lovely woman. Always had a smile for everyone."

"Pack's alpha and the cemetery tour woman sounds like a weird pairing." My gaze snagged on a group of handkerchiefs printed with dog faces. Ah, well. In for a pair of flip-flops, in for a new wardrobe. At least the stuff was cheap. I added the handkerchief to the pile. "Is it true Hutton's mother broke them up?"

He began ringing up the items. "If you want to know about that, you should ask Veva."

13

Veva. I searched my memory for the name. "Veva Daly? The tarot reader?"

"Her shop's at Marquesa. She and Charlotte were best friends. Bag?"

"I see. Wait, do you have a tote?"

"Over there."

I chose the least visually offensive one, and he added it to my bill before snapping the tag off and putting my purchases inside.

"Do you know if she's open tonight?" I asked as I paid. Thank the good Earth the place was cheap.

"It's Saturday evening, lady."

"Got your money, back to 'lady,' huh?"

His smile was open, wide, and I was tempted to count his teeth. "Have a good day."

"May many tourists find comfort in your tees."

He acknowledged my blessing with a solemn nod of his head, and I left his establishment. Night had fully fallen outside, and the people on the streets were getting rowdier, with honks of cars mixing with the loud music coming from the open bars and restaurants. I hitched the tote high on my shoulder and made my way to Marquesa Street.

The street was more sedate than Bosko's, with fewer bars and restaurants and more proper shops. A lot of tiny specialized stores lined the sides—dolls, suits, clocks, jewelry stores, candles, occult, crafts, and the like. Veva's parlor, Cards & Destiny, was a tiny thing, easily missed if you weren't looking for it.

The curtain behind the single window was drawn, but the neon sign read open, so I pushed the door open and found myself in a darkened room with shelves lining the walls and an old wooden desk serving as the counter at the far end. A chime not unlike the Tea Cauldron's tinkled in the air as the door hit it on the way in and then on the way back out.

"Welcome." The heavy curtains hiding the doorway into the back parted open, and a tall woman walked into the room. Her hair was tucked under a small turban and she wore high-waist jeans, a white blouse, and a pair of comfortable sandals. Her lips stretched into a warm, welcoming smile. "Ah, the new witch. Avery, is it?"

"Hope Avery, ma'am." I stepped forward and offered my hand.

Her grip was firm and friendly. "None of that. Please call me Veva. About time we met."

"I haven't seen you at the PBOA's meetings."

"Ah, yes. I don't like going downtown. I send Marcel instead sometimes. He owns the shop next door."

That'd be the one with the creepy ceramic dolls. I suppressed a shudder. Talk about haunted locations. "I'm sorry it took me so long to come around. It's been busy."

She eyed the tote bag. "I see Bosko's hand at work. Did he send you?"

"Caught," I confessed with a grin. "But I did mean to visit at some point."

"It takes two to tango, honey. It's not like I've gone to drink tea at your shop, is it?"

"When you put it that way…"

She walked up to the curtains and beckoned me to follow. "Since you're here, let me give you a reading. Let's get to know each other better."

I examined the blackboard listing the prices for the different readings. This research trip was proving to be more expensive than anticipated, but hopefully whatever I discovered would be worth its weight in gold.

Except, of course, words carried no weight.

"Come, Hope," Veva urged.

I followed her through the doorway and she ushered me into a small side room containing a round table and two chairs. She had me sit on one and made use of the other. A worn tarot box lay on the side, which she opened to reveal a lovely set of cards.

As she shuffled, I studied the rest of the room. A few framed photographs and drawings decorated the walls, most featuring Veva herself. My gaze fell on a photograph of her and a young woman dressed in a police uniform.

"You're Officer Brooks's mother?" I asked in surprise.

"Aunt."

"No wonder you haven't come to the shop." Officer Brooks had probably told her I was missing some screws.

"I make my own opinions, Hope. Now, concentrate."

I returned my attention to the cards in her hand. She put the stack on the middle of the table and I parted it into thirds. She joined the small piles deftly and placed the three topmost cards on the soft, dark red cloth covering the table.

"Why did Bosko send you to me?" Her tone was sharp.

Warm and sharp in a way that made you want to confess all your sins because you needed someone to have your back, no matter what.

"Nothing bad." I successfully resisted the urge to spill all my secrets. "I'm curious about what happened between Cavalier's mother and Derek Hutton's dad."

"Ah, I see." She gave me a knowing look, and I felt myself blush.

"He said you might know more about it." I decided to go with my main theory. "I come from a line of witches, and I'm not used to shifter stuff. I've done some research since I moved to Olmeda, but the whole notion of true mates seems hard to believe. Makes me think Ian's parents were already in trouble but didn't tell anyone, and Hutton's mother happened to come by right before they made their breakup official."

"Shifters can be weird," she agreed.

As usual, the itch to ask what kind of paranormal creature she was rose unencumbered. Perhaps Dru would know.

Tapping the first card to my right, Veva said. "This is your past."

"Fitting."

"You'll find so many things fit like a puzzle when you really pay attention."

I couldn't tell if she'd guessed my mental meandering or if it was simply good life advice. "Let's see it."

She flipped the card—death.

"I know what that means," I said with no small triumph. "Rebirth. Me opening the shop."

Veva shook her head. "Count on the witch to take the fun out of it."

"You're right, you're right." I flipped the card back. "Let's do it again."

She grinned and turned the card.

A gasp of horror escaped me, and I pressed a hand to my chest. "*Death?*"

"Sometimes the card can be taken quite literally," Veva said with a smile. "Death does not always mean the end of life itself. Death surrounds us no matter where we are, no matter what we do. We walk among the buildings built by those no longer among the living. We use tools developed by people long dead. Our society is forever haunted by the ghosts of the past. You are here, digging up the past of someone dead. You involve yourself with someone who lives among graves. You live in a house where death occurred not long ago." She tapped the card. "Death is what brought you here, Hope Avery."

Bagley's death. Grandma's death. My eyes filled with tears, and I blinked them away.

Veva's voice softened. "The why of your past will help you understand your present. It's what's formed you, what drives you. Sometimes it's a good thing." She shrugged lightly. "And sometimes it isn't. Knowing the why allows you to judge whether your current choices are the correct ones, or if they're driven by the wrong force in your past."

I swallowed the lump in my throat. "You think I should stop nosing around the past?"

A cheery laugh escaped her. "No, hon. Life would be unendurable without gossip."

Relief made me a little giddy. "So, you know what happened between Ian's parents?"

"Oh, but I do." Her fingertips rested on the middle card. "This is your present."

"If it's death again, I'm flipping the table and leaving without paying."

"That's sweet, but I know where you live."

We grinned at each other, then she flipped the card.

"The Two of Coins." She studied me thoughtfully. "You are

new in town, eager. You have taken in too much, and perhaps too soon. Your attention is divided. For some, this invigorates them, but for others, it might bring them down. Which one are you?"

I thought of the shop, of Dru, of Key, of the dark magic business I'd inherited from Bagley, of Hutton and his problems, and Ian and his refusal to help. Was I juggling more than I could handle?

"Was that what separated Ian's parents? It was too much to handle for Charlotte, being with a pack's alpha?"

Her eyes rolled skyward. "Lord, but you're insistent."

"I've heard that complaint before." I gave her a sheepish smile.

"Let's finish the reading first, and then we can talk about Cavalier's parents." Without preamble, she flipped the last card.

The lovers.

"Oh, Mother," I groaned, burying my face in my hands.

Veva nodded in contentment. "Look at that, the cards *do* know it all. Love is in your future. But it's not always in the way we expect."

I peeked between my fingers. "It's not?"

"Sometimes it means romantic love, sometimes it means a choice. The opportunity for love is there, but it's up to you to claim it. Just because the option is there, it doesn't mean you need to take it." Her lips pursed for a moment. "Linking yourself to Ian Cavalier might not be the best choice."

My cheeks heated again. Apparently, my friendship with Ian hadn't gone unnoticed. "We're not linked that way."

She tapped the card with a perfectly manicured nail and said what my inner voice had silently added, "Not yet."

"Pretend he was interested in me that way." I kept my voice as nonchalant as possible. "Why would it be a bad choice? Because he's a bounty hunter?"

"Bounty hunters are bad news, but no."

"Then why?"

"That family comes with heartbreak."

"Don't tell me Derek Hutton also broke some poor soul's heart." My attention sharpened. "So it's true? Ian's father really did break his mother's heart? That other woman waltzed in and, boom! Fated mates?"

Her fingertips rested on the card. "The future is never guaranteed. It's built on the choices you make in the present, and romantic love does not escape those."

"But people made it sound like fated mates couldn't be escaped."

"There is always a choice. It might tear something out of us, but the choice is there."

I made a face. "Even if he hadn't broken up with Ian's mother, she'd have known his 'true mate' was out there. She'd always fear that he would leave her."

"Love does not always make us think rationally."

"This tarot reading is not very uplifting."

Veva laughed. "It's not meant to be. It's meant to make you think."

"And you think me and Ian—" I cleared my throat. "*If* Ian and I were to go down that road, it might be a bad thing."

"All choices have consequences. It might work out, it might not. What does your gut say?"

"My gut is currently on time out."

Her smile broadened. "Then I guess you'll have to listen to something else."

I worried my lip, concentrating on the card and thinking beyond Ian and my possible future relationship. Something Veva had said stuck out—*the opportunity for love is there. It's up to you to claim it.* But what if it wasn't there, but you still claimed it? Like, say, the girl who'd come to me for a love potion. Or her sister, whom Bagley had actually given a real love potion.

And suddenly, I knew what had happened between Ian and Hutton's parents.

"Son of a witch." I shot upright, sending the chair cluttering backward. I hurried to straighten it and dug into my wallet. "Sorry. I need to go."

Veva looked disappointed. "Are you sure? Don't worry about that." She waved my money aside. "On the house."

"Thank you. Please come visit the Tea Cauldron soon."

"Will do," she called after me. I rushed out of the shop and all but ran home.

"Bagley," I shouted, dumping the tote on the counter.

"So noisy," came the complaint from a book on the merchandise shelf. "Keep your voice down, child."

I came to stand in front of it. "Did you, or did you not give Hutton's mother a love potion for the alpha?"

A giggling noise poured out of the book's spine. "Oh, you finally figured that out, did you?"

It explained everything. The supreme coincidence that the alpha's true mate happened to waltz in, the whirlwind courtship and unceremonious dumping of Ian's mother, the fact that Hutton had no alpha powers even though he was clearly fathered by the same person as Ian and Ian had no trouble with his—Ian's father had been under a spell when they conceived Hutton.

"The spell interfered in the passing of the alpha power." Dark magic always screwed things up in some way. Always.

"I'm afraid so," Bagley said mournfully. "I warned her it might happen, but she didn't believe me."

"That's why Hutton came to you for the alpha potion—it was his mother's idea, wasn't it?"

"You're doing so well, dear. Look at all that thinking power! All those theories! All on your own."

"Oh, get lost."

A cackle rose in the air. "Get me a new body, and you'll never have to hear from me again."

"Over my dead... Never mind." I took the book with me into the kitchen and tossed it onto the counter. I needed to do something about the witch; some kind of spell that would force her to re-spawn in the same object rather than one at random.

Or one that would get rid of her once and for all.

But that was a worry for another time.

In my eagerness to show Ian that his parents' breakup hadn't been as bad as he thought, I'd discovered it was a million times worse. The witch could be lying, but everything fit so perfectly, it made me wonder if Ian hadn't already guessed.

Part of me hoped he hadn't, and the rest wasn't about to tell him—nobody would appreciate learning their father had been spelled into a relationship and a family.

Unfortunately, that left me back where I'd started—with a resounding rejection and no other way to save Hutton's dwindling alpha powers.

14

A FRETFUL NIGHT of little sleep had made things abundantly clear—if I wanted to save the pack from the evil dark-magic using twins and keep it in the hands of the other evil-out-of-necessity dark-magic user, I needed to up my game.

I hoped Grandma would forgive me.

Ian arrived at around ten, Fluffy and Rufus in tow.

"Leave the dogs out here." I indicated the backyard, refusing to meet Fluffy's round, innocent eyes. What I needed to do couldn't be done in her presence—her goodness was too strong, and I didn't want to disappoint her.

She let out a small, sad whine when I closed the door in her face, but I hardened my heart.

"All right, I'm here." Ian stuck his hands in the front pockets of his jeans and leaned against the wall of the hallway. "What was so important that you needed to meet me 'with all urgency?'"

The sleepless night also reinforced my decision not to disclose my discovery about his father.

Like me, Ian must've wondered why Hutton needed a potion for his alpha powers when they clearly had the same father. He might've arrived at the same conclusion about Hutton's mom and a potion interfering with the process. But then, maybe not. I had no way of knowing, and I wasn't about to make things harder for him—or myself.

If he didn't know, telling wouldn't help my case, and I'd be introducing a huge heap of extra pain. If he already knew, it would only remind him that Hutton seemed to be following in his mother's footsteps and make my job all the more difficult.

Did that make me selfish? Probably.

Would Ian forgive me if he didn't know the truth and found out I'd kept it from him? Probably not.

The lovers' card came to mind. The choices of the present influenced the opportunities in the future. After this mess with his brother, Ian and I might not even have a friendship. How utterly depressing.

"Well?" he asked.

I forced myself to stop thinking about tarot cards, sad little animals in the backyard, the growing guilt weighing my heart down into the pit of the abyss, and everything that didn't have anything to do with Hutton's potion.

"The twins visited the shop," I said in a grim tone.

"No, they didn't."

I filled my lungs with enough air to last a deep dive. "They did. Wanted to know if I had freezing potions, or worse."

A faint smile curved one side of his mouth. "No, they didn't."

"They threatened me if I didn't help them with the potion."

"No, they didn't."

"How do you know?"

"Because you'd have called me right away."

I sneered. "I don't always call you right away."

"You called me the moment you saw that post in the dark web."

"That was different."

"You're trying to pressure me into helping with the alpha potion." He leaned in and his voice cooled. "It's not going to work."

"Not even if it puts me in danger?" I asked just as coolly.

"The twins don't know who you are."

"Hutton does, and you know what he'll do."

"He'll do nothing because if he does, they'll think he's trying to shift blame from losing his pack."

Ah, how I longed to strangle him. Why did he always have to be so clinical, so...prepared? Like a goddamn boy scout.

Time for plan B—the big guns.

"You leave me no choice." I crossed my arms and tapped a finger against my biceps. "Are you sure you don't want to help?"

"Throw your best shot." By the tone of his voice, he couldn't wait to hear it.

So be it. "If you don't help me, I'll add you to the dark web marketplace as a hitman."

It would've taken a way less observant witch than me not to sense Ian's barely contained anger at the mere suggestion he might be confused for a hitman. It should've taken a way less scruple-free witch to bring it up, yet here we were—Ian, me, and all the bad karma I'd be eating for the rest of my life.

"Do that, and I'll be contacting the Council about Bagley." His smile grew colder. "I will survive. You won't."

"Then I'll tell the mage why the shop got closed down, and he loves his dark magic potion. He'll make your life impossible."

"Until I tell him how you cheated him, made him look like a fool with fake blood and a can of energy drink."

That's what I got for telling him my tricks. I tilted my head. "Why should he believe a hitman over his new favorite witch?"

"You think he has survived this long by not being paranoid?"

Mentally, I kicked a rock. Outwardly, I was the face of pure serenity. "Fine. What about the strays, then?"

"What about them?"

"They might not be around for much longer if the twins take over the pack. They don't seem the type to allow free-roaming shifters to stay near their territory."

"How would you know? You've never talked to them."

"The kind who needs to cheat to win a territory is not the kind who'd be kind to outsiders."

"Unless all they want is the land to sell."

A crack appeared in my blasé expression. "And you'd be fine with that?"

"Doesn't involve me."

"You'd be fine with me having to pack up and leave?"

"Why would you pack up and leave when things are getting interesting?"

"Because Hutton will tell the Council about me, and all the excuses in the world aren't going to help if he shows them that listing for the shop. Nothing will happen to him, everything will happen to me. They might jail me. What about our deal to figure out Bagley's dark magic users? To bring them to justice or fool them into using good magic?"

His hand landed on my shoulder, and he squeezed lightly. "Don't worry. If a shift of alpha happens, Hutton won't last long enough to tattle on anyone."

"And you're okay with that? With Hutton being killed?"

"He has been using dark magic. He should reap the consequences."

I studied his expression, searching for any hint of regret, of bluster, of something that might indicate he didn't really believe what he was saying. When I couldn't find it, I switched to plan C.

The beyond-big guns.

Straightening, I held his amused stare.

"If you don't help, Fluffy will be *so* disappointed."

He blinked. Then it was his turn to search my face, my eyes, and my very soul.

With a soft exhale, he ran a hand through his hair, dislodging wavy locks from the hair tie keeping it gathered at the back of his head. He seemed to weigh his options for a few interminable seconds before facing me again.

"Be completely sure this is a favor you want to ask of me because you only get one."

I refused to drop my gaze. "I'm sure."

"Why?" He sounded genuinely baffled. "Why put all this effort to help him?"

"Because it's the right thing to do." I touched the center of his chest. "And deep inside, you know it too."

———

We were in the downstairs kitchen, and Ian's skin felt incredibly warm and solid under my fingers as I positioned his arm over a small glass bowl. With my other hand, I grabbed a sharp knife disinfected for the occasion and positioned its blade against the inside of his forearm.

I'd had one or two daydreams about all the things I could do with this bit of lovely, prime forearm estate, but somehow slicing it open hadn't come to mind.

"I hope you're up to date on your tetanus shots," I said with forced cheer.

Thud.

That was the sound of my joke landing with all the success of a flying cement block.

I concentrated on the blade. Now that it was time to do the cut, I found myself hesitating. I had done this before a couple of times, but only on myself. Cutting another person—cutting Ian—felt like a whole different matter.

His other hand wrapped around mine, and he guided the knife down in a fast, sharp move. A line of red appeared on his skin, and blood beaded immediately. It ran down the length of the cut and began dripping into the bowl.

The man didn't even flinch.

The man might as well be made of ice, the way he stood by my side, emanating waves of displeasure like an A/C unit set to frigid.

Plink. Plink.

I squirmed, my gaze fixed on the small puddle of blood forming at the bottom of the bowl. The weight of his stare was another dagger slowly making its way between my shoulder blades.

"Stop looking at me like that," I murmured.

"What else am I going to do?" His voice, cold and implacable, made things worse. I should've kept my mouth shut.

Being this close to Ian should've been another most excellent occasion, but the tightness in his posture made it clear how little he wanted to be here, and the blood seeping out of his arm made my stomach churn with unease.

Without a word, he took my hand and sliced through the cut again. I looked up in surprise.

"Shifter."

Which meant improved healing. I closed my eyes tight as realization hit—I might have to cut his arm several times before I got enough blood.

"I'll survive."

The hint of wryness in his tone should've encouraged me —the first hint of defrosting—but I was too deep into a self-flagellating spiral to take real notice. Using his hate of being mistaken for a hitman had been too low a blow. Forcing him to do all this when he clearly didn't want to was awful on my part.

This bloodletting might not be technically unwilling, but it was getting awfully close.

I wanted to hug him and tell him how sorry I was, but as Grandma used to say, if I were truly sorry, I wouldn't have done it in the first place.

Ian reopened his cut.

"Wow, this sucks." I winced, and part of me took comfort in the weight and warmth of his hand covering mine. Which was selfish and messed up and right on course with the morning's theme.

"Not as much as the favor you owe me now."

Definite defrosting in his tone now. One might even call it "edging on gleeful." I eyed him warily, but his features were still inscrutable.

"You're going to make me mow the whole cemetery, aren't you?"

"No. Your stray can do that."

"She's not my— Never mind. You know what?" I stepped back and opened my arms, offering myself on a platter. "Take your best shot. I deserve it."

He perused my figure slowly and the flutters in my belly fought with the shiver of unease creeping up my spine. "I'll think about it. Are we done?"

I checked the bowl. "A little more. Just to make sure." Because if I ever needed more of his blood, it'd definitely enter unwilling territory. So unwilling the blood might crawl right back into his body.

"Tell me about your bounty hunting days," I said. "Regale me with a story."

Maybe that'd help with the mood.

"I once hunted a witch. He tried to stab me."

I swallowed hard. "I see. What happened then?"

"He failed."

"And you captured him?" I asked tentatively.

"I ran him over with my car while he tried to run away."

"Did that really happen or are you trying to scare me into never putting myself between open space and your SUV ever again?"

His smile was fast, feral, and deeply disturbing. "Oh, it happened."

"Lovely." At least he was smiling, and every smile I could squeeze out of Ian was a huge win. I checked the bowl. "This is enough."

Carefully, I put the knife in the sink and grabbed a piece of gauze to press on his cut. Ian gently dislodged his arm from my hands, and the sense of loss hit me by surprise. Loss and regret. He was nowhere near being done forgiving me, and Grandma's saying or not, telling him I was sorry now would make things worse.

He understood that while I held all the sorrow in the world, I'd still do it all over again, anyway.

I moved the bowl to the portion of the counter holding my potion-making equipment. I'd already prepared the basics— clear quartz and other intent-focused crystals forming a circle, herbs, my favorite moon water foundation tonic, and a mortar and pestle ready with a mix of ingredients that interacted with blood or power. I scooped some of the fine powder with a measuring spool and placed the potion glass, already half-filled with the foundation tonic, in the middle of the circle.

A potion like this needed three stages of spelling. The intent poured into the magic had to be exactly the same during each stage, otherwise, the ingredients wouldn't react with each other, and you'd end up with a layered drink instead of a true potion.

Another tricky part was that beyond the three spells holding the same intention, they also had to be of similar power. The crystals making the circle were more for my sake than the spell's. With my crappy level of magical power, I was going to need all the help focusing. Not just because of the amount of power required to do the spell itself, but because I burned out fast. Doing one spell was fine, but three in a row?

Now, that was going to test my limits.

"It's a marathon, not a sprint," I murmured.

I sprinkled the powder into the basic tonic. It made beautiful swirls as it sank slowly.

A tingle began inside my chest, almost ticklish as it ran down my arms and wound around my fingers.

Power can't be bought.

Power can be *gifted*.

Gifted by the will of blood.

The words were inconsequential, nothing but a conduit between a witch's brain and their magic, a way to put will to magic. Power left my body as if poured right into the potion bottle. A wave of dizziness hit me, but I stood my ground. Things had to move fast now before I passed out.

Inhaling deeply, I took the bowl with the blood and tipped it carefully over the bottle. It would've been easier to mix the potion into another bowl, but potions lost effectiveness with each subsequent transfer.

Ian's blood ran down thickly, then dripped into the potion.

My hand tightened around the bottle. One hand, double the power, but, in the end, it must be exactly as before.

Power can't be bought.

Power can be gifted.

Gifted by the will of *blood*.

The tickling on my left hand intensified, power zapping through the contact with the warm glass, mixing into the potion, into the blood as it fell into the liquid.

Sweat broke out on my forehead, and I blinked to clear my vision. Carefully, I set the bowl aside and inserted the stopper for the bottle. One more spell to go. My legs felt wobbly. Next time, I was making these sitting down.

Holding the bottle with both hands, I poured in what was left of my magic, matching the intensity and focus of the last two spells.

Power can't be bought.

Power can be *gifted*.

Gifted by the *will* of *blood*.

The last of my power poured into the mixture, hopefully making all parts interact with each other to form a stable potion capable of keeping Hutton's borrowed alpha power alive for a bit longer.

I snatched my hands back, scared some last vestige of magic might mess things up, and my knees buckled.

"Oops," I said on my way down, my brain struggling to catch up. The room was covered with a strange, cozy glaze that made it look extraordinary in all its commonness.

Strong arms caught me, then gathered me against a solid chest. I murmured in contentment and burrowed into it. So warm. Such a wonderful smell.

"Ian?" I asked drowsily.

His grunt reverberated right down his chest and into my ear. We were moving now, going up a set of stairs.

"I just need a little rest, then I'll be fine," I mumbled into his Henley.

"Sure."

I heard the squeak of one of the hardwood boards, and then

I was placed on a soft surface that dipped under my weight. My bed.

I stared into Ian's lovely green eyes. Perhaps it was my sudden tiredness, but they didn't look frozen over. They looked warm and soft and inviting.

"Thank you," I said. "I'm sorry."

He straightened with a snap, his hands abandoning me like I was a hot potato. Yum, potatoes. Later, maybe. After a short nap.

With a huge yawn, I turned onto my side and closed my eyes.

15

THREE HOURS LATER, I was nursing an extra-strength energy drink from the stack I'd bought for Brimstone and Destruction's fake potions when Hutton deigned to come in. My gaze drifted to the masses of tourists walking by the shop. What a sad, sad sight. Sunday afternoons had been a good moneymaker so far, but I hadn't wanted to keep the shop open while I used my magic.

The reminder made my mood plummet.

Ian had left without leaving a note or a text or anything. He'd taken the dogs with him too. I supposed I didn't deserve for Fluffy to cleanse my house and my soul. I'd have to live with my high-handed, failed attempts at bribery and blackmail.

Getting back into Ian's good books was going to take patience, perseverance, and a full-on miracle.

"Yes, I have the potion," I said before Hutton could get out a word. "This way."

I marched across the room, my grim mood mixing with my tiredness and the energy drink's caffeine in the worst possible way. Hutton followed me into the kitchen and stood expectantly.

"Here you go." I retrieved the bottle from the counter and dropped it into Hutton's waiting hands. Seeing the fruit of my labors and bad karma cheered me up a little.

I'd made the potion. I was helping the local alpha keep his pack.

Not a drop of dark magic involved.

And it was okay to bask in my accomplishment. There would be time later to deal with the repercussions.

"What's in it?" he asked.

"Blood," I said simply. He didn't need to know it was his brother's. "Only way to keep the other potion going."

Hutton unplugged the cork stopper and sent it flying. Ignoring my glare, he brought the bottle to his mouth and chugged the potion in one go. My stomach rolled along with his Adam's apple.

When he was done, he tossed the bottle my way and looked at me expectantly.

I clutched the bottle close to my chest. "Well?"

"Well, what?" he snapped.

"How are you feeling?"

"Like I just drank a shot of blood."

I wasn't sure where to look. "Right."

He began pacing the small space, irritation seeping out of his every pore. "How long until it starts working?"

"Should be immediate."

"How immediate?"

"You should be feeling the effects soon."

"I feel nothing."

Prickles of unease ran up my back. "Soon-ish?" I said, more to comfort myself than him.

He stopped right in front of me, looming like a medieval tower complete with a dragon spewing fire on top of it. "What did you give me, witch?"

I placed the bottle on the counter with a loud thump. "A potion to help you keep your alpha powers."

His eyes narrowed. "Did you poison me? Are you working for one of *them*?"

"No, and I don't appreciate the lack of trust."

He laughed harshly. "Trust? I don't trust you as far as I can throw you, witch."

As a shifter, he could throw me pretty far, but this was not the moment to point that out. "Are you sure you're not feeling any different?" I peered into his eyes, a watered-down version of Ian's green, searching for signs of something. Demons' eyes turned red when the glamour potions faded out. Maybe Hutton's would turn yellow like a wolf's if my potion worked out?

He stepped back, scowling. "What are you doing?"

"Do your eyes turn yellow with alpha power?"

"The hell?"

"I'm not well-versed in shifters," I admitted. "Is there any way to tell if you're an alpha beyond the lack of overall power vibes?"

"You'd have to be a shifter." He sneered as if being a witch was so below being a shifter, we belonged to different planets.

"Well, that doesn't help you right now, does it?"

The sneer fell right off. "You did something wrong. Did you mess up intentionally?"

"I didn't." But the probability that the way I'd created the potion was flawed from the start was a very real one. The whole thing had been built on guesses—the types of herbs, the amount of blood, the magic's intent itself. This is why there were spellbooks.

"You need to make another one."

I rubbed my forehead, a headache building behind my eyes. "Are you sure it's not working? You might not feel any different

—the key is for it to keep what alpha powers you have left going."

"It's. Not. Working." He planted his pointed finger right on my sternum. "You better make the potion again or—"

I pushed his hand away. Clients didn't get to go anywhere near second base. "Yeah, yeah. You'll tattle on me to the Council, etcetera, etcetera."

His mouth fell open in outrage. "I don't tattle."

I turned him around and pushed him toward the hallway. "I'll get your potion, don't worry about it."

He stalked to the back door, sending me a last glare over his shoulder. "You better. And make it soon." A troubled look crossed his face. "Meetings start tomorrow. I've been able to stay away until now, but the moment I'm in the other alphas' presence for long, they're going to notice. I can't... I can't lose my father's pack."

My heart squeezed at the worry in this voice. What must it have felt like growing up knowing you'd take over a pack? Having all those people depend on you? All that pressure. No wonder he was being such an ass about it. "I'll do my best."

"You do that."

He slammed the door behind him.

What an absolute mess. I could've really used Fluffy right now.

Except Ian was never going to let me see her again.

Dragging my feet, I returned to the kitchen and surveyed the fruit of my labors—the herbs and crystals, the clean knife and bowl, and the mortar and pestle still holding the powdered ingredients. The empty potion bottle.

I opened the faucet and let water fill the sink. The familiar gurgles echoed behind the wall.

"Goldfish ghost, I need your wisdom."

Something thudded twice.

I contemplated the round pipe for a few seconds, then nodded to myself.

"You're right—if one must fail, one must fail upwards."

As much as I wanted to blame Hutton for rushing me, I was the witch here. It had been my decision to go ahead with a spell instead of waiting until I had more data. Who did I think I was? If all spells were so easy, there wouldn't be a need for experts in the field.

Lilian Valenti hadn't gotten back to me, and why should she? I was a nobody, and she was a top-of-the-field expert.

"Sacrifices," I told the faucet, "must be made for the greater good."

I had already sacrificed a chunk of my and Ian's friendship, so what was a piece of my pride compared to that?

Sitting on the bottom step of the stairs, I pulled out my phone and dialed Tammy, my ex-witch-boss.

"Ms. Summers's phone," said a hurried voice. Not Tammy's. Probably her new witch intern.

"Hi, is Tammy around?"

"She's busy right now. Can I take a message?"

"Who is that?" asked a familiar voice in the background.

"I don't know, Tammy," said her intern.

"It's Hope Avery."

"She says it's Hope Avery," the intern repeated.

"Who?"

I rubbed my eyes. Chances were Tammy remembered me as You. "I interned for her a few years back."

"She says she interned for you a while back." A long pause ensued, then, "I'll get back to you."

"No, wait! It's urgent."

"I'm sorry. Tammy is busy right now."

"If she's busy with me, she won't be busy bugging you," I pointed out.

Another pause. Then, "I'm sorry, Tammy. She's very, very insistent. You should take this."

There were a few muffled sounds, then my ex-boss's cultured voice came on the call. "Hello, Abby. How wonderful to hear your voice again."

"Avery. Hope Avery."

She chuckled. "Of course, of course. What can I do for you, dear?"

"I was hoping you could put me in contact with Ms. Valenti."

"Lilian? Whatever for?"

"I need to consult her for a spell, but I think I got the wrong number. I'm sure you can convince her to talk to me for old time's sake?"

Unless they were no longer besties, in which case —awkward.

"What kind of spell? Anything I can help with? Is it for the Council?"

From the tone of her voice, the Council was about to get a chillingly polite call about using new witches for their spells instead of highly established ones like herself. As I'd just witnessed, she wouldn't remember my name two seconds after we hung up, but why chance her bringing me up?

"It's a private business. Nothing Council-related." I chose not to tell her I'd gotten the shop either, in case she kicked up a fuss about that too. "It would be such a huge favor if you could give me her private number."

"I'm not giving her number to strangers."

"A good deed a day keeps the sins away."

"Excuse me?"

"Something my grandma used to say." Except her version mentioned wrinkles. "I know you're a very busy woman, and I understand your concerns, but this is really urgent. Being your intern was such a...transformative experience. I wouldn't be the witch I am today without you."

"That's so sweet of you to say." Her voice warmed up.

"Some of the best months of my life. Seriously."

"Hush, now." Giddiness all but reeked from the phone now.

"You're a gift to the community. The fact that you still take on interns with your busy schedule is something else."

"Someone has to do it," she said humbly. "I have the time and the knowledge, so why not? I'll tell you what, Abby—I'll love to pass your phone number along."

"Oh, I wouldn't want to bother..."

"Nonsense! I'll give it to her right away. She's free on Sundays, anyway. It's her cleansing day. She does nothing but lie on the couch sipping lemon water and watching TV."

"Are you sure? I don't want to impose..."

"Yes, I'm sure. She'll be miffed, but I'm more than capable of dealing with her bad moods."

"Oh, that's not good. Perhaps it'd be better if the call came from me directly? That way she won't blame you."

"I don't know..."

"I promise to delete the number as soon as I'm done talking to her. I wouldn't ask this favor if I had any other option, but there's no one else who can help me, Tammy."

"Yes, I suppose that would be all right." She chuckled. "I do hate bothering her on Sundays."

"Taking the blame for the disruption is the least I can do."

"You're so sweet." She changed the phone to speaker and rattled off a number.

Oh, wow, we were doing this *now*. I scrambled to open the notes application and type it down. "Seven, oh, eight?"

"Seven, oh, nine," she chided.

"Thank you *so* much, Tammy. You're a real lifesaver."

"I do my best, love. That's all we can do."

With those sage words, she ended the call.

As I took a few minutes to fill my lungs and clear my thoughts, one thing became crystal clear: I had royally screwed up. The call had been so much easier than I'd expected. I should've called from the start. Why had I let my pride stand in the way of business?

Grandma would be so disappointed.

The thought gnawed at my heart.

"A path taken late is better than a path never taken," I reminded myself. "Giddy up, Buttercup, you're not done."

It took five rings for Lilian Valenti to pick up, and I almost fell off the step in relief when she did.

"Who's this?" Her voice was rough and annoyed. Her Sunday lemon water was in dire need of some honey.

"It's Hope Avery. Tammy gave me your—"

"Robin, *no*. What are you doing, man? Go to your right. To your right." A sharp inhale filled the air. "That's *left*!" The sound of fake gunfire in the background made me wince. "Aaand, we're dead. Bless your stupid little heart, Robin, and lift both your hands. What? Yes, I'm serious. Are they up? Okay, now make an 'L' with your thumbs and index fingers. See the one that's not written backward? *That's your left*. No, *you* go screw yourself. Never mind, you already do that every break. Yeah, I sure *dare*. Goddamn newbies," she muttered. Her voice grew closer as she lifted the phone to her face. "Who's this? I don't recognize the number."

I dropped my left hand and its cute L. "Hi, sorry to interrupt"—your relaxing Sunday cleanse—"I'm an old intern of Tammy and—"

"Which one?"

"Does it matter?"

"Guess not. What do you want? I'm in the middle of ranking."

"I was hoping to ask for your advice about a high-level blood potion."

She grunted. "What kind of blood potion?"

"Nothing illegal," I assured her. "No dark magic."

"Sure. Whatever. What kind of potion?"

I wondered if she and Bagley were old friends. "I'm trying to make a potion to improve a shifter's well-being." Presenting my case in a way that didn't ring alarm bells was key, both in case she tattled to the Council or was actually a dark magic user. "She's been feeling sick whenever she shifts back and forth, but nothing seems amiss on her human tests. I think there's an imbalance of magic once she's shifted, and I was hoping that by using her sister's blood, it could reinforce her own power, boost it up, so to speak."

"Hmm." The sounds of the game stopped abruptly. "Are you sure the problem is with the power itself and not some physiological issue?"

"I ran several tests with wards. It's definitely magic-related."

"The sister is willing to donate her blood?"

"Yes." I crossed my fingers tightly because, at this point, why not. "Absolutely. I went ahead and tried a potion, but it had no effect."

"Tell me what you used."

I told her the ingredients, the method used to spell the potion, and the spell itself with slightly changed wording.

She harrumphed. "That's the issue right there. You only used the healthy sister's blood."

My attention sharpened. "Oh?"

"There's been several studies about shifters. Their magic runs different from other paranormal species."

"I checked some of them at Montel's library, but they weren't of much use."

"Ragford's book?"

"Yes."

"That man shared one single brain cell with his cat. His 'studies' were an excuse to play around with blood and think himself some kind of Van Helsing."

"I see."

"By the nature of their shifting, the magic shifters carry in their blood doesn't last long outside their bodies. It retains some power, but it's mostly inert." Not good for dark magic, then. That was a relief. "Dark magic can harvest some of its power in the long run, but it will never contain the same magic levels as other paranormals. However, if the blood is fresh enough, there is no difference, really, in any kind of magic."

Assuming, the perennial sin. "I see."

"In this case, your potion was missing two key ingredients — Give me a second." There was some clatter as she put the phone down, and I thought she was getting some research book from her private collection. Instead, there was some muttering and a series of pings. A few moments later, she returned to the call. "Sorry. *Someone* thinks I give two shits if they leave the team."

"That's rough."

"You tell me. Anyway, your potion. I'm going to be straight with you because I need to get back to the game: the ingredients you used need some adjustments, but you need to mix both sisters' blood, and the sister with the problem needs to ingest it right away. That's the only way the potion has a chance of working. You also need to be super specific about how you manifest or verbalize your intent. There cannot be any doubt in the magic. It needs to be as tight as a fist." She then gave me a list of herbs and measures to try.

"That's very helpful. Thank you."

"One more thing."

"Yes?"

"Write the experiment down and send me the notes. I want to take a look at the prognosis for the shifter and any changes or improvements you record for a month. Check once daily for the first two weeks, then every other day."

"I'll make sure to give you a full report." Sister Wolf was about to make a miraculous recovery, no further potions necessary. Iron deficiency, I decided. When in doubt, blame iron deficiency.

"Great."

Lilian cut the call, and I stared at my phone as my brain processed her advice. Not one, but two shifters' blood. One who would kill me if he discovered his brother knew his secret, and the other who, at the moment, disliked me immensely. And they'd have to give it freely, together, at the same time.

No problem.

A LOT of brainstorming and a power nap later, I stood by the counter of the shop, a plate of grilled ham and cheese sandwiches at the ready.

Someone knocked on the back door.

"It's open," I shouted.

There was a creak and soft thuds as Ian made his way through the hallway. At the same time, a harsh rap on the front door's glass told me of Hutton's arrival.

I stared hard at the golden crust of the bread, the scent of browned butter filling my nostrils as I took a few deep breaths.

"You can do this, Hope. This is naught but a tiny hurdle. Hurdles are not walls. They can be scaled, taken down, and have huge open spaces underneath."

With a nod to myself, I gestured for Hutton to enter.

He opened the door and walked into the shop, his brow creased with obvious displeasure.

"Witch," he said in greeting, then stopped abruptly at the sight of Ian stepping through the bead curtain covering the archway. "You."

Ian came to a halt, black boots planted wide, arms folded

over his chest. He didn't say a thing. He simply gave his trade-mark granite stare.

I lifted the plate. "Sandwiches?"

They turned toward their exits in unison.

I dropped the plate on the counter and grabbed the back of their shirts. "Wait!"

Hutton yanked himself out of my grip, glaring at me with a mixture of incredulity and outrage. "Why is *he* here?"

"Let's all be adults," I said in an appeasing tone.

Ian reached back and gently disentangled my hand from his long-sleeved tee. He didn't say a thing, simply stared at us.

A flicker of unease showed in Hutton's expression as he glanced at Ian for a second. "What is this about?" he hissed. From the strange widening and narrowing of his eyes, he was trying to send me a message. I assumed he was either trying to warn me about telling Ian anything about his problem or using Morse code for *you're dead, witch*.

"We all have a problem here—" I began.

"I don't," said Ian.

"—and we're going to solve it together." My smile was wide and encouraging. Not a hint of over-sweetness or fakeness.

"Did you tell him?" Hutton's glare was still trying to fry me on the spot.

Ian snorted. "I didn't need her to tell me."

Hutton put his hands on his hips, digging deep to keep from wrapping them around my neck. "This is none of your business, Cavalier. Whatever you think you know, forget it. It doesn't involve you."

"But it does," I said. "Family must stick together."

Hutton made a sound of disgust. "Family? I don't know this guy."

"What better time than now, then?" I said excitedly.

That one might've been slightly forced.

"You're nuts. Enjoy the Council jail."

"Oh, my." Bagley's voice filled the shop. "Family drama. How wonderful!"

"What the hell?" Hutton cried, jumping back and scanning the shop with wild eyes. "Who was that?"

"Where?" Ian asked calmly. There was a small but encouraging hint of sufferance in his voice.

"I'm starting to feel grateful you destroyed my spellbook, child," Bagley said with something akin to wonder. "This is a lot more entertaining than I'd thought at first."

I pointed at the acrylic charms on the merchandise area of the shelf behind the counter. Ian gathered all with ease in his big hands and stalked into the back.

"Don't throw them into the trash," I called after him. They were a dear remnant of my online shop, and they sometimes sold.

Hutton grabbed me by the shoulders and shook me slightly. "What. Is. Going. On? Who was that?"

I bit my lip with indecision, but I supposed the cat was out of the bag now. "That's Bagley. She haunts the shop."

His eyes bulged. "She what?"

"She did a dark magic spell on herself hoping to cheat death, then when she was murdered, her soul stuck around. She haunts different objects now. We can break the object or take it out of the room for her soul to lose that tether temporarily, but it always snaps back."

"Bagley was murdered?"

Funny that he'd focus on that instead of the dark magic or the haunting. "Vicky pushed her down the stairs. She thought she'd get the shop."

"The witch who tried to kill you weeks ago?"

From the expression crossing his face, he regretted not letting her finish the job. "The one and the same."

He rubbed his chin and scanned the room. "So the old witch can't hear us now?"

"No," Ian said, returning to the room and resuming his position of crossed-arms sentinel. He addressed me next. "Your pipes are still making noises."

Hutton scrunched his nose with disgust. "What are you, her handyman?"

"It's a ghost goldfish," I said. "You don't need a handyman for that."

"The f—"

"It doesn't matter." It was my time to cross my arms and glare at them both. "We have a problem, and I've figured out how to fix it."

Ian leaned against the archway, the bead curtain clattering under his weight.

"I don't have a problem," he repeated with glacial indifference. "I have no interest in"—he unfolded one arm to point at me and Hutton—"that."

"Oh, yeah?" I said, unimpressed. "Then why are you here?"

He shrugged. "Cu—"

"Curiosity?" My brows arched. "Are you really going to go with that, Ian?"

His eyes narrowed at the sound of his name. I'd read my share of romantic suspense, courtesy of my sister, and I knew all about negotiating tactics. Use first names, show them you're a real person, make a human connection, listen to their needs. I didn't think "how can I help you?" was going to work in this case, but who knew? The rest might.

"There is a reason you came here," I continued. "After our talk earlier, you should've sent me straight to voice mail, but you picked up and came over without question." I'd spent a good twenty minutes making a list of things to use to convince him to come. The fact I hadn't needed to use it was telling. Had my words about family and things that were right to do finally reached him?

"I thought I was coming for dinner." Ian looked at me in mock betrayal.

"That might've been my opening salvo, but we both knew it was an excuse. Also..." I grabbed the plate of sandwiches and offered it to him. "Dinner."

He huffed a laugh and picked one, ate it in three bites.

"This is wonderful, and congratulations on your dating life," Hutton said, the sarcasm heavier than a house, "but can we skip the bullshit? You figured out a potion that works this time?"

"The potion didn't work?" Ian asked, although he must've guessed as much because...duh.

"No," I said, wondering if either of us was going to acknowledge the giant elephant Hutton had dropped into the room. Whatever vibes were going between me and Ian, we were nowhere near dating. Or were we? Did Ian think we were? I doubted he did after this morning's fiasco. Did I want him to think dating was a possibility? I was here for the shop, not a love life. But the jolt to my heart when I'd seen that Lovers' card... Nope, too much. Time to compartmentalize. I cleared my throat. "I contacted a potion expert and got advice on how to make one that works."

"You told someone else?" Hutton hissed.

He went to grab my arm, and probably bury me in the backyard, but I batted his hand away. "No, I didn't tell them. For the Mother's sake, stop being so jumpy."

"Jumpy?" He reared back in disbelief. "Seriously? It's my pack we're talking about here."

"Should've thought about that before you started taking the potion," Ian put in smoothly and not ungleefully. "You only have yourself to blame. Take responsibility like an adult."

I rounded on him. "Oh, *now* you break your vow of silence?"

He scowled. "I don't have a vow of silence."

Hutton snorted, then grew serious. "The potion was necessary. The others wouldn't have accepted me without the alpha powers. They'd have gotten suspicious... They'd have thought there was something wrong with me."

"First of all," I said, "I already told you—you don't know that. I know you guys like your Neanderthal traditions, but being an alpha is more than your blood."

Hutton looked taken aback. "We don't have Neanderthal traditions."

"You really need to stop focusing on the wrong thing. Anyway, now it's too late, I guess. If they know you've been lying, they might not be happy about it."

"You think?" Ian said wryly.

Hutton's jaw clenched. "No, they won't. And the other alphas will press the advantage. I'll be gone for sure."

"And that," I said, "is a problem." I rounded on Ian. "If you say it's not your problem, I'm bleaching all your clothes white."

Ian clamped his mouth shut, a small curve rounding the corners of his lips.

"I don't care what happens after the meeting," I continued, "but for now, we need to see this through. The twins or another alpha taking over the pack is bad. The pack is part of Olmeda, and we need to protect them. I know you guys dislike each other, but what happened between your parents is not your fault. Hutton—Derek—needing a potion to keep his alpha powers is not his fault. It's tradition's fault."

"It was his decision to follow tradition," Ian said.

"Please, as if you don't know what peer pressure is."

"I don't. Will you enlighten me?"

"Seriously, Cavalier?" Hutton ground out. "Why did you come here?"

Because, hopefully, something akin to brotherly love existed somewhere deep, deep beneath his stony expression. A yearning to know his brother, to know what it would be to have a relationship with him. The reason he'd stayed in Olmeda. It might take a lot of climbing rope, some squeezing, and a degree in cave exploration, but I was sure it could be found.

"I was curious," Ian insisted, his gaze pinning me in place. I saw brutal honesty there, but also an opportunity. He was giving me an excuse to do this potion without him having to step off his high box.

I wasn't about to look this gift horse in its nonexistent mouth. My voice brightened by a few levels. "Aren't you curious about this new potion of mine?"

"Wait," Hutton said. "He knows about the other potion?"

"He does." I led the way into the kitchen. "I used his blood to make it."

Hutton cursed. "Gross."

"Not any less gross than drinking a random person's blood. What did you think Bagley put in her potions, red eggnog?"

Hutton shuddered. "I try not to think about it."

"Wait until you hear what the new potion requires."

"Jesus, what does it take?"

"Your blood, too."

"Oh, all right." He sounded relieved.

I had already set up the circle and mixed the herbs per Valenti's instructions, so I only had to grab clean bowls for the blood and a new bottle for the potion. With the ease of many bored hours waiting for an online order to come in, I spun my spells knife and looked at them expectantly. "Who wants to go first?"

They both offered their arms in unison.

They glared at each other.

I tapped the knife on their arms. "Eeny, meeny, miny, mo, something something, I choose you." The blade's point landed on Ian's sleeve.

He smiled wryly. "I don't think that's how it goes."

"Who cares?" Hutton said, exasperated. He moved away to give Ian space. "Do it already."

All kinds of different, naughty meanings of that phrase came to mind. *Compartmentalize, Hope.* I concentrated on rolling Ian's sleeve up his forearm, the warmth and texture of his skin under my fingertips not helping in the least.

The sight of my blade positioned against his flesh once again was a bit of a cold shower startling me awake. The knowledge that Hutton was giving us the evil eye helped my blush dissipate from my cheeks and neck.

Bleeding someone else wasn't any more fun the second time around.

As before, Ian closed his hand over mine, aware that I was having a horrible time gathering up the courage to cut him, and sliced downward.

"I should take nursing courses and learn how to take blood samples," I muttered.

Ian's blood beaded and ran down his arm in a single deep red rivulet. Disgusting. Fascinating.

"We got a nurse in the pack," Hutton said. "She can teach you."

"Do you have enough power to make the potion?" Ian asked.

"I took another quick nap. I should be fine."

Hutton's brow creased. "What's wrong with your power?"

"It's a little weak," I said.

He scowled. "How weak?"

"Do you want your potion today or not?" I asked, annoyed now.

"Yes."

"Then not that weak."

I caught the edge of Ian's smile and returned one of my own. A minute later we were done recutting and rebleeding—ugh—him, and I pressed a clean gauze pad to his healing wound. Ian stepped aside, and Hutton took his place, his sleeve already rolled up. He was wearing a checkered shirt. Very rustic. Very pack.

Touching his skin felt completely different from touching Ian's. It was warm and firm and...alien. Like I was touching a lifelike mannequin. The mental comparison didn't make it any easier to make the cut.

With a sigh of irritation, Hutton copied Ian and guided my hand sharply down. Blood immediately ran down and into the waiting bowl.

"This makes the blood more willing," I murmured. Sweat dampened my lower back as each drop of blood lost the fight with gravity and fell to its death. To think witches everywhere did this all the time. To think dark witches did it to unwilling participants. To think Bagley had done that to kidnapped people in the upstairs bathtub.

Later, I'd ask Shane and Alex to come deep clean the bathroom again.

Once the bowl had about the same amount of blood as Ian's, I gave Hutton another square of gauze and got ready to make the potion.

"Wait," Ian said. He disappeared into the shop and returned with a stool.

I sent him a grateful look and sat down by the spell circle. I retrieved more basic tonic from the lower cupboard and filled the new potion bottle one third of the way.

"What's that?" Hutton asked.

"Be silent," Ian bit off.

"Watch your tongue, Cavalier."

"Aww, look at you two—your first sibling squabble."

Hutton clenched his teeth so tight his dentist was going to send me a gift basket for Christmas.

"I need to concentrate," I said. "This is a tricky spell." Remembering my role as a witch was to not only help the community but also guide them, I added, "I need to imbue the potion with magic four times equally—once per ingredient, then a final time for the whole mix. Any distraction might make me misjudge the amount of power or might change the intent of the spell. I only have one shot at this, unless you want to wait until tomorrow, because this one's going to knock me right out."

Hutton nodded with understanding. "Thank you."

The words made me sit straighter, prouder, as I focused on the potion bottle. It was bigger than the last one, to account for the extra dose of blood.

First, the powder. I used a bigger measuring spoon and dropped it into the bottle.

Brothers in blood.

Brothers in soul.

Brothers with the *gift* of power.

Power shared with *will*.

Magic tingled, suffused my arms, my hand, my fingers, the glass bottle, and the liquid inside. The specks of powder shimmered and settled like diminutive sparks making their way across a clear sea.

Next came Ian's blood. I concentrated all my magic in the hand holding the bottle.

Brothers in *blood*.

Brothers in *soul*.

Brothers with the gift of power.

Power *shared* with will.

My shoulders sagged, and I was thankful for the stool under my butt. Two spells to go still. Had I used too much magic? To me, it felt nearly the same amount as with the last potion, but perhaps the naps hadn't been enough to rebuild my magic. I should've waited at least a day.

Too late now. I'd simply have to use all my reserves and plan better next time.

"Failing upward."

If they heard my whisper, Ian and Hutton didn't comment as I lifted Hutton's bowl and dripped his blood into the bottle, repeating the spell in my head with the emphasis on the *Brothers*.

The second dose of blood slowly mixed into Ian's, settling into a strange three-layered potion. I grabbed the stopper and plugged the bottle tightly, then held my hands around the glass. Same amount of power, overboard on the intention. Here went nothing.

Brothers in *blood*.

Brothers in *soul*.

Brothers with the *gift* of *power*.

Power shared with will.

The mixture shimmered, the layers suddenly swirling into each other. I shook the bottle slightly to help the process, feeling as if everything that I was had been sucked right out of me, leaving me a husk capable of movement but little else.

I pushed the bottle across the counter, scared I might drop it if I tried to lift it up. "There you go."

Hutton snatched it from my fingers. My vision blurred, and I blinked repeatedly to clear it up. He chugged the potion down like a champ, slamming the bottle down when he was done.

Power exploded inside the room, making my skin prickle

with the need to fight or flight. Hutton's face brightened with delight. For a moment, he looked young and happy and free of worries.

"It worked," he said in wonder.

I snorted. "Of course it—*oh*."

Ian caught me before I slid right off the stool.

"Call Dru," I mumbled. "Open tomorrow." The slam of my back door startled me awake. "What...?"

"He's gone," Ian said.

"Rude."

He helped me into an upright position. "Can you walk?"

I attempted to stretch a leg forward, but my muscles felt like jelly. "Maybe I'll sleep down here tonight."

With a snort, Ian bent to sneak an arm under my knees and lifted me into his arms.

"You came back," I murmured against his chest. "That was nice."

"You owe me two favors now."

I patted his shoulder weakly. "Keep dreaming. No promises were made."

He dumped me rather unceremoniously on the bed.

I bounced with a small giggle, then snuggled into the covers. "I knew you would come around to helping your brother."

Ian tugged the covers from under me until I rolled obediently, then pulled them over my exhausted body.

"I didn't do it for him."

Then who? I wanted to ask, but it felt so warm and cozy in my bed cocoon, I made a mental note to ask him tomorrow. Because tomorrow would be glorious. The hurdle had been dealt with, and everything was going to be okay.

17

A WARM, wet tongue licked me awake. I pushed the furry head away from my cheek with a wince of disgust, then recognized the texture under my hand. Gasping, I opened my eyes.

"Fluffy!"

I sat up on the bed, still in yesterday's clothes, and Fluffy pawed at me, huffing and wagging her tail in excitement.

"Good morning, Fluffy." I hugged her close and allowed her vitality to sink into me. "Did Ian bring you?"

Was he sitting in my kitchen, waiting for me to wake up? The image produced a warm tingling in my chest. There were worse fates than having Ian use the only chair upstairs, sipping some coffee, and checking his email on his phone as he waited for me to leave the bed.

I pushed off the covers and left the bed eagerly, but the floor was empty. The background music we used in the shop sometimes drifted up the stairs. Dru must've opened the shop, but I wouldn't find Ian down there. That wasn't his style.

Fighting a pang of disappointment, I returned to my bedroom and checked my phone. A text notification increased the butterfly population in my belly by about a million.

Good morning. Take good care of my girl.

His girl was busy sniffing around the base of the dresser. Had he brought her this morning or yesterday after I'd passed out to keep guard over me? Either way, he deserved a thank-you call. Maybe even a thank-you lunch with a thank-you peck on his cheek. Ian might've been mad at me for forcing his hand with the potion, but we both knew he had done it of his own volition. I had nothing on him except our easy friendship.

A silly grin spread across my face even as my phone rang in my hands. I accepted the call automatically and asked a breathless "Hello?" expecting Ian's deep tone to come from the other side.

"The potion is *fading*," came Hutton's low, angry voice.

I lowered the phone and confirmed the name on the screen. The butterflies inside me died a fast, painful death, leaving behind a growing sense of dread. "What?"

"The potion isn't working anymore."

"But that's not possible. It worked yesterday."

"Well, it's broken now." The ire in his voice was palpable. It slapped the last vestiges of sleep right off.

"Oh, no."

"Is that all you have to say?" he demanded. "'Oh no?'"

I bit my lip and paced the small room. "What are the symptoms?"

"The symptoms are *it's not working anymore*."

"So your alpha power is not there?"

"It's back to what it was the day before yesterday. I can't talk to the alphas like this, and they're going to know something's off."

I didn't understand it. The potion should've lasted days, weeks even. A depressing realization dawned on me—*I* was the problem. The potion had worked, but my power was too low to make it last beyond a few hours. I had failed Hutton. I had failed my client.

And I had failed Grandma.

"I'm going to figure out something," I told Hutton.

"You better, because if I go down, I'm taking you with me."

I rubbed my face, thinking hard. If my power was the problem, I'd have to figure out how to have another witch do the spell for me without them knowing what they were actually doing. Almost an impossibility since intent carried so much weight in spells. And even if I managed to wangle a favor, finding that witch would take time, and time was something Hutton didn't have.

I needed kitchen paper and some tape.

Changing clothes fast, I refilled Fluffy's bowls, gave her one more hug, then hurried to the downstairs kitchen.

Hutton's potion bottle lay where he had slammed it on the counter yesterday. To my immense relief, it still had some potion left. Not enough to have made such a strong difference in its effect time, but maybe enough to give him a short, temporary boost. I mixed a bit of moon water to liquefy the hardening blood and sent in a bolt of magic to reactivate the mixture. The potion wouldn't be as effective now that hours had passed from its creation, but, hopefully, Ian's remaining alpha power would make a difference and keep it alive longer than otherwise.

Dru was sitting behind the counter, reading something on her phone, and an older man sat at the table by the window, glancing into the street while sipping a mug of tea.

"Good morning," I said in a whisper. "Thank you for opening."

"Ian called me. Said you passed out and I'd need to open today." Her glance flicked toward our customer. "You made a special order?"

"Something like that." It sucked to keep Dru out of the

loop, but this was Hutton's secret. It was bad enough that I'd told Ian against his explicit wishes.

"I passed by yesterday and you were closed. You didn't answer my text. Is there something…*dark* going on?" Her whispering became so low I barely heard her.

"Just some business with Ian. I went on a recognizance mission about his parents," I added, knowing the rumors of me asking around might reach her.

Her face lit up with interest. "What did you find out?"

Oh, nothing much, really. Only that Hutton's mother might've given his father a love potion, therefore breaking a genuine love match and leaving her child without alpha powers, screwing the pack, and, by extension, half of the paranormal community of Olmeda, probably. "It was all as you told me. Hutton's mother waltzed in and the Cupid of Matehood shot his arrow." I pressed a hand to my chest. "Straight in the heart."

"Meh."

One day, Dru was going to discover how much I'd lied to her during our short acquaintance, and she was going to rip out my tongue with her demon claws. "Yeah, nothing too exciting. It was a shock to most people, but that's about it." I decided to give her a nugget of entertainment because she deserved it for opening on her off day. "Oh, and I got my cards read by Veva Daly."

That perked her up. "Really?"

"It was quite insightful."

"What did they say? Riches and a boyfriend in your future? Bounty-friend?"

"Ha-ha, very funny." I pursed my lips in mock disapproval, but some amusement escaped anyway. "No boyfriends, but deepening relationships." I pointed at her. "Including you. Also a lot of death in my past."

"You don't say."

"That one was a bit obvious," I agreed. "Maybe she cheated."

"Don't let anyone hear that unless you want Brooks to put you on her shit list."

"Veva's reading was of superb quality and opened my mind to all the possibilities lying in front of me."

Dru smiled slyly. "Better."

"Can you—"

The door of the shop opened, and Key walked in, scanning her surroundings with a nervous glance. She gave us a tentative smile when it found us. "Good morning."

"Good morning," I said brightly.

Dru grunted.

Key approached the counter, eagerness replacing her initial shyness. "Mr. Cavalier doesn't need me today. I was wondering if I could hang around for a bit?"

"Of course," I said warmly. "Want something to drink?"

"Sure," she blurted, startled by the offer. "Green tea?"

"No problem." I busied myself preparing it. "You have some studying to do?"

"Oh, nothing like that." She licked her lips, then gave me one of her puppy-eyed stares. "I was hoping to learn more about the shop. In case you can afford to hire me soon."

"Ah." I focused on the steeping tea, conflicted. The chances of me earning enough to hire her were slim, but it was hard to say no to such eagerness. She reminded me of Fluffy when she was like that—all innocent hope. Hard to say no to your own name. "I guess you can stay for a bit, as long as you don't get in the way," I added to appease Dru's stormy expression. "But I need to be honest with you—the shop isn't making enough money to hire you too. It might take until the holidays. That's why I put you with Cavalier."

"I know, but in case?"

Dru shook her head and went back to her phone.

I set the mug of tea in front of Key. "I gotta go, but I'll be back later." An excellent idea popped into my head. "You can check on Fluffy upstairs if you want."

"Mr. Cavalier's dog?"

"Yup. You'll love her."

With that, I retrieved the potion from the kitchen and rode Bee-Bee to the shifter compound.

The same shifter was on guard duty. He was busy on the phone and simply opened the side door and waved me inside.

No guide for me today, apparently. I snuck through before he changed his mind and forced me to wait, and made my way up the road to the main building. The front lawn was abuzz with hushed conversations as several shifters stood in groups and couples, some talking loudly, others with their heads down and close, talking in inaudible whispers.

I took a path running the long way around, not wanting to intrude by marching straight through. Some shifters I recognized from my last visit, and a couple of the closest ones nodded my way as I passed by. I returned the greeting, unable to keep my gaze from roaming the gathering.

Was this what an alphacon entailed? Politics on the lawn? I suddenly recognized one of the shifters, and I dropped into a crouch behind the low hedge separating the path from the lawn.

One of the twins was here.

What were the chances he'd recognize me? If it were me trying to take over someone else's pack, I'd have investigated the local paranormal community.

And if it were me trying to take over someone else's pack with the help of dark magic, I'd have paid special attention to the local dark magic community. My shop was there on the dark web marketplace for all to see, and there were plenty of photos of me on the shop's social media.

If they saw me, they'd wonder why I was here, especially if someone had told them of my visit a few days ago. They might suspect something was amiss and make trouble for me and Hutton.

Awkwardly, I made my way to a small thicket of trees, keeping low the entire way, and only when I found cover behind a thick trunk did I chance standing up.

Luckily for me, Ian picked up right away.

"I'm busy today," he said without preamble. "Keep Fluffy until tomorrow."

"Ian, I need help," I whispered, daring a fast look around the tree. The twin was now giving me his back. Excellent news.

"What happened?" Ian asked sharply. "Where are you?"

His fast reaction warmed my heart. "I'm at Clawstone Park. The potion I made for Hutton is fading."

"Is he threatening you again?"

Sweet of him to jump to that conclusion instead of asking why the potion was a failure. "No, nothing of the sort." Kind of. "There was some potion left in the bottle so I'm bringing it to him to act as a boost, but there's a bunch of shifters on the lawn in front of the main building and one of the twins is here, and I think he might see me."

"Where are you now?"

"Hiding behind a bunch of trees."

He barked a laugh.

"Hey, thirty seconds ago, I was crouching behind the hedge. This is an improvement."

"Are you sure you can't make it around without being seen?"

"On my fours or crouching like in a video game, I might, but I'm thinking it might be a tad suspicious if someone catches me."

"A tad."

"What do I do? Hutton really needs this potion." Should I go back to the entrance and leave the potion with the guard? But who knew how long until he gave it to Hutton, or how many hands it'd pass through to get there.

"Wait until a shifter you recognize comes close by. Ask them to find Grier or Lim."

"Who are they?"

"Hutton's seconds. They'll get the potion to him."

"Hutton won't like them linking him to a potion. They might get suspicious."

"Make something up."

"Why don't you come and give it to him, show some brotherly support?"

He hung up.

Tch.

It took about ten minutes of patient waiting for someone I recognized to walk close enough that I could signal him without earning the attention of the other shifters on the lawn.

He didn't find my hiding spot weird and made no comment about my need to talk to one of Hutton's seconds, simply left to search for them. I wondered how many shifters got into trouble and hid in the bushes until someone brought one of the leaders. It stank of accidentally getting locked outside your house in your underwear and waiting for a neighbor to bring you a robe and number for the local locksmith.

Fifteen minutes later, the shifter returned with another familiar face. My mouth went dry. It was the shifter who'd been joking around with the twin outside the gate the day I'd come to talk to Hutton.

"I'm Grier. Luis says you need me," Hutton's second said.

I straightened, holding the potion close to my stomach. "Yes, sir."

His attention kept straying toward the lawn, a suspicious glint in his eyes. Probably checking for signs of trouble. "Well?"

"I, ah…" I glanced at the other shifter.

Grier jerked his chin toward the lawn, and Luis made himself scarce.

"I need to deliver something to the alpha, but don't want to interrupt the meetings," I said.

He focused his suspicions on me. "Something?"

Oh, Mother. What if he went and told the twins about the potion? It was too late now to ask for someone else or tell him it was all a mistake. I better make this good or the entire plan would blow up in my face.

"It's a potion I forgot to deliver last time."

"A potion."

"Yes, it's urgent that he gets it as soon as possible."

He studied me closely, and I could see the wheels turning in his brain. "What kind of potion?"

"It's for his rash."

"His rash?"

"Yeah, you know." I circled the apex of my thighs. "Down there." Shifters healed fast, but some ailments would always require outside attention.

He jumped backward and coughed. "I see."

"Very sensitive stuff. He wouldn't want anyone else to know. I trust you'll give it to him right away?" I held out the potion.

He eyed it like it was full of cooties.

"It's perfectly safe," I assured him.

"All right." He snatched it out of my hand and shoved it inside his jacket pocket. "Anything else?"

"Nothing. Tell him to drink it right away and he should start feeling relief instantly."

"Will do."

He stood there like a sentinel, and I realized he was waiting for me to leave. If I were a shifter, my literal tail would've been right between my legs as I slunk my way back toward the entrance, keeping my face averted from the shifters in the lawn and all but running until the cover of trees surrounding the main road hid me from view.

Stepping outside the gate brought no comfort or relief. I didn't think Grier would find the potion suspicious—or want to dig into it—but the fact that he had been so friendly with one of the twins was a complication.

As I rode Bee-Bee to the shop, I tried to remember how Hutton's second and the twin alpha had looked that morning. Had it been more of a polite joking around—an alpha's second trying to keep an enemy alpha in a good mood—or had it been more like old friends re-acquainting after a long absence? I couldn't decide.

Hutton had said the alphas had friends in the pack, and that made them dangerous. It didn't get any more dangerous than being friends with one of the top leaders. The whole situation was rolling downhill fast.

I brought the Vespa into the backyard and closed the gate carefully. To my surprise, Fluffy was out, the back door standing ajar.

"Hello, beautiful," I cooed, delivering some much-wanted attention. "Have you been a good girl? Never mind, you're always a good girl."

Fluffy yipped softly and rubbed against my hands. The temporary lifting of my spirits at her company was much appreciated, but the underlying tide of dread didn't abate. Should I tell Hutton I'd seen one of his seconds talking to one of the twins that day? They had been talking in the open, so Hutton might already know their level of friendship. Still, assuming anything had yet to take me down the correct path, so better to warn him.

I sent him a fast text and stepped inside the building. The bead curtain was drawn aside, and the shop appeared empty. No clients, no Dru. Nothing but some strange scraping sounds coming from behind the counter.

Rats? Hissing in a breath, I stepped around the counter, ready to throw my phone at whatever rodent had thought to intrude into my beautiful shop.

Key was on her knees behind the counter, using a screwdriver to pry my witch supplies cabinet open.

18

HONESTLY, I would've preferred the rats.

I didn't know if my heart could take another betrayal.

"Hello," I said.

Key screeched and whirled to face me, mouth gaping. The screwdriver clattered noisily to the floor, and Fluffy barked in excitement, thinking this a new game.

"Fluffy, stay." I put my hands on my hips and scowled at Key. "What are you doing?"

She focused on my sneakers. "Nothing."

"Where's Dru?"

"She left for an errand."

"Did she, now?"

Key nodded, but her shoulders tensed.

"Did you happen to make up this errand so you'd get a moment alone in the shop to rummage through my stuff?" The reason for Key's insistence on working at the shop—and disappointment when she couldn't—became crystal-clear. "Was you needing a job an excuse to get into my supplies?"

Her head whipped up. "No! I need a job, but..."

"But?"

Her mouth drooped. "Nothing."

"Go sit at a table."

"What?"

I arched an imperious eyebrow, one of the few things I'd learned from Tammy. "You heard me."

Silently, she got to her feet and marched around the corner to sit on the bench side of the table furthest from the window.

Fluffy trotted forward to sniff the screwdriver. I picked it up before she could slobber over it and placed it on the counter. I would've flipped the open sign to closed, but Key had already taken care of that. Smart.

With a sigh, I made us some tea and brought it to the table.

"Are you going to tell me why you were trying to break into my supplies cabinet?"

Key squeezed her mug and her mouth tightened into a locked line.

The river of truth never ran straight, I reminded myself. "How did you get Dru to leave?"

"I told her one of Uncle Jeremy's friends at the bank was having a meeting about what to do with Mr. Lewis's old place."

I swallowed that with some tea. Not only the fact Key was aware of Dru's hopes to take over the other shop, but that someone as suspicious as Dru had believed her so easily. Our dreams and our brains didn't always communicate as they should.

"She's going to kill you."

Key's expression grew shifty. "I wasn't planning on sticking around."

"Bet you weren't." I sipped more tea, putting my thoughts in order. "What were you looking for? Why not ask me?"

"I can't afford you," she whispered.

"Afford me for what?" I had a good inkling, but at some point my luck had to change.

"A potion."

This was harder than baking good muffins. "A potion for...?"

She mumbled something. Next to us, Fluffy barked.

"Fluffy says to spit it out so she can get happy play time."

Key's expression grew defiant, her spine straightened, and her chest puffed out. "I want a potion to change my magic power."

Something only dark magic could come close to achieving. "You know about my shop's side business."

"Yes." She watched me warily, as if she expected me to jump at her and spell her body into the next realm. "Uncle Jeremy told me about it."

"He knows you want to change your power?"

"No. My, uhm, family likes to use dark magic for...uh, stuff. He thought that since I'd moved here, I should know where to get my fix."

"Have you used dark magic before?"

She shook her head vehemently. "No. Never."

Her tone sounded sincere enough. Once more, I chose to trust my gut. Third time's the charm. Never allow the disappointments of the past to stand in the way of your future.

Trust cautiously and you'll be rewarded.

My affirmations book hadn't told me the reward could include getting stabbed repeatedly in the back, but that was my bad for not asking.

"What were you hoping to find in my cabinet? I wouldn't keep a potion like that lying around."

"I just wanted the ingredients."

"Why? You're not a witch."

She seemed to shrivel into herself. Oops. The whole power thing truly was a sore spot, apparently. I commiserated at some level. "Do you want to be a witch—a spirit mage? Is that why you want to change your power?"

"I want to be a fire mage like my uncle."

"Being an earth mage is not so bad."

"It effing sucks."

"You could sell your services to the police or private investigators like we talked about. The whole cadaver dog thing."

She choked on her tea.

"Going around the forest looking for buried corpses," I continued. "It'd be so useful. You could get a dog like Rufus and use him as an excuse for your powers."

"I... I think I'd rather be a fire mage."

Ah, the obstinacy of youth. "Dark magic is never that simple. There are always consequences."

"No, there aren't. It's never harmed Uncle Jeremy."

"Oh, it has," I said darkly. "Just because you haven't seen his soul, it doesn't mean it's not rotten to the core. What kind of person takes pride in consuming something created from the pain of others?"

"That's not—"

"That is what dark magic is—unwilling blood. Unwilling pain. Do you think people sell their blood to dark witches? Selling it is a willing action. It'd render the magic moot. No, dark magic is made without consent. That leaves an imprint on your soul, no matter how many lies or tales you tell yourself."

She lifted her chin stubbornly. "Then that's my problem."

And now, somehow, it was mine too. "Why not buy the stuff online?"

"Too expensive."

"Let me get this straight. You have a spell for a potion to change your magic power?" I waited for her nod. "And you were hoping to steal blood and other ingredients from me to try the spell yourself?"

"No, I wanted to find something to blackmail you into doing the spell for me."

"Smart," I said, impressed.

She drew circles on the table. "Uncle Jeremy told me what he pays you. There is no way I can afford your fees."

Uncle Jeremy needed to tell me *where* he paid me because so far I'd yet to find the mythical account Bagley had used for her dark magic payments. Could Ian help me with that? I should ask him to use his contacts to dig into Bagley's finances.

"But if you do this for me," Key continued, still focused on the surface of the table, "I swear I'll pay you back. Fire mages get paid well."

"I'm not sure arson is a better career than cadaver dog." Ignoring her wince of disgust, I pondered how to convince her she didn't need dark magic in her life. A placebo wasn't going to fly—fireballs were hard to fake—and if she had a spellbook with a dark magic spell, there was no stopping her from trying her plan with another witch. A real dark magic witch would not take her attempts at blackmail as nicely as I had. My backyard might not contain any corpses at the moment, but Key would make a good addition to another witch's. Her earth magic might actually improve a witch's herb garden.

A truculent but realistic fate.

I kept that to myself.

"I will help you."

Key tensed like a bowstring. "You will?"

"But I need to see the spell first."

And if I was crossing my fingers behind my back, I was sure karma and Grandmother would understand these lies. It was this or have Key end up in an early grave.

"I'm not sure..."

"Your plan included me using your spell anyway. What's the problem?"

"Are you going to charge me?" she asked, a note of wariness creeping in.

I considered this for a moment. "Yes." If I didn't, she'd grow suspicious like the teen with her love potion. "We can arrange a payment once I see the spell."

She thought about my offer for a few moments, then reluctantly agreed. "Okay."

I jumped out of the chair, startling her. "Great. Grab Fluffy's leash. I'm going to call Dru and tell her to come back."

"I'll wait outside." Key hurried into the back to find the dog's stuff.

Fluffy looked at me, tail wagging supersonically.

"It's going to be okay, Fluffy." I brought out my phone and dialed Dru's number. "Nothing one of Grandma's sayings can't fix, you'll see."

———

Dru arrived shortly after, looking like Mount Doom about to erupt.

"Hope, I swear to God almighty if you don't explain yourself this minute, I'm going to strangle you to death."

"Key misheard something but didn't have your number," I explained soothingly. "She's very sorry and will make amends."

Dru cursed me, Key, the shop, and the dog.

Fluffy let out a happy bark.

"I will end you, you small furry creature," Dru told her.

Fluffy barked again and pawed at her jeans.

Dru crossed her arms and looked away. "Whatever. I'll deal with the girl later."

"You'll stay until I'm back?"

"Yes, but you're paying me double overtime since it's my day off."

I gave her a fast hug. "Thank you!"

Dru swatted me off. "Good Lord, get off me."

Blowing her a kiss, I left the shop through the back, Fluffy in tow. Once outside, I attached the leash to Fluffy's harness and gestured for Key to lead the way.

After I made sure neither Shane nor Alex were on sentinel duty.

Key lived in one of the satellite neighborhoods of old Olmeda. It was a darker, run-down zone—the losing side to the battle of tourist attractions. A few shops were open, but most had their shutters drawn or had fallen into clear disrepair. The streets held a heavy, loud silence that made me glad we'd brought Fluffy along and left the Vespa home. I had the feeling it wouldn't have survived long parked outside.

"Here." Key stopped by an old three-story whitewashed building with rivulets of rust running down from narrow windows and a barred gate protecting the front door.

The inside wasn't any more promising. A narrow, tiled hallway poorly illuminated by a window at the back extended in front of us, with a couple of worn doors lining one side and the stairs going up the other. We took the steps up to the third floor, and Key unlocked one of the old wooden doors.

"This is my room," she said defensively.

I studied the bare-bones bed, the cracked tiles on the uneven floor, the plastic chair in one corner with a small pile of clothes on top, and the duffel bag and open suitcase next to it. A round mirror hung on the wall right next to a hook holding Key's toiletry bag. A lighter cross shape on the yellowed white paint of the wall above the bed hinted there had been a crucifix there at some point. The window was narrow and opened into the side wall of the next building.

Fluffy immediately set herself to sniff everything at floor level.

"It's a room," I agreed.

Key's hands clenched into fists. "The door has a bolt and the bathroom's clean."

"Excellent qualities when looking for a place to live."

Her lips firmed. "Are you laughing at me?"

"I'm not. How's the rent?"

"I can pay it."

"How come you don't live with your uncle? You two seem close."

"I like to be independent." She made a face. "He has dates all the time."

"Yikes. Awkward."

"The walls of his place are very thin."

I lifted a hand, warding her off. "Say no more. I can't take it."

She laughed and sat on her bed. The springs complained with a high-pitched squeak. "This is better than it looks. The block is safe, and there are no drug dealers in the building."

"Other paranormals live here?" I guessed aloud.

Key nodded.

It wouldn't have surprised me if Alex and Shane lived in a similar place. "All right, where's the spell?"

It took her a couple of seconds of hesitancy, but then she left the bed, knelt by the open suitcase, and moved clothes and plastic bags around.

"Why do you hate being an earth mage so much?" I asked, curious. The walk over had been tense at first, then I'd been too worried about the feeling of a dozen pairs of eyes on our backs to raise the subject.

"Earth is a shitty power. Everyone knows it."

"It's all about how you use it. You know, my power is low, but I can still do potions fine." Except when they didn't turn out fine and threatened to bring the local alpha down. But that was then, and this was me trying to convince Key to stick to the path of good rather than evil.

"It's different."

"How so?"

She paused her search and sent me a frustrated glare. "I can't do anything!"

"Lies. You searched my backyard and helped Ian's business."

"That doesn't count."

"Doesn't count for what? Do you really want to spend your life being an arsonist for hire and ending up with a bounty on your back?"

Her face paled. "Are you going to tell Mr. Cavalier?"

"I might if you lie to me again. Why risk so much to change your power?"

"It's none of your business."

Since I needed to know to convince her to do things other ways, it sure was. "It is if you want me to do this spell for you."

"I need to avenge my parents, okay?" she half-shouted in frustration.

A gasp of disbelief escaped me. "What? I thought you said you lived with your dad..."

Her face crumbled. Oh. Oh, no. Had he died recently? I hadn't been raised to be an unfeeling monster. "I'm so sorry, Key. That's awful." I clenched my hands so I wouldn't drop by her side and hug her tight. Her body vibrated with unwelcoming tension. "Tell me about it."

"It happened a long time ago. I was a kid."

"Did you...watch?"

She nodded stiffly.

My heart hurt for her. At least I hadn't been present when Grandma had died, and she'd died from a heart attack, not murder. "You know who killed him?"

"Yes. My uncle put a bounty on the murderer, but he was never found." Her hands sank into the pile of clothes in the suitcase. "I think the man paid the bounty hunters to look the other way.

"You should talk with Cavalier. He'll straighten things out. Maybe the bounty is still active. You don't have to avenge him yourself."

"I'm sorry," she whispered.

"Why?"

She spun and threw something at me.

19

THE STREETS WERE DARKENING with the lovely purples of dusk. Fluffy trotted happily by my side, stopping to sniff a bush or a piece of wall here and there. We were a bit far from the shop, but I didn't mind the extra exercise. There was something about the atmosphere at this time of day that filled me with energy. I itched to do something different. Something spontaneous.

"What do you think, Fluffy? Should we invite Ian for dinner?" He deserved a treat for leaving Fluffy as my emotional support animal.

Fluffy yipped in agreement, and I almost began skipping with contentment. We'd stop by the grocery for some fresh, juicy, dog-approved chicken on the way, I decided. Mentally, I ran through all the takeout places on the way from here and home. Should I grab Chinese today? Pizza? Where was I anyway?

I checked my phone's GPS. How had I ended up walking Fluffy so far off from the Tea Cauldron? Something teased my brain. A delivery of some sort?

That felt off. I checked the solitary street surrounding us. This place didn't feel right. Why was I here?

Fluffy made a concerned sound when I stopped in my tracks.

"Something's not right." I turned to glance at the street we had taken. Boarded lower windows on the nearest house, iron rods protecting the glass on the one across. There was little traffic, vehicular or human, and a general sense of uneasy expectancy hung over the buildings, like a warning to check my surroundings and the spaces between the houses. My left hand pressed against my jeans pocket, but it was flat and empty. My last freezing potion lay in my nightstand drawer back home.

Potions. Why did that set off alarm bells in my—

Memories rushed in, and everything clicked into place.

Oh, I was going to murder Key.

"Let's go, Fluffy." I sprinted the way we'd come, startling the few passersby into jumping out of my way. By the time we'd made it back to Key's building and ran up the stairs, I was out of breath. Luckily, Key had forgotten to bolt her door, so I was able to make a grand entrance, slamming it open against the wall and looming on the threshold like a sweaty, panting goddess of war.

"What do you think you're doing?" I rasped as loudly as my poor lungs could allow.

Key fell back from the shock, scrambling backward on her hands and butt. "You're back!"

"I am."

Fluffy backed me up with a sharp bark.

Key ran a hand over her face. "Shit."

The clothes on the floor and chair had disappeared, the toiletry bag was gone from the hook, and the suitcase was full to the brim. The duffel bag lay open on the stripped bed. Brought her own sheets. Smart.

No, Hope. No admiring the lying, backstabbing stray.

I pointed at her. "Did you use a memory potion on me?"

Her shoulders sagged, and she looked ready to cry. "Yes." Guilt filled her eyes as she finally met my gaze. "I'm sorry."

I kicked the door closed with the heel of my sneaker and sat on the bed. Fluffy stood guard at my feet, ready to defend me to death. Just not warn me someone had used a potion on me. Or that my best friend was a murdering villain. Ian and I needed to talk about stepping up her training.

The memory of Vicky was a sour stab to the gut. "Do you have any more potions?"

Key shook her head. "No."

Having learned my lesson, I pushed the suitcase away from her reach.

"How much did it cost?"

Now she really did look about to cry. She named a number that made me also want to cry and added, "I bought it online."

"You got scammed."

She winced, but I was in no mood to be nice or kind.

"Lesson one of the magical world: check your henchmen."

"Your what?"

"The people you depend on to do your evil deeds."

"I didn't mean to..." She trailed off, her gaze finding mine then flitting away.

"Didn't mean to what? Wipe my memory clean of our encounter? Make me forget I caught you trying to break into my supplies cabinet?"

Key opened and closed her mouth, then whispered, "I'm sorry."

"Promise me you'll never do something as dumb as using dark market potions. You don't know what you're getting or how much damage you're inflicting. Memory potions of this kind can do serious harm, and they can act erratically unless they're made with the person's blood."

She pressed her lips tightly.

"Next time, it might not be me coming to talk to you but someone going straight to the bounty hunters."

"Are you going to tell Cavalier?" she asked in a fearful rush.

I studied the tense line of her shoulders, the way her hands clamped on her thighs. "I don't know. I'm thinking about it."

"Please don't."

"Depends on your explanations. If you wanted to use the memory potion on me, why not bring me here directly instead of appearing so reluctant?"

Key seemed to admit defeat. Turning, she leaned against the wall opposite from me and clutched her hands on her lap.

"You'd have been suspicious if I brought you right away," she admitted.

Probably not, but who was I to destroy her expectations? "You counted on my curiosity about the spell to convince me to come."

"Uncle Jeremy says he hasn't met a dark witch who can resist learning about a new spell."

"I'm not a—" I cut myself off. If I admitted the truth, Key would tell her uncle, and I didn't need his wrath on top of Hutton's. Another thought struck me. "Are your parents actually dead?"

She bit her lip. "My dad's back home. My mom left when I was little but is still alive."

A willingness to believe others was not a fault, I reminded myself. It was a strength that would reward me someday. Some day that wasn't today. "Do you even have a dark magic spell?"

"Yes!" Her voice filled with excitement, as if she was glad to show she wasn't one hundred percent a liar.

"Show me." I lifted a threatening finger. "No tricks."

"No tricks," she agreed. Slowly, she got to her feet and reached for the mirror. She felt underneath and tugged something off, then offered it to me, hands trembling slightly.

It was a thin notebook. An old one with gray cardboard covers and a black ribbon tying it closed. I took it from her and examined it carefully. It looked like something a school student might've used a long time ago, with three straight lines on the cover marking a spot to write one's name and subject matter.

"It was my grandmother's. It has all kinds of spells."

I untied the ribbon carefully and flicked through the contents. The pages were full to the brim with tight, neat handwriting. The notebook might not have many pages, but Key's grandma had made good use of them. I retied it closed and stuck it under the back waistband of my jeans because I didn't have my tote with me. Key wasn't getting it back until I'd time to study it.

She watched the spellbook disappear. "But..."

"You can have it back later." Ha, look at that—for some reason, I didn't feel so guilty about lying to her anymore. And speaking of lies... "You don't actually want a spell to change your power, do you?"

"I do!"

I brought out my phone.

"What are you doing?" she asked.

"Calling Cavalier."

Her hands closed around my phone. "Wait, wait."

Fluffy yipped and wagged her tail, probably expecting one of us to throw the phone into the corner for her to fetch. The dog had eventually growled at Vicky and even bitten her, so maybe Key wasn't so bad underneath her lies.

Or maybe I was trying to fool myself. But if Key had really wanted to harm me, she'd have used a freezing potion, then shanked me, not a memory potion, then tried to run away.

"Don't make me use magic on you," I warned.

Key snatched her hands off mine.

"What are you really after?" I asked.

She rubbed her eyes with the heels of her hands and cursed softly. I allowed her to stew in her internal debate for a bit longer, and just as I was about to tell her I'd help, she began speaking.

"I'm in debt with someone."

"Who?"

Her lips twisted in disgust. "A shifter alpha."

Oh, Mother, it better not be Hutton. "Which alpha?"

"The twins."

It took me a good few seconds to digest that. "What kind of debt?"

"I thought they had information about someone, so I traded in a favor."

The desperation in her voice wasn't fake. This time, I was sure she was telling the truth. "How old were you?" Something in her tone told me this debt had hung around her neck for a while now.

"Sixteen."

What kind of alpha demanded a debt from someone so young? The kind who resorted to dark magic to take over other people's packs, that was who.

"Why would you do that?"

She slipped back to the floor, as if all strength had suddenly abandoned her.

"They said they knew where my brother was."

"But it was a lie?"

"Yes."

How desperate she must've been to agree to such a reckless deal. A favor for information you had no way of corroborating. "You got scammed and now you owe them whatever they choose to charge you." That was what "favors" were after all.

"I saw the potion post on the requests page, and I thought..."

"You thought you'd get the potion for them and get out of the debt. But how? You're not a witch."

Key glanced at my waist. "There's a spell for a potion like that in the spellbook. I have some spirit power."

"And if you couldn't make it, you could try to sell the spell itself to them?" I guessed.

She nodded glumly.

Not a bad plan. "Tell me about your brother."

"Why?" she asked suspiciously.

"I need to understand everything or I can't help you."

Her mouth formed a circle of surprise. "You're going to help me?"

"The enemy of my enemy is my friend."

Understanding dawned. "You're planning something against the twins."

"I'm helping someone. Now, why is your brother missing?"

"It's complicated."

"We have all day." Or like, about an hour before Ian got tired of me not answering his text messages about the Clawstone Park potion drop.

"My parents separated when I was little," she explained. "I stayed with my dad's side of the family."

"Your mother took your brother? How old was he?"

"He's a few years older than me, and not exactly."

"Oh?"

She glanced at the window, then the door, as if checking nobody was eavesdropping. "I'm not sure where he went."

"You can't ask your mother?"

"She doesn't remember him."

"How's that possible?" After a moment, I answered myself, "A memory potion."

"Yes." Key's expression tightened. "I wasn't supposed to remember him either."

"But the memory potion didn't work as expected?"

"It faded. I think because of my earth affinity."

Or poor quality like the one she'd used on me. I was starting to see why evil hadn't progressed further in the world. Crappy outsourcing—an evildoer's Achilles' heel.

But beyond that, memory potions of this magnitude were volatile and unpredictable. Whoever had the genius idea of using one on Key and her mother should've prepared for this eventuality. I harrumphed silently. Mages. Always assuming someone else could do the dirty work for them.

"I started remembering things," Key continued, eager now to share her tale. "Not much, but the sense of playing with someone. Of a familiar presence here and there, and the love I held for them."

"What did your dad say?"

"I've never asked him."

"Why not?" I asked, taken aback.

Key shuffled forward and sat on her heels. "What if he was the one who gave us the potion? He might've given me another one. I couldn't risk it."

"I see your point."

"I did some digging and got someone to look up birth records for me. That's when I discovered I had a brother. I asked Mom first, but she didn't know what I was talking about and assumed I was talking about one of my cousins."

"She didn't tell your dad about your questions?"

"Oh, no way," Key said matter-of-factly. "Mom and Dad hate each other. Mom would rather eat dirt than to talk to him."

I nodded in agreement. "Seen it happen."

"I looked up my brother's name, but it went nowhere."

"Whoever wanted his presence gone would've given him a new name." I hesitated, then spoke kindly. "You know, there's a possibility that they wiped your memories of him because he's, well, passed on."

"I thought of that," she said, unperturbed, "but if he were dead, they'd have told me that instead of buying such an expensive potion. I also have a feeling that he's out there, alive. Like an itch in my soul I can't scratch. There has to be more to his disappearance than death. So, I kept digging and found a place that likes to hire young mages for shady stuff."

Because her brother would've needed a job, and mages loved to use their magic for their employment. "Let me guess, the twins used that service."

Her expression grew dark. "Yes. They told me they knew exactly who I was talking about—a mage a few years older than me who was a loner and never talked about his past."

It wouldn't have occurred to sixteen-year-old Key that every young mage who used that service would've been a loner who never talked about their past.

"They lied," she stated in a flat, cold voice.

"Does your uncle know about any of this?"

"No. We're close, but I can't trust him." She leaned forward, all sad, pleading eyes. "Please don't tell Cavalier about this?"

"He might be able to help. Bounty hunters have a lot of resources."

"They'll arrest my dad for using a potion on me. They'll find out about Uncle Jeremy and everyone else."

"I'm reasonably sure he can keep that part off the books."

"*Please* don't tell him. I'll disappear and he never needs to know a thing. I swear I won't come back."

She was breaking my heart. "Do you have anywhere to go?"

"I'll find something."

Besides her duplicity, Key had appeared happy with Shane and Alex, eager to be useful in any way. But it wasn't fair to Ian if I stayed quiet. Key *had* used a dangerous potion on me. He needed to know the risks if she kept working for him. I would willingly assume the risk of hiring her, but my budget wouldn't, no matter how I twisted it.

My phone rang, and I checked the screen.

I'd overestimated Ian's patience by about forty minutes.

Sending Key a look of warning, I answered the call and brought the phone to my ear. "Hi, Ian."

20

"Did you deliver the potion?" Ian asked.

I glanced at Key. She looked like she was about to barf.

"I did. I made some interesting discoveries."

Key inched toward her suitcase, but I blocked her way with my leg.

"Did you, now," Ian said.

"I'll tell you about them later. How about dinner?"

"Sounds good. Your place."

The call cut off, and I pondered talking into the phone longer just to see how much sweat Key could produce. But that would've been mean, and I'd like to think I'm a better person than that.

Paying it forward like any good witch worth her salt.

"Don't worry." I lowered the phone. "My 'interesting discoveries' are about someone else."

Key sent the door a longing glance.

"What are you going to do after we deal with the twins?" I asked.

"I'll pack and go somewhere else."

"Even though you have nowhere else to go?"

"I'll manage."

"Or..."

She eyed me warily. "Or?"

"You could stick around, as long as you promise not to touch dark magic."

"Why?"

"Because it's bad for your soul and it comes at the expense of someone else's will."

She blinked a few times. "No, I mean, why would you let me stick around?"

"I feel bad for you."

Her expression soured.

"You can stay if you promise not to use dark magic," I continued, "and you help me deal with the twins."

She grew alert. "How?" Her voice lowered to a whisper. "Do you want to kill them?"

That was what Bagley would've done, I was sure. "Not quite. I'm thinking more like beating them at their own scamming business."

The twins wanted a potion. I made potions. No one said the potions had to work as intended.

"You want to scam them?" Key sounded dubious.

"Fake potions are one of my specialties." Perhaps not the smartest thing to declare, considering her uncle was one of my clients, but it sounded like something a dark witch would do.

I turned on my phone and browsed the requests listing. My heart sank a bit. "That's not good."

Key sat by my side and tried to peek into the screen. "What is it?"

"The listing's gone."

The page had a couple of other posts but not the one Brimstone and Destruction had linked.

"That means they got the potion," Key said in a defeated voice.

Fluffy put her paws on my knees, and I lifted her onto my lap. Her weight and softness helped me focus.

"When did you see the request?" I asked.

"Last week."

"I got the link on Saturday, so that means it's been two days maximum. Would they have deleted the post when someone offered the potion or on delivery?" Key knew more about these kinds of deals than I did, so I'd defer to her expertise.

"They probably got contacted by several people. Once they chose a trusted seller, they must've taken down the post." She thought about it for a few seconds. "For a potion like this, they must've paid a deposit first, then took the post down once the deposit was confirmed by the seller. No point in deleting it before that."

"And the seller wouldn't get started on the potion until they had confirmation the payment had gone through."

Key nodded.

"So, two days ago or less, they got someone willing to make the potion for them." I returned to the main marketplace listings and checked the area around Olmeda. No other dark magic sellers popped up, which made sense because Bagley would have ended anyone who dared start a dark magic business in her area. "No other sellers nearby, so they must be importing it somehow. For a potion like this, it'd take at least one day to gather ingredients." Aka fresh blood. "Then they'd have to ship it. They must be using some sort of private carrier. If we could intercept the delivery before it gets to them..."

"You think they don't have it yet?" Key asked.

"Chances are they don't, given the time frame. Where do the alphas stay while they're in town, do you know?" It wasn't with the pack itself, and I remembered Sonia mentioning something about living quarters for the alphas during the PBOA meeting.

"You want to check their rooms for it?" Key's attention was fully glued to me.

"As a last resort. It's a lot of risk." Fluffy nudged my arm, and I scratched the top of her head. "And it might not be easy to break in without being noticed. They might've brought a few of their shifters with them in case there's any trouble."

"Then how do we know if they've gotten the potion or not?"

"Do you have any local contacts beyond your uncle?" I asked.

"Only Uncle Jeremy."

"Where does he get his stuff?"

Key's gaze locked on mine.

I cleared my throat. "Aside from me."

"I haven't got a clue." Her face brightened. "But I can ask?"

I considered the pros and cons of that. The two of them appeared to be close, so I didn't think Brimstone and Destruction would think anything of her asking.

"Go ahead."

She brought out her phone and scrolled through her contacts list. The call rang for a few seconds before it went to voice mail.

I shook my head, and she cut the call. Not the kind of question you wanted to leave for someone else to overhear.

"I know of a club he likes to go to a lot," Key said. "We could go there?"

"You think the club might have ties to illegal magic?"

"Yeah." There were zero traces of doubt in her voice, and about a ninety percent occurrence of *why do you even have to ask?*

Like-minded people did like to stick together. Just look at

me and Ian and Dru and… And perhaps I should stop while I was ahead.

Placing Fluffy back on the floor, I grabbed her leash and got to my feet. "Let's do this," I said with renewed energy. "Lead the way."

Key remained seated. "Are you really going to help me?"

"Of course."

"*Why?*"

"Because it's the right thing to do." And one had to lead by example.

———

For a Monday evening, the weblike streets forming the Guiles and Romary area were surprisingly lively. Visitors and locals ambled from bar to bar, if at a much less crowded pace than on the weekends, and there was an electrifying energy in the air that made me want to stick around and see what happened next.

"Over there." Key pointed to a narrow side street crossing this section of Guiles Street.

"Dark alleyways," I murmured as we approached. "Right on brand."

"Uncle's crowd can get stereotypical," Key admitted.

"You've been here before?"

"Once. I was curious." She scrunched her nose. "It smells of sweaty, drunk people."

Something to look forward to. "I expected better of your uncle." Drunk and smelly did not agree with the mage's suave exterior.

"Maybe they have a VIP room."

"Maybe it's his hidden identity. Vampire during the day, drunken fool at night."

Key let out a nervous laugh. She was all but thrumming by my side. "He's not a vampire."

"Then why does he love to drink potions made with people's blood?"

Key stumbled, and I grabbed her arm to help straighten her. Fluffy woofed in concern.

"I... He..." She seemed at a loss for words.

"Never thought of it that way, huh? Makes you wonder, doesn't it?"

We took the corner into the narrow street as Key muttered, "*Not* a vampire."

I hid my grin and fished for my driver's license. The club was a hole in the wall guarded by a beefy security guy. Likely a demon or a berserker. The facade of the building was painted black, as was the metal door behind the bouncer. A couple of neon signs announced more establishments farther up the street.

The bouncer watched us suspiciously and inspected my license in the weak light illuminating the door. He returned it without a word, then checked Key's.

"You're good." He handed Key's license back, and I arched my eyebrows. No way Key was twenty-one.

Key returned my look with blank innocence.

"The dog can't go in," the bouncer added.

I gathered Fluffy in my arms. "She's my emotional support animal. She goes with me everywhere."

As if to demonstrate, Fluffy licked my cheek.

"I don't see a vest," the guy said, unfazed.

"I forgot it at home."

"No vest, no enter."

I stood straighter and lifted my chin. "Do you know who I am?"

Key leaned in and whispered, "She's *the* witch."

"Whose bitch?"

All at once, two paths burst open in front of me. On one, Key would use her magic to open a hole under my feet and return to dig me back out in about a hundred years. Option two consisted of taking life's lemons and making the best lemonade this side of the equator.

Grandma had been a great fan of lemonade.

"Don't be mean to Fluffy," I told the bouncer airily. "She's a good girl."

Key stared at me, awestruck.

The bouncer crossed his arms and scowled. "I don't care if she's the best pet in the world. No vest, no enter."

I hauled Fluffy against me with one arm, then dug into my pocket. I found a couple of bills and brought them out. "I got twenty. You?" I asked Key.

Key checked her pockets. "Ten."

We looked at the bouncer hopefully.

His expression didn't change. "No vest, no enter."

I wasn't about to leave Fluffy alone outside, and I wasn't about to allow Key to go in alone, so I transferred the dog to her arms. "I'll be quick."

"Wait, what do I do?" she asked, struggling with the mass of energetic fluffiness.

"Wait by Guiles. I'll find you. And take good care of Fluffy, or Ian will chase you to the end of the world."

Key swallowed visibly. "Yes, sir."

The metal door behind the bouncer opened into a small hallway that led into a big, darkened room. A series of booths filled one wall, and a long bar the other. The rest was filled by a series of small, tall tables. The space was half empty, and nobody paid me much attention past a fast first glance. There were no overt signs of paranormal power, but if Brimstone and Destruction liked this place, I calculated that about half the people present had to be involved in the morally dubious side of the magical community.

I approached the bar, sniffing as I did and catching a mixture of beer scent and sweat. Probably meant to be cozy, like the lack of good light, and not remind me of old, unclean truck stops.

"Hello, there," I told the bartender—a tall, gaunt man with salt-and-pepper hair.

He whipped a dishtowel over his shoulder and walked up to me. "What do you want?"

I surveyed the offerings on the wall—a selection of liquor bottles at different stages of fullness, and a few draft beer taps. "Soda, please."

"No, I mean, what do you *want*?"

I blinked, then gasped in delight. "Ooh, we're using code!"

"Lady, you're in the wrong place."

Oh, look, my favorite endearment. "Do you happen to be friends with Bosko?"

He became immediately suspicious. "Why? Did he send you?"

"You two sound like you should be friends."

"If we are, it's none of your business."

So they were. Interesting. I should start a chart—knowing everyone's relationships in town would help my role as the local witch. "I'm looking for a special delivery."

"I'm not the post office."

"That's true. I heard you're much better."

"Get to the point or I'm kicking you out of here."

"Jeremy the mage told me you're the guy to ask about getting things delivered from out of town."

"Jeremy who?"

"Brimstone and Destruction."

He snorted with disgust. "Brimmy needs to keep his trap shut."

I crooked my finger invitingly. The man planted both hands on the bar's surface but refused to budge forward.

It would take more than this refusal to give in to deter me. Making my voice louder, I said, "He said you know of every delivery that gets into town."

A few heads turned our way.

The man smirked. "Nice try, lady. I know nothing."

"Is that a real 'know nothing,' or an 'I have to be a client and then you might know something?'"

He lifted a hand with a shrug and reached for one of the bottles. It looked fancy.

"A drink might loosen my tongue."

I touched his hand where it rested on the bar. "A spell might, too."

He leaned in, fearless. "Try me."

This wasn't going as I'd planned. With a heavy sigh, I cut to the chase. "I only want to know who to talk to for getting spells delivered into town. You can tell me, or I can ask someone else. It might take me all night, but I'll get the information. On the other hand, you'll get a bad review."

"Ask Brimmy, since you're friends and all." He jerked his chin toward the hallway. "Out."

I pointed at the bottle. "What if I drink some of that after all?"

"Too late. Get lost."

As I made my way to the exit, head held high because *hurdles, not defeats*, one of the women at the high tables stopped me.

"Wyatt's an ass. If you want to know something, ask at Rena's."

Then she turned away as if I didn't exist.

21

KEY AND FLUFFY waited for me at the corner of the street, eyes vigilant and alert. One pair of them, anyway. The other was just the usual doggy excitement.

"You got a name?" Key asked, trying to read my face.

"I sure did," I told her triumphantly.

Her face filled with hope. "Who?"

"Rena's. It's a bar, I think."

Her excitement dimmed a little. "Oh."

"Each new name we learn is a step up the ladder," I told her. "And if the steps ever stop, then you shuffle sideways until you find another ladder."

"And if the ladder breaks?"

"Then you climb with your hands and feet."

She stared at her hands but said nothing. With a family like hers, she'd probably had to climb her fair share of walls. Any other advice I gave her would sound patronizing, and the goal here was to encourage her, not have her resent me.

Rena's was a bar on Romary, doors wide open and loud pop music spilling into the street. The man standing by the entrances took a cursory look at our licenses and allowed us in, making no comment about Fluffy.

The inside was brightly lit, with a bunch of normal tables and chairs and a small karaoke stage in a corner, currently off-line.

Did Ian really serenade a bunch of strangers on his nights off? My heart constricted with yearning. Key was a fine companion, but I wished I was here with him instead. His solid presence was a port in the storm, a haven of safety.

No matter how much we disagreed, how much we argued, and how much I had to blackmail him into doing things, I knew I could count on him. Fluffy's presence at our feet was proof of it.

Ian would know how people got their illegal potions and spells delivered into town, but that would mean giving up Key's secret.

I had to learn these things on my own—Ian was a safe port, but I couldn't depend on always being able to reach him. This was not the Ian and Hope show. It was the Hope Avery tales of wonder and adventure, local witch and pillar of the community, discretion guaranteed.

I'd give it one more try at discovering how the underground potion delivery system worked in Olmeda, then I'd figure out how to ask him about it without involving Key.

"Cute dog," the bartender said, peering over the bar. "What's his name?"

"Bi-Bi," I said.

Key didn't react, thankfully. I didn't relish the idea of Ian learning we'd gone around asking about illegal stuff with his dog in tow.

"Adorable." She had a handsome face and shrewd eyes. Her midnight-black hair had been gathered into a ponytail, and she wore jeans and, I noticed with approval, a T-shirt with *Rena's* written in cursive matching the logo outside. I should bring Dru here, show her the wisdom of my ways. "What can I get you?"

Key opened her mouth, but I cut her off. "Two diet sodas, please."

She didn't blink at the request. "Coming right up."

"I wasn't going to get drunk," Key murmured.

And I wasn't about to put the place's alcohol license in danger—unlike the mage's club, they were being nice. I might need to come around in the future. Besides, alcohol was expensive and there was only so much I could claim for tax deductions.

The woman opened two cans and poured the contents into tall glasses in front of us. "Two diet sodas."

I drank mine greedily and welcomed the refreshing, cold bubbles running down my throat all the way to the center of my chest. Bliss.

Key sipped hers slowly, scrutinizing our surroundings. Aside from us, there were a few customers on the other end of the bar and a group of loud women occupying two of the tables. Girls' night or bachelorette bar hopping? I didn't spy any white veils.

I put my glass down and wiped my mouth with a napkin. "Someone at..." Oh, oops, I didn't remember the name of the other bar. "The sketchy black-metal-door club in the one alleyway recommended this place."

The bartender made a face. "That place's a dump."

"It's not as cheerful as yours," I agreed diplomatically. "They said you might know about *deliveries*."

She cocked her head. "Deliveries?"

"You know." I shrugged one shoulder nonchalantly. "*Special* ones."

Her attitude cooled instantly. "Are you looking to score drugs? We don't allow that shit in here."

"No, *no*," I said hastily. Key began coughing by my side. "I'm looking for, uh, *private* delivery services."

A crease appeared between her brows. "Like a messenger service?"

"Yes! But for...you know."

"You know—what?"

I gestured vaguely, encompassing the bar, the city, and half the globe. "*Stuff.*"

Her baffled expression told me she had no idea what I was talking about. Either her acting abilities were off the charts, the code for supernatural stuff in Olmeda was a lot harder to crack than I'd assumed, or she was a normal bartender and clueless about any underground paranormal delivery ring. Had the woman at the other bar lied? What would be the point?

"Could I speak with the manager?" I asked with my most disarming smile.

Her return smile was toothy and slightly mean. "I'm the manager, sweetheart." She studied us closely. "Are you guys cops?"

Strangled noises came from Key's whereabouts, but my attention remained fixed on the bartender. "No, not cops. I'm the local... I run a tea shop nearby."

"Huh. Is that so?"

"Yeah, I opened recently. I'm getting familiar with the local establishments."

"Are you?"

Key tugged at my sleeve. "We should go," she whispered.

Glancing at my phone, I checked the time and saw a text notification from Dru promising to skin me alive and something else that got cut off in the preview. "You're right. It's gotten late. Oh, do you have a small plastic bag?"

The bartender seemed to find the request somewhat suspect, but she dug behind the bar and handed me a ball of opaque yellow plastic.

I thanked her, paid with a hurried goodbye, and we scurried toward the exit.

Once outside, I rescued Key's grandma's spellbook from the back of my jeans and put it into the bag.

"What do we do now?" Key asked, anxiety clear in her voice.

"We're going to have to call..." A man lurking across the street caught my attention. His eyes met mine and held on. He had been at Brimstone and Destruction's pub. One of the people at the bar. "Come."

I dragged her and Fluffy across the street and approached the stranger.

"You were at the bar," I told him without preamble.

He tipped an imaginary hat. He wore faded jeans and a light blue flannel shirt. I could see him on top of a horse, staring thoughtfully at the mountains while chewing tobacco. As if he'd read my mind, he spat to the side. Gross.

"You guys looking to score some magic?"

I prayed my distaste didn't show on my face. "From out of town. You know where this stuff gets delivered?"

He dipped his chin. "I know a guy."

"Will you take us to him?"

Appearing to consider my question, he gave us a slow perusal. I refused to cross my arms in a defensive posture and held on to Fluffy's leash tighter as she attempted to sniff the spit on the ground.

"Sure, will do." He turned and walked away.

We followed, exchanging wary glances. When he turned into another street, we didn't say a word. Same when he led us down a smaller alleyway, and we squeezed by some dumpsters

to arrive at a small opening behind some houses, barely illuminated by a weak street lamp way in the back.

All perfectly normal.

He definitely wasn't bringing us into a dark corner to
mug us.

The man surveyed the space, then rounded on us, eyes
flashing red. "Give me your jewelry, wallets, and phones," he
hissed, showing us his clawed hands.

"Key," I said, stepping aside and gesturing toward the man,
"do your thing."

Key looked like a deer in front of my words' headlights.
"What thing?"

"Your mage thing."

Since, as we've already established, my last freezing potion
was back home.

The man snorted. "Mages. Right."

"I need earth," she whispered in frustration.

"Oh. Hmm." I pondered the situation. Wasn't asphalt
made with rocks? Maybe the petroleum interfered with her
magic. "Go find some."

Her gaze flickered from me to the man. "You sure?"

"Yep."

She ran back toward the dumpsters and squeezed through.

"Hey!" The man rushed forward. "Come back here!"

I reached over and grabbed his shirt, stopping him from
following Key. Fluffy began barking furiously.

"Who do I talk to about deliveries?" I let the man go when
he whirled to face me and narrowly avoided a claw to the arm.
Fluffy launched herself at his leg, but he kicked her aside. Fluffy
yipped in pain.

My heart jumped into my throat. "Fluffy, back," I ordered.

The dog stood her ground and growled as deep as a fluffball
could. Relief that she was still on her little paws warred with a

wave of anger. What kind of monster mugged two innocents, *then* kicked their dog?

The man took a step toward me, but one look at my face had him changing course toward Fluffy.

"Fluffy, run!"

Fluffy shot toward me, and the man cursed. Hah. No hostage for him. It would be just me, his sharp claws and superior demon strength, and my crappy power.

Realizing if I had any potion on me I'd have already used it, and if I were anything but a witch, I'd have used my powers, he stalked my way, triumph gleaming in his reddish eyes. "Now, little witch, let's not get more hurt than we need to, eh? Give me your stuff and you and the pup can go."

"I need the information."

He spat again. Good Mother Earth, did demons really salivate that much? I'd have to ask Dru.

"I don't know what you talkin' 'bout."

The exaggeration in his drawl mixed with the sneer on his face belied his words and made me want to punch him.

But I was a good witch, I reminded myself. I aimed for peace, not violence.

"I think you do," I said. "I think you came to sell us the information but then thought, what's the point when I can just rob them?" I lifted my hands in an appeasing gesture. "Tell you what—you tell me who's in charge of deliveries, and I won't tell the bounty hunters about this small misunderstanding."

He barked a laugh. "Like they gonna do anything."

"You're mugging people with your demon traits right out. They're not going to like that."

"You let me worry about that, little witch. Hand over your stuff."

I cracked my knuckles. "Come get it."

An Oakes-Avery witch might not want to start fights, but she sure as the Earth was round would end them.

The demon rushed me. I threw the plastic bag with the spellbook aside and called on my magic, feeling it rush into my fingertips.

His swipe was slow, as if he was unconcerned that I posed any kind of threat. I dodged it easily and planted one hand on his flank. My magic sparked with intent.

Sleep.

No time to get fancy.

The demon didn't stop. The fabric of his shirt was too much of a barrier—spirit magic worked best flesh to flesh.

Jumping back, I nearly crashed into one of the walls, putting myself into a neat corner. He followed, an unhinged grin pulling at the corners of his mouth. Adrenaline—the most powerful potion of all.

It rushed through my veins, too, almost overpowering the tingling of my magic along my skin. He swiped again, faster this time, and I barely avoided his claws. I tackled him from the side, but it was like moving a building, and I did little more than hang on to him so he couldn't spin and turn me into minced meat.

"Fluffy," I gasped, "assist!"

Growling echoed through the alleyway, and I heard the patter of Fluffy's paws and the rustling of her leash against the ground as she ran to us. The man cursed and tried to kick Fluffy again, but I threw my weight to the side, trying to tip him over. He nearly lost his footing but managed to stay upright as we shuffled and hopped sideways like a couple of fumbling drunks.

"I'm going to kill you," he roared.

"Tell me the name," I shouted back, panting. Sweat ran down my back, and my arms were hurting. I dared to move one upward, feeling around for any spot of naked skin. My fingertips came into contact with something warm and slightly rough. The base of his neck? It didn't matter. I forced all my magic into my fingertips.

Down.

The demon flinched. His knees buckled.

My arms turned into instant jelly.

He regained his balance and elbowed me hard. I stumbled backward. My hands tingled like their circulation had been cut off, and I curled my fingers, trying to return some life to my digits.

The demon turned on me, rubbing the base of his neck, the bumps of his horns now peeking prominently through his short hair. "Witch..." He licked his lips, as if savoring every moment of pain he was about to unload on me. "You shouldn't have done that."

I grinned. "It's only the beginning." As long as I was standing, I had a chance.

"Hey," came Key's voice.

We whirled toward the opening of the alley, and the demon got a handful of dirt in the face.

He clawed at his mouth and neck, making strangled noises. With a choking sound, he fell to his knees, and I helped him go the rest of the way with a solid push from my foot. Key didn't move, a deep furrow of concentration creasing her brows, her mouth compressed into a tight line.

"Hold him down." I blinked away a drop of sweat.

The dirt left the demon's mouth and nose and formed a ring around his neck. He tried to push himself off the floor, but the dirt held him glued to the asphalt.

Gingerly, I stepped closer and began patting him down. Phone, keys, and...

"Oh, what's this?" I retrieved a small flat bottle from his

front pocket and held it up for Key to see. Her focus didn't move from the demon.

"Give that back," the demon garbled against the ground. Fluffy came to sniff his hair. "Get that thing away!"

"Fluffy, don't bite." The glass of the bottle was tinted a dark color, but the liquid inside swished around easily. I lowered it into his field of vision. "Is this a potion? I bet it's a memory potion, isn't it? You were gonna rob us, then use it to wipe our memories. How many times have you done this? Memory potions aren't cheap. I bet you get them in bulk from somewhere else, don't you? Maybe an accomplice from out of town?"

"Screw you," the demon snapped.

I held out the potion to Key. "Can you hold this while I call Officer Brooks? I bet she'll be interested in the prime suspect of a series of local robberies."

"Wait!" The demon struggled again. "What do you want to know?"

"How do you smuggle potions into Olmeda?"

"There's a guy in the Crawler."

"Name?"

He glowered.

I waved my phone at him. "Name?"

"Jones. He's always hanging around the bar."

"Is there anyone else?"

He tried to shake his head but only managed to bump his temple into the ground. "If you want something from out of town on the down-low, that's your guy."

"Even if you bought it through the dark web?"

"Yes," he gritted out.

"Who's your potion dealer?"

"None of your business." His voice turned into a growl.

Trying to get another name out of him would take too long, so I took a photo of him to send Ian later.

"What are you doing?" he demanded.

I pocketed my phone, put the potion and his stuff in the bag with the spellbook, and patted his shoulder. "If I were you, I'd think about leaving Olmeda."

Fluffy barked with happiness as I retrieved her leash. Straightening carefully, I stretched my muscles. My legs had lost some of their wobbly quality, so I was reasonably certain I could make it out of the alleyway on my own. A chair, a drink, and a snack sounded heavenly.

"Can you hold him down enough for us to get away?" I asked Key in a whisper.

She nodded curtly.

"Then let's go." I pulled at her arm, and she turned to follow me.

Behind us, the demon began cursing at us. We hastened our steps until we burst onto one of the well-illuminated, decently populated streets.

I hung on to Key's arm, a bit winded from our semi-run. Her muscles trembled under my grip, betraying the rush of adrenaline still coursing through her veins. Fluffy trotted along, tongue out like nothing was amiss.

"See?" I said cheerfully. "Earth magic is so useful. Much better than fire; less ash to clean after. Fewer burned bodies to deal with."

Key made a strangled noise, then a choked laugh.

I patted her arm. She would be okay.

22

WE ASKED a man selling trinkets in a corner, and he directed us to one of the side streets off Romary. Like the first bar we'd visited, the Crawler appeared to be a literal hole in the wall—a wide-open door with a burly, intimidating man standing guard.

"Berserker for sure," I murmured, eyeing him.

Unlike Brimstone and Destruction's haunt of choice, this one appeared more upbeat. The entrance was brightly lit, and music escaped the open door, along with the high-pitched sounds of someone attempting to carry a tune. The place even had two wide windows, if currently shuttered.

The bouncer straightened at our approach, towering well over us.

"Hi," I said in greeting and dug for my driver's license.

The man shook his head.

"No?" I asked, confused.

He pointed to a large metal sign by the door. A witch hat silhouette had been drawn on the upper corner, followed by a wolf's head shape and an elliptical head with upturned large eyes. A red circle with a line across was stamped on top of each.

"No witches, no wolves, no...aliens?"

The bouncer shrugged. "Can never be too careful."

"How do you know…?"

He glanced down, and I followed. A set of thin lines lit up in lovely shades of purple under my feet. A very complicated, very powerful, utterly shocking kind of ward—I hadn't known such a magic-type-detecting spell could be done. Another thing to research later, even if its creation would be well beyond my power.

"Neat." I looked up again. "But I really need to go in."

"No witches."

"I run the local witch shop. I'm not a tourist."

"Them are the rules."

Crossing my arms, I tried to stare him into submission. "Does the PBOA know about this?"

"Why? Are you going to tell them?" He leaned down until our noses almost touched. "Are you going to go cry to Mommy Sonia? Boo-hoo, the mean berserker doesn't let me into a private establishment?"

Sheesh, when he put it that way… I stepped away from his mocking expression and motioned for Key to huddle closer.

"What do we do now?" she whispered.

Key might be able to sneak in—mages and witches were often considered different paranormal kinds, even though they used the same power source at their core—but I didn't want her to go in alone. She'd shown she could take care of herself, but I wanted people to remember me as the one asking the questions, not her. She didn't need any more trouble on top of the twins' debt.

And maybe I was feeling protective. Maybe because of the whole dead grandmother link. Maybe because seeing her work with Shane and Alex had convinced me she'd make for an excellent member of Ian's small stray pack, extra fur or not.

It was too bad that being shifters, neither Shane nor Alex

could help us now. And I had promised myself one more try before I called in the big guns. Who, then?

I smiled slowly. Of course.

Dru answered on the fourth ring.

"Hope? I'm going to kill you. You owe me big time."

"Consider today's shifts as triple overtime pay." I cringed at the mental calculations that brought up. At this rate, I was going to have to go into dark magic for real rather than try to wean people from using it. "I need another favor. Are you free tonight?"

"Why?" came the immediately suspicious reply.

"I need you to come get into this bar and ask a man about some things."

"Why don't you do it yourself? Did you get carded and forgot your wallet?"

"They don't allow witches or shifters— Oh, son of a witch!"

Key jumped, startled.

"What?" Dru asked, alarmed.

"That demon lied!"

"What demon?"

"Never mind, I'll call you later."

I ended the call and squeezed the phone in my hands, wishing I was strangling the demon's neck.

"What is it?" Key asked.

"The demon sent me to a place he knew I couldn't enter, and if they don't allow shifters, how would the twins get in there to conduct business? What kind of smuggler conducts business in a place half the paranormal community can't use?"

Key's mouth formed an *o* of understanding.

I took in a long lungful of air, then released it slowly. "I need to call Ian."

Fluffy yipped. Key's shoulders sagged in defeat.

"I won't tell him about the memory potion," I reassured her. Not yet, anyway.

Key hung her head in sad acceptance of her fate.

Ian answered in two rings. He said nothing, letting me make the first move.

"Ian? I need a favor."

His silence continued for a couple of seconds. Noises and scrambled sounds filled the background.

"What is it this time?" he asked dryly. "A tooth for a power potion? Half a finger? My left kidney?"

"Sarcasm doesn't suit you," I told him primly from my high horse. "I need some information about Olmeda's illegal dealings."

"Why?"

"The twins might've gotten someone from outside town to make them the potion. I wanted to know who can deliver it. Nobody's telling me anything useful."

"Why didn't you ask me first?"

"I can't depend on you for everything."

"And yet, here we are."

I toed the worn stone of the sidewalk. "I had to try."

"What did you learn?"

"That demon thieves like to scam people," I muttered.

He laughed. One of his deep belly-laughs that made me instantly envious that I wasn't there to watch it happen in person. "You can't trust thieves—a good lesson to learn. What's your plan?"

"Intercept the potion, slip them a fake one, watch their plan crumble into pieces, then set it afire and watch them leave town with their tail between their legs."

"Succinct."

"The best kind of plan. Will you help?"

Fluffy started barking excitedly and pulling at her leash. I followed the direction of her scrambling and my mouth fell open in shock.

Ian and Rufus were strolling our way, the big man and large dog completely at home among the increased late-evening revelers.

Key moved to stand behind me, and I sensed the tension in her ratchet up sharply.

"It'll be okay," I reassured her in a whisper.

Ian came to a stop in front of us, dressed as usual in all black, his hair held back with an elastic tie, a few tempting loose strands framing one side of his face. Rufus sat on the ground while Fluffy went ecstatic at his arrival and pranced back and forth until he deigned to greet her with a nudge of his snout against her head.

"Hey, Cavalier," said the bouncer from behind us.

I whirled in surprise. "You know him?"

"I told you I like to do karaoke," Ian said placidly.

"How come he's allowed inside?" I asked in outrage. "He's a shifter."

The berserker grinned. "Bounty bros over woofing woes."

"That makes no sense!"

His smile widened. "It does to me."

Ian took hold of my elbow and dragged me farther down the street. I kept my gaze locked on the bouncer's, promising retribution. He pointed at his eyes, then at me.

Good luck getting your potions, I mouthed.

He pouted exaggeratedly and traced an invisible tear down his cheek.

Key giggled by my side, and the sound lifted my spirits enough to forgive the bouncer. The man was only doing his job.

So what if he ever came for a potion and ended with a blue tongue for a month? I'd be doing my job too—a witch had to earn some respect in the community.

Turning, I kept a normal pace with Ian.

"How lucky that you happened to be in the neighborhood," I said. "Were you out trying to catch a paranormal getting their hands dirty so you can haul them to bounty hunter jail?"

"That's not how bounty hunters work."

"It should be." Then demons wouldn't be out and about mugging people. "Why are you here?"

"I've been searching for you. You weren't at the shop, and you promised dinner."

I felt a small stab of guilt. "It's not dinnertime."

He stared me down in his best granite impression. "I like to arrive early."

It sounded like an excuse. "Were you worried about me?"

"The twins might've discovered you're helping Hutton."

"Aww, see." My heart turned into mushy goo. "You *do* care."

"There was also a high probability you were planning to do something stupid."

He looked at me like he had been proven right, which only showed how much he still had to learn about me.

"How did you know to find me here of all places?" I asked.

He answered with the blunt truth, as he usually did. When it suited him. "I followed your trail."

"How?" My fingers immediately moved to my pockets. "Did you bug my phone?"

He snorted. "I have a dog."

Fluffy yipped in agreement, and I didn't have it in me to tell her he was referring to Rufus. "Handy."

"Very."

I studied his face, but he was giving nothing away. "When did you catch up to us?"

Had he followed us from the moment we'd left the shop, or after the call from Key's room?

"Just now. Took us a while to find your scent."

I wasn't sure if I should fully believe him or not, but I decided to give him the benefit of the doubt.

"Why didn't you tell me about your plan from the start?" he asked.

"I didn't know if you'd help or if you'd interfere." I reached for Key's arm and gave her a reassuring squeeze. "Girls gotta stick together sometimes."

He glanced at us. "Just the two of you?"

"I called Dru before you. I thought about inviting Sonia to the party, but her presence might've been counterproductive."

"The PBOA has its cons," he agreed. "Did you learn anything else besides not trusting thieves?"

"That Fluffy needs an official emotional support animal vest."

Fluffy yipped.

Ian rubbed his chin. "Not a bad idea. Rufus gets tired of waiting in the car sometimes."

The male dog's head tilted up at the mention of his name, and his dog walk took on a dignified air. Ian absentmindedly reached down to scratch behind his ears.

"Don't worry, Fluffy," I told the other dog following me obediently. "You're awesome too."

She stopped to sniff a puddle of vomit.

"What makes you think the twins got their potion?" Ian asked.

I checked our surroundings, saw nobody sticking close to us, and explained my Sherlock Holmesian deductions. "The twins' request got deleted. That means they got someone to send them the potion from out of town, but I can't be sure if they got it yet or not."

"They might've simply changed their minds about it," he pointed out.

"But what if they didn't? Hope for the best but don't ignore the worst."

"I'm not sure that's how the saying goes."

"Put your best foot forward and you shall be rewarded."

"There is a message for me in all this, isn't there?"

"If you can't say anything nice, say nothing at all."

He flashed me a smile. "That one sounds about right."

"I like to be prepared." I tried not to preen at the warmth in his voice. "Knowing who here imports potions from out of town will tell us if they got the potion or not. I was following some leads, but nothing has panned out."

"What will you do if they got the potion already?"

"If they got it already, the idea was to, uh, visit their lodgings and replace it with a fake."

"Breaking and entering an alpha's premises is not a good idea," Ian cautioned. "Especially given your success history."

I turned to Key, who looked a lot more alert and a lot less shocked. Excellent. "Don't listen to him. I take every failure seriously and use the lessons learned toward the next attempt."

"Good god," Ian muttered.

"What else am I supposed to do? Wait for the twins to roll in and take over your brother's pack?" The edge of resentment in my voice startled me.

As if he'd heard it, too, Ian pressed his lips to stop himself from uttering one of his blunt responses. One like "yes."

"No hints on the website about who might've accepted the request?" he asked.

"None. Everything seems totally anonymous." For good reason. "And no delivery services in the area."

"Something like that goes by word-of-mouth recommendations rather than a storefront."

That was probably how Bagley had operated too. Me? I liked to test new things, apparently, and shout my business in the dark web marketplace. "You don't know anyone who imports illegal magic?"

He regarded me with amusement. "I don't involve myself in illegal dealings any more than I need to."

"Ahh. The mythical status quo."

"They stay in their lane, I stay in mine."

"Bet it helps you sleep at night."

"It helps avoid waking up with a knife in my back."

"All right, point taken."

"Uhm," came Key's shy, eager voice. "I could try to call my uncle again."

Ian narrowed his eyes. "Why would your uncle know about this?"

I stepped into his line of vision. "He knows stuff."

"He's from Olmeda?"

"Comes and goes." I waved his question aside and turned to Key. "Try him."

Key swallowed and brought her phone up. Would Ian put two and two together—my fire mage dark magic user, the new earth mage stray, and the uncle who had knowledge of Olmeda's illegal stuff? It seemed glaringly obvious when put that way.

And was Hutton still patiently waiting for me to figure out how to fix *his* potion?

The thought came out of nowhere, and with it a sudden realization.

I touched Key's arm. "Hang up."

Key did, looking at me expectantly. Ian stepped up to make a tight triangle among the three of us.

What if the twins had gotten the potion *and* already used it? What if that was the reason my alpha potion had faded so fast when it had felt so strong at the shop?

"How exactly does an alpha take over someone else's pack?" I asked. "Is there a vote or something more old-fashioned? Do they fight for it? Dru mentioned an official challenge."

"The pack members can request a vote," Ian said. "Official challenges rarely happen nowadays. The losing pack might reject the new alpha, making the fight useless."

"But if they have the support of one of the alpha's seconds in command, then that would give them a good chance of being accepted, right?"

"It's a more direct route to change alphas than voting," Ian admitted. "If the pack leadership looks for strength in their alphas, a challenge would skip a lot of politics."

Accidents happened in fights, even if you had superiority. Making sure your opponent was as weak as possible would ensure a victory. I took a hold of the front of Ian's black Henley. "I think they might already have used the potion on Hutton. We need to warn him."

Ian held my gaze. "Call him."

Oh, that was right—I had his number. I brought up my phone and tapped on his number. It went to voice mail. "He's not picking up."

Without a word, Ian called someone on his phone.

"It's Cavalier," he said in a somber voice. "Where's Hutton?" His jaw clenched. "Where?" A pause. "Thank you."

He lowered the phone and met my questioning gaze.

"A challenge has been issued."

23

"THEY CHALLENGED THE ALPHA ALREADY?" Key asked as we hurried toward Ian's SUV. He hadn't exactly offered to give us a ride but hadn't barked when I'd demanded to know where he was parked.

"Time is golden. Why waste it?" I said. "Come in, get the leadership out of the way, and check if any of the other alphas are going to complain. *Will* they complain?"

"Doubt it," Ian said, not even breathing hard at our fast pace. "They won't get involved in direct challenges."

"Even if the twins used potions?"

"No proof."

Ian was right. Even if someone had kept a screenshot of their listing, there was nothing in the post tying it to them, and any witness, like good Uncle Jeremy, wouldn't get involved in someone else's problems.

We reached the car and piled in—me and Ian in the front, Key sharing the back with Rufus, Fluffy in her lap.

"Where's the challenge happening?" I asked, securing my seatbelt. Ian turned on the engine and shot out of the parking spot. Key cried out in distress, but I craved the speed. The faster, the better. The knowledge that Hutton was facing the cheating pair of alphas, that my potion hadn't been strong enough to compensate for theirs, was eating at my insides, its saliva flowing through my veins like pure adrenaline.

Faster, I willed the car. *Faster.* Late evening traffic filled the streets, hampering our speed.

"Right on the edge of pack territory," Ian said.

The stonier his expression, the more he cared, I'd learned. Part of me wanted to break out the party poppers and cut out a flag garland spelling *Finally!* The rest of me couldn't get past the need to teleport to the challenge and stop the proceedings. How could something that affected so many people be settled in such a fast, brutal way?

"Who did you call?" I asked. It must've been someone in the pack to get such a fast answer.

"An acquaintance."

The need to throw a party rose again. I *was* right—Ian cared more about his brother than he liked to admit. Why else keep a contact in his pack? That wasn't something someone who liked to stay in their lane would do. Someone who outwardly hated the packs and wanted nothing to do with them.

"I don't know what you expect us to do once we get there," Ian said. "We can't stop an official challenge."

"I'll think of something. Maybe Key can help Hutton cheat back, get the twin fighting Hutton to stumble."

Key's eyes grew wide with alarm in the rear mirror.

Ian harrumphed. "Hutton cheated first."

"You had to get that in, didn't you?" Can take the brotherly hate out of the man, but can't take the man out of killing the mood with reality. I didn't mind. The banter helped me focus on something other than the need to scratch at my arms, to free the nerves and adrenaline and fear crawling under my skin.

"I like to be fair."

"You're a bounty hunter, not a judge."

His hands tightened around the steering wheel. "Forget it."

Surprised at the abrupt coolness in his voice, I tried to take my words back. "I bet you're not just a bounty hunter, but a *great* bounty hunter. Got a wall full of medals and all." Ian's lips formed a thin line. "Plaques and recommendations and the whole thing." By now, his upper and lower jaws might as well have been fused together. "With a bank account to match. The best bounty hunters are the ones who get to retire early, right?" Oh, good Mother Earth, I was making it worse. I racked my head, searching for a way to turn back time. Could I use the memory potion from the demon? No, too dangerous. Ah! I knew just the thing. "Look, a doggy!"

Rufus and Fluffy let out low woofs from the back seat. Ian glanced at the sidewalk, then at me. The ghost of a smile turned up his lips, and he relaxed slightly.

I kept my mouth shut for the rest of the drive.

He took us to the cemetery, and, for a few moments, I was afraid he had lied and had no intention of taking us to the challenge. Then he drove past his gate and I sighed with relief. Getting scammed by strangers was one thing, but I'd rather not add Ian to the list.

We came to a stop by the small patch of forest rear-ending the pack's territory into the street proper. I was glad it wasn't the cul-de-sac Vicky had used to try to kidnap me.

"The fights to the death happen right by the cemetery?" I remarked as I unbuckled the seatbelt. "How convenient."

"We do have a few shifter graves."

"Seriously?"

Instead of answering, he opened the glove box and retrieved two items from within, one a holster that had a particular shape.

"Is that a gun?" I asked, a little scandalized. Firearms and paranormals didn't often go together, and if they did, it was frowned upon. Those kinds of things attracted undue attention.

"No," he said, stepping out of the car. "Rufus, Fluffy, stay."

I shoved the bag with Key's grandma's spellbook and the demon's stuff in the glove box and closed it, then got out of the SUV. Ian was strapping the—it *had* to be a gun—to his belt, but it was hard to see since he had killed the car's lights and the spot had no street lamps to illuminate it well. He threw me the second object, and I caught it easily. A flashlight.

By the time I found the button to turn it on, Ian had already gone into the trees. Key and I followed him, the flashlight making the trip a lot easier. The thing was powerful for being so small. It felt like it could illuminate all the way into people's souls.

After a few minutes of following a thin trail—or so Ian called it; I reserve my opinion—we stepped into a man-made opening. The ground was clear of trees and stumps, the underbrush gone, leaving behind a covering of grass and other small, leafy vegetation. Two huge lamps installed on the nearby trees lit up the night, revealing a gathering of five men and a couple of women.

Hutton and the twin shifters stood in the middle of the opening.

"Oh, goodie, we're in time," I exclaimed happily. "Thanks for waiting."

The trio didn't switch their attention; the others had been looking our way since before we'd entered the clearing.

"Is this why you were stalling?" one twin said with a sneer. "Need the grave man to take care of your corpse?"

"I wasn't stalling," Hutton answered coolly.

One of the male shifters on the sidelines gave us an almost imperceptible nod of greeting. I recognized him as the man who'd come with Hutton to deal with the shifter hitman three weeks ago. Grier was in the group as well, studying us with a slight frown creasing his brow.

"Can we get this over with, then?" the other twin asked. Without waiting for an answer, he began stripping.

"Yes, *please*," the first twin said. He also took his light jacket off.

Snarling, Hutton took a hold of the back of his long-sleeved T-shirt and pulled it right over his head.

One guess as to why they were getting naked.

"Wait." I stepped forward. "Why are they all shifting?"

Everyone turned toward me.

"It's an alpha challenge," one woman explained, not unkindly, which I appreciated. "The alphas fight for the territory."

I pointed at the twins. "But they're two and he's one. How's that fair?"

"Close family members are allowed to join. Up to the defendant to call on his own."

Ian's presence felt like a huge magnet behind me. From the gleam in the twins' eyes, they were perfectly aware that Hutton would never ask, and Ian would never join. B- on their research, six out of ten.

Because they hadn't dug deep enough.

I turned to Ian.

His expression was flat. Flatter than an open can of soda forgotten for a week.

I wriggled my eyebrows encouragingly and tilted my head toward the center of the opening. *C'mon, big guy. You can do it.* If I threw the flashlight at the trio of alphas, would he run after it and then get stuck having to help?

With a slow, heavy exhale of air, he uncrossed his arms and walked up to the trio.

"Luckily for Hutton," I said triumphantly, "he also has a brother."

Ian came to stand by Hutton. "Derek."

Hutton's focus didn't waver from the twins, but he acknowledged his brother with a gritted, "Ian."

Wonderful. Now the twins would reconsider their challenge and go back from whence they'd come.

The three men continued to strip.

Ian caught my look of confusion and smiled grimly. "Once a challenge has been issued, there's no stopping it."

"Can't they simply apologize and move on?" I concentrated hard on Ian's chest as the sounds of zippers filled my ears.

One twin snorted. "Keep dreaming, woman."

"Step back," one of the other shifters told me.

Key tugged at my arm, and I returned to the edge of the trees, my limbs feeling as if I'd just spent the whole day making potions. This wasn't part of my plan. The whole thing was supposed to be stopped, not...

Growls rose in the air, the sounds of snapping and popping echoing in the opening and creating a mark in my memory I'd never forget. In the blink of an eye, the three naked men had turned into wolves—two huge gray ones and a slimmer black one.

Ian hadn't even touched his belt buckle.

Shift, I mouthed in panic the moment he glanced our way. I didn't think anyone was about to wait for him to join the fray in his wolf form. The twins were throwing off so many alpha power vibes it was a physical wave pushing against my skin.

Ian's mouth kicked up at the corner, but he didn't make a move to strip. Was he being shy? That didn't fit with him—he'd shown no bashfulness the couple of times I'd caught him home without his shirt on. Then I remembered Dru's words about him so long ago—Ian never shifted.

Seriously? I mouthed. I could understand his hatred of shifters stopping him from shifting on a day-to-day basis, but this was taking it to the extreme. He was going against two wolves. He had no armor, no protection against their claws and teeth. He was going to get absolutely mauled.

My pulse began to pound in my ears. I patted my pockets, searching for anything that might help. The demon's memory potion? That might confuse the wolves long enough for Ian to do something, *anything*.

I had nothing on me aside from that, and I'd left it behind in the SUV. No freezing potions, no smart wards pre-laid on the ground, no way to give him a hand. *Nothing*.

Ian shook his head, as if guessing the panicked course of my thoughts. Perhaps he had. Perhaps he'd noticed the bulge of my hammering heart as it tried to claw its way into my throat. I didn't care if it was against the rules—this was an outrage! How could he simply stand there, fine like a daisy, like this was not a matter of him about to get turned into burger meat?

The growling intensified. One twin and Hutton were nose to nose, their mouths open into snarls, saliva dripping between their sharp teeth. The second twin advanced toward Ian, head low but calculating yellow eyes fixed on him, deciding where to hit first.

What did it matter? Ian didn't stand a chance!

Hutton and his twin leaped at each other, turning into a gray-and-black furry blur rolling on the ground. The second twin rushed Ian.

My heart stopped.

Ian dodged the teeth and used his hands to slap the wolf's snout away from his torso. The twin turned swiftly and lunged. Ian kicked him in the head and sent him rolling sideways. I gasped for air. Was that it?

No, the twin got back onto his fours and shook his head,

looking no worse for the wear. A yip of pain and a howl of anger came from the other side of the clearing, registering in my senses but not my thoughts. All my neurons were busy with Ian's fight. No space for anything else.

If he gets badly hurt, it'll be my fault.

If he dies...

My brain recoiled from those unpleasant words, kicked them to my stomach, where they were happy to roll and throw a party straight out of Hell.

The twin stalked toward Ian again, slowly, slyly, as if letting Ian savor the last breaths of his life.

Ian took his gun out and shot at the wolf.

A loud *t-t-t-t-t-t* erupted from the gun, and the wolf reeled back.

What the heck?

The *t-t-t-t-t-t* noise came again, and the wolf shook as if electrified. That was when I noticed the thin wires connecting the wolf to the gun in Ian's hand. A stun gun? It took another long shock for the twin to fall on its side and lie there immobile and panting.

Ian stepped forward and nudged him with his boot. Content with the results, he unplugged something from the end of the gun and returned the weapon to its holster.

The faces of the other shifters showed the same open-mouthed shock mine did, but nobody stepped forward demanding Ian's head for cheating. They simply picked their jaws up and switched their attention to the two other wolves.

"Holy crap," Key murmured, awestruck. She'd been gripping my arm, and I hadn't noticed until now. "That was *so* cool."

I appreciated the teachable moment—you didn't need fancy powers to win fights. I should thank Ian later. If I ever got my vocal cords to work again.

A high-pitched howl tore my attention from Ian to the fighting wolves. Blood shone wetly on the fur of the smaller black one, but he'd clamped his teeth on the gray one's throat. The big wolf tried to shake Hutton off, but the alpha had a firm grip. Blood flowed from the wound, coating the twin's fur. His howls turned into yips, and the yips turned into whimpers. The thrashing slowed into a twitch.

I averted my eyes and made Key turn away. Plenty of others here to stand as eye witnesses. The shifter world could be harsh—there was no hiding from that, nor should we, but the sounds of a slow, agonizing death and the pungent scent of blood were enough of a reminder. Of a warning.

Only when silence fell over the clearing, when the alpha power vibes lowered to unrecognizable levels, did I look back. The one twin lay bloodied and still on the ground. Hutton made his way to the second, clamped his teeth around its throat, and shook him violently until a loud snap reverberated against the trees.

I tensed, shocked by the unexpected brutality. So much for not being a witness to death. Although, I consoled myself, that ship had sailed when the shifter hitman had attacked me weeks ago and the shifters had brought him down in front of me. This one shouldn't add too many nightmares.

Would Ian let me sleep with Fluffy tonight?

The clearing erupted into cheers, almost making me jump out of my skin. The remaining shifters whooped and punched the air above their heads. Hutton returned to his human form with another series of disturbing snaps and pops, then put on his jeans and nothing else. Bleeding gouges marred one arm and part of his torso, his skin covered by a sheet of sweat. His breathing was labored, his face a mask of stone rivaling Ian's best.

A couple of shifters came forward to pat him on the back, but he held up a hand.

"Grier," he said, "go deliver the news to their pack." He breathed in deeply. "Don't come back."

Grier's shoulders slumped, but he nodded and disappeared into the forest.

Did that mean don't come back to the clearing, or the pack? Common sense told me the latter—nobody wanted a second in command who actively worked to give your pack to someone else. In older times, he might not have made it out of the clearing.

The two wolf corpses lay like beacons of light on the disturbed ground.

"They'll take care of them," Ian said.

The urge to hug him close was overpowering. So, I did. One fast—one second, five at most, maybe ten—squeeze, good enough to reassure myself he was still solid and whole, and done.

He oomphed, his fingertips barely alighting on my shoulders before I was pulling away.

Okay. I could breathe again.

A group of four shifters entered the clearing with a couple of tarps and got to work on transferring the dead twins onto them. I wondered if they had a special pit where they kept throwing all these dead people. Better not to ask, or I might get to see it firsthand.

"You're tricky," I told Ian.

He shrugged. "I learned a lot during my bounty hunter days. We should go."

Hutton caught my eye.

"Give me a moment." I left him and Key and made a circle around the shifters and dead wolves to reach the alpha. He was putting his T-shirt back on, momentarily alone as his crew cleaned up the place and spoke into their phones.

"Will the twins' pack retaliate?" I asked.

He shook his head. "It was an official challenge, witnessed by others not in my pack." He glanced at me. "And you."

I shivered at the reminder and lowered my voice. "I think the twins used their potion on you. The effects should disappear within a day or two. There is a chance my potion will remain strong. At least for now."

"Good." A snarl of pain curled his mouth as he pressed a hand to his torso. His T-shirt gained a damp spot.

"Do you need something for that?" Wounds inflicted by paranormals like wolves or demons took longer to heal, the magic counteracting a shifter's innate fast healing.

"We have medics in the pack."

He had told me that before—the nurse who could teach me how to draw blood without the need of slicing instruments.

"The witch—Bagley," he whispered, so low I could barely hear him. "Has she told you how to make my potion?"

Hutton and Ian were a lot closer in temperament than they liked to admit—both blunt, both liked to get to the point. It was heartwarming. "I don't deal with Bagley. She'll take as much as she can and leave me with nothing in return."

He grunted in agreement, probably used to having to haggle the price for his potion. "She talks about her clients much?"

"Not at all."

"But you took over her business."

The dark magic one, he meant. "Of sorts."

"I expect you to do better, then."

Ian and Hutton might be similar, but I much preferred his big brother. "I'll do my best," I told him dryly. "About the Council meeting..."

"I'll cancel. They're not needed anymore."

Relieved, I moved to go back to Ian and Key, but he stepped in front of me.

"Next time I tell you not to involve my brother, don't."

My glance switched to Ian, then back to him. "You need his —" I stopped myself. I couldn't whisper as low as him, and shifter ears were sharp. "You need his support as alpha."

"I don't want him involved."

"Even after that?" I gestured toward the shifters heaving up the heavy, wolf-filled tarps.

"He doesn't need to know any more," Hutton insisted, glowering at me.

It suddenly made sense—his questions about Bagley, his insistence Ian stay far away from his dark magic dealings even though Ian already knew about the alpha potion. Hutton knew, or had guessed, the reason his powers were not what they should be. He knew his mother had used dark magic on his father.

And he didn't want Ian to know.

Oh, my goodness. That was the sweetest thing ever. A little brother keeping secrets that would destroy his big brother's heart.

I patted his uninjured arm. "Your secret is safe with me. Witch-client confidentiality."

The look on his face told me I should escape before he reminded me of how I'd absolutely ignored that so far, so I hurried around him and went back to Ian and Key.

Key was admiring Ian with nothing short of complete idolatry, and when we began our way back to Ian's car, she held me back and whispered, "I think I want to be a bounty hunter."

Oh, boy.

24

IAN DROPPED Key at her building, waited until she went inside, then drove me home.

We sat in the SUV, idling in front of the shop in a thick silence, so heavy it held me down against the seat and stopped me from jumping out. Or maybe it was the events of the whole day finally catching up to me, turning my legs into soft butter. I wanted to remain inside the SUV, keep roasting in this silence, hug it like a warm blanket, and go to sleep with my head on Ian's shoulder.

Unfortunately, Ian would probably rather sleep in his bed.

"Are you okay?" I asked tentatively.

"Yes. You?"

Would he have nightmares about today? I knew I would. The what-ifs had a way of sneaking up on you.

What if he'd been hurt?

What if he'd died?

"Life is a risk," I murmured, studying his profile. "No point in dwelling on what didn't happen."

He turned toward me, reached up, and held my chin so I couldn't look away. "My decision, my risk."

His thumb ran across my lower lip. I held my breath.

"No regrets," he said.

"No regrets," I agreed against his questing thumb.

For a moment, I thought he might lean in and kiss me, but he retracted his touch and faced ahead. "Keep Fluffy for a couple of days."

Fluffy yipped, her tail thumping against the back seat.

My heart filled to overflow. "Really?"

"Yes."

I glanced at the dogs. "You hear that, Fluffy? You get to sleep with your favorite person!"

Ian snorted. "I'll call tomorrow."

Following an instinct, I leaned in and kissed him soundly on the cheek, then retrieved the bag from the glove box, got out of the car, and opened Fluffy's door. She was all too happy to jump out.

Ian waited for us to get inside, and then some, before driving away. The shop was drenched in darkness, and I held still for a couple of minutes until my eyes adapted while Fluffy went ahead toward the back, the clacking of her claws against the hardwood floors filling the house with the warmth of life.

Home—what a wonderful, wonderful place.

"Well?" Bagley demanded eagerly. "Did you get that young woman's spellbook?"

"Nope."

"Are you sure?"

"Very sure." Technically, it was the young woman's grandma's spellbook. Not that I should feel bad about lying to the ghost of an evil, murdering witch.

"Dang it, child. Research is important. How are you to evolve your spells without inspiration?"

"You mean steal ideas from other dark witches?"

"Witches are meant to share."

She sounded so disappointed in me it was hard not to chuckle. "And if in the process you steal their spellbooks so they have to start over, all the better?"

A loud sniff came from the direction of the water urn, and I seriously hoped she hadn't taken over that. Could her evilness seep into the water, or would I have to unplug the whole thing and drag it out of the room and back?

"I won't dignify that with an answer," Bagley said. "Now, tell me about the young alpha. Did you attempt one of your weak potions on him? Are you ready to learn the secrets of powerful magic?"

I checked the bolts on the door and walked to the back. "Not yet. Good night, Bagley."

"*Ms.* Bagley. Youth these days..."

Her voice disappeared as I crossed the invisible barrier between the shop and the rest of the house. If the old hag ever hoped to earn my help, she was going to need to get over her disappointment with the ways of the new generations. And my lack of power.

Not that I'd ever tell her—her wicked witch ways kept me from growing complacent.

"Ready for a shower and bed?" I asked Fluffy.

Fluffy lolled her tongue and wagged her tail.

A long shower, one long Dru phone update, and some leftovers later, I sat on my bed and studied Key's grandma's spellbook. Fluffy sniffed it, but I gently pushed her head away.

"No sniffing sources of evil, Fluffy. It's bad for the soul."

Fluffy rested her head on her paws and watched eagerly.

The notebook looked harmless lying on my cream-colored blanket. Who could guess so much harm could be contained inside?

Hutton's mother's use of dark magic had prompted Hutton's need for a potion to remain alpha. Hutton's status as alpha had prompted the twins' use of dark magic. The twins' use of dark magic had ended with me holding on to Key's dark magic spellbook.

Once unleashed, dark magic spread like rot, poisoning the lives of everyone who came in contact with it.

The only way to stop it was to cut it at the root. To burn it to the ground.

This spellbook should be in my fire pit, not resting on my bed.

But I couldn't make myself destroy it. It belonged to Key, not me. Who was I to decide what to do with it? I wasn't Key's mother or guardian. It wasn't my place to make that decision for her. If someone had burned Grandma's spellbook, they would have taken half of my soul with it.

On the other hand, I was Olmeda's official witch. I had a responsibility toward the well-being of the community. The existence of this spellbook threatened that. I already had one dark witch haunting the place. Did I need another source of dark magic hanging around?

"No point in deciding before you know the contents."

Until I was sure there was actual evil inside, how could I make an informed decision?

Fluffy agreed with a soft yip.

Carefully, I untied the ribbon holding the spellbook closed and opened the cover. From page one, the thing was chock full of tiny writing and drawings. No elegant family tree to start things with—Key's grandma had gotten right down to it. I checked the back of the cover and found a name: Amber Stone.

The find cheered me up. Things couldn't be so bad if the woman had left her name so visible.

I flipped through the pages, fighting to read the minuscule cursive writing. Spells for growing herbs better suited for magic, spells for different everyday potions like the ones I sold at the shop, spells for poisoning without leaving obvious traces, spells for putting your clients in a trance, spells for marking your tarot cards. Spells for subduing demons and spells for...keeping your dead pets looking alive? I tried hard to forget that one as I skipped to a freshly dog-eared page.

Accidental, or had Key specifically marked it? I skimmed the contents and found the reason for the marking—a power spell. Key hadn't been lying after all. Her grandma had written down a spell to mess with someone's power. And it only required a good dose of blood from a different, powerful paranormal type. I buried my face in my hands for a few minutes. I could ignore the unethical dealing with clients, the murdering possibilities of the poisons, and the vaguely disturbing pet ones, but not this. This one was dark from start to finish.

You could use willing blood to make a harmful potion—that was how you made freezing potions—but the reach would be limited. To make any real dent, the blood had to be unwilling.

Peeking through my fingers, I read the spell instructions again, hoping to salvage the situation, and my gaze snagged a series of notes written around and underneath, as if Key's grandma had been brainstorming and had run out of normal page space. It theorized which paranormal types most opposed each other, and which complemented each other. She went through different ideas, and it felt as if I was reading a horoscope or a tarot reading. The contents of someone's soul had been important to Key's grandmother, cheating her tarot clients or not, and, being a spirit witch, I commiserated. I kept on reading.

And there, at the end, in a scribble so twisted I had to turn the book in a complete circle to read it, was the solution to Hutton's problem.

———

The morning was deliciously chilly, the sun already bright, the shop open downstairs with Dru in charge, and Ian and Hutton stood in the middle of my upstairs kitchen.

It made for a bit of a cramped space, but I wanted no chance of my magic being accidentally discovered by doing the spell downstairs. Through the window into the backyard, I could see Fluffy running playful circles around a very put-upon Rufus.

"Well?" Hutton demanded. He looked worse for the wear—eyes rimmed in red and a stubble darkening his lower jaw. It looked good on him, gave him a rugged edge rather than his usual handsome pretty visage.

He still had nothing on Ian's enticing harshness, though.

"Long night?" I asked.

Hutton grunted. "We celebrated."

"As you should."

Ian crossed his arms. "You found another way to do the potion?" He was wearing a soft, thin black sweater, and it made me want to pet him like a cat.

"Sort of. It won't be a potion but a direct exchange of power."

That got their attention.

"How?" Hutton asked.

My mistake had been in trying to use a potion from the start. No non-dark potion could produce such a change in someone's power. But, following her own theories about blood opposites, Key's grandmother had theorized that if you used direct blood-to-blood contact, the power would grow exponentially. Unfortunately for dark witches everywhere, and fortunately for the world, both sides would need to be willing, as it would require a power exchange, not simply bloodletting.

"I'm going to use Ian's innate power, using my magic as a conduit, and direct it into yours. It should keep what alpha power you still have from Bagley's potion activated. Hopefully. It should last a lot longer than any potion I can come up with, even without others messing with it."

"That's a lot of 'shoulds.'" Hutton didn't sound convinced.

"Take them or leave them or tell your pack you're not an actual alpha."

He shook his head. "No. Not so soon after the challenge."

"Then it's the shoulds or the byes." I lifted a shoulder. "Your choice."

"Jesus. Whatever." He rolled up his sleeve and offered me his forearm. "Do it."

I looked at Ian. "You?"

Wordlessly, he also rolled up his sleeve.

"Gotta be the hand this time." I bit my lip apologetically. "Sorry."

Hutton snarled. Ian scowled. Couldn't blame them—cuts in the hand hurt a lot more—but it was the best way to make sure their open wounds would come into direct contact.

"Here, let's do it over the sink." *And let's hope the ghost goldfish in my pipes isn't a vampire.* I directed them to stand on each side of me, picked up my knife, and offered it to Hutton, handle forward. It wasn't about me being squeamish about the whole slash-and-dice situation—I wanted this exchange to be a hundred percent willing.

But mostly the slashing part.

He grabbed the knife with a shake of his head and sliced fast and deep into his palm. I winced at the sight, then motioned him to pass the blade to Ian. Ian repeated the motion on his own hand.

Once they were both bleeding freely all over my sink, I indicated they shake hands.

Hutton hesitated, a look of doubt crossing his face.

"What is it?" I asked sharply.

"Perhaps you're right," he said. "I don't need to do this."

I gasped with delight. He had finally seen the wisdom of my ways! "Do you mean it?"

He snorted and clasped Ian's hand. "Hell, no. After lying all this time? They'd quarter me alive." A hint of wicked amusement curled his mouth.

"Jerk." They were so clearly brothers that it made me want to roll my eyes. Instead, I held their hands in mine.

My magic rose, wonderfully tingly, wonderfully awake, and eager to perform. Low power, great enthusiasm.

"Raise your alpha power," I murmured.

Ian's magic filled the room. Its pressure mixed with my magic, leaving every inch of my skin over-sensitized and thirsty for more. It seeped into my lungs, rested on the tip of my tongue, raised my awareness of him as someone to fear, someone to give my loyalty to.

I concentrated on the warm hands under mine and focused my intent.

Blood shares with blood.

Power shared to power.

Through mine.

Let it bond. Let it remain.

I felt a jolt pass through their held hands.

"Shit," Hutton whispered in surprise.

A second kind of alpha power grew around us. It felt like Ian's but with a slight twist. A dark, ugly twist that filled me with unease.

Bagley's alpha potion, rotting away and poisoning the air. Leaving a foul taste in my mouth.

I stepped back and wiped my forehead. "It's done."

Ian immediately took my elbow and tried to guide me to the kitchen chair, bleeding all over the linoleum floor.

"I'm okay," I told him, holding firm. "I didn't have to use that much magic."

"This feels different from the potion," Hutton said.

"Hopefully, that's a good sign." I handed him a piece of gauze and used another on Ian's hand. Magic had coursed through these wounds—they wouldn't heal as fast as they would otherwise.

"I'll let you know." Hutton cleared his throat. "Thank you."

I grinned at him. "And free of charge."

He nodded sharply and left for the stairs.

Opening my first aid kit, I took out the medical tape and busied myself treating Ian's wound, making sure it was clean, and securing the gauze with some medical tape.

His alpha power hadn't gone down, and once Hutton was out of the room, I felt it envelop me, cleansing away the foulness of Bagley's magic. I inhaled it in, bringing the scent of the man along with it. The warmth of his skin felt amazing under my fingertips, the reassuring solidity of muscle and bone.

"How did you come up with this blood-to-blood theory?" he asked.

How much to tell him? I pressed the gauze against his palm, hoping to stanch the bleeding. "I found another witch's notes. They were helpful."

"The book in the plastic bag? You got it from Key?" he asked, never one to miss a detail.

"Yes, her grandmother's spellbook."

"Ah."

I squirmed under the weight of that single, pointed word. With his scent in my lungs, his power tracing my skill, and the way his deep voice liked to wrap around my heart, if he asked whether the notes were dark magic related, I'd end up blurting the truth.

"Key has been very helpful, and she really knows how to use her magic. She helped me with the demon and never complained. I think she'll be a great addition to your business." I stopped before I also told him that for the price of one Key, he could also get a set of knives and a carrot peeler. I dared a glance at his face, but the intensity in his eyes had me glancing back down at his hand. "Alex and Shane seem to like her."

He said nothing, perhaps wondering how far into the ground I was going to dig in my attempts to keep Key on his payroll.

"You didn't shift during the fight."

"I didn't need to."

I glanced up again, this time holding on to his intensity, no matter how fluttery it made me, now nervous, how eager, how it made me feel as if I was the only thing in the world.

"Is it true you never shift? Ever?"

"Yes."

Watching his lips form the curt word made mine go instantly dry. "Is it because of your father?"

"I don't like shifters."

"That would be like not liking yourself, and you're the type of guy who definitely likes himself."

His sudden smile nearly stopped my heart. "Is that a compliment?"

"Self-assurance is always a compliment," I agreed.

"Did you decode Bagley's ledger?"

It took me a few moments to realign my brain and understand what he was asking. Bagley's ledger. Right. The one I'd taken back under the excuse of having obtained the code. "Not yet."

He touched my hand with his free one. "When you do, don't tell Hutton. He doesn't need to know about his mother."

I didn't have to fake my shock. Ian had known? "I don't..."

"You're smart, Hope. All this research on blood and alpha powers and potions. You know why he didn't inherit the power."

His faith in me made me humble. Him wanting to protect his little brother threatened to turn me into a puddle. "You're right. I guessed it. Bagley dropped some hints as well. I won't tell him."

"Good." His fingers rubbed the top of my hand. "You know, this healing thing would go faster if you kissed it better."

My entire being stilled. His eyes held a sort of promise that sent deliciously thick lava pooling into my lower belly.

"No kisses without dates." Light, playful words that did nothing to slow the thumping of my heart.

He arched an unimpressed eyebrow. "We've had five dates already."

We had? "How? We're not dating."

His free hand landed on my hip, and he tugged me closer. "You cooked food for me, and I deemed it acceptable. I asked you to dinner, and you deemed it acceptable. We're dating."

"Oh, yeah?" My voice came out breathless. "When was our last date?"

"Yesterday," he said, all seriousness.

I let out a surprised laugh. "How was that a date?"

"We went pubbing and then I took you to a show. It was a date."

Oh, my goodness, this man. "Fine, fine." I kissed the top of my index finger, then pressed it to his hand. "There. Kissed all better."

He dipped his head toward me. "That's weak."

"So is your date game."

"I'll try to improve."

His lips touched mine, and I immediately pressed upward, closing my eyes and rolling onto my tiptoes. Anchoring myself on his arms. Arms that went around me and held me tightly, keeping me close to the increased pounding of his heart. His lips tasted of morning coffee and mornings spent lazing around in bed. Of late nights and entangled sheets and laughter and tenderness. Of Ian, standing by my side, silent, secretive. Inviting me to open up his heart, look into his soul, and agree to everything he had to offer.

He broke the contact, and I stepped back, touching my lips in wonder. "Maybe we're dating after all."

"I knew you'd see it my way." His smile was slow, dangerous, and deliciously wolfish.

Too dangerous. If we kissed again, we might not stop, and I needed some time to get used to the idea that my late-night dreams might become reality.

"Speaking of, uh, stuff, I got something to give you."

"Oh?"

I cleared my throat. "It's from the demon who tried to mug us yesterday. Maybe the bounty hunters can do something about it? I took his photo too."

"Show me."

I went into the bedroom to retrieve the demon's phone and my gaze fell on my bed.

No, Hope. Don't go there. Later, not now.

Tearing my gaze away, I searched for the grounding presence of Grandma's spellbook on the dresser. I reached for it, my fingerprints grazing the risen threads of the embroidery on the cover, but no familiar sense of comfort filled my veins at the touch.

Instead, a strange sense of unease crept into my stomach. A sudden weight of foreboding so unfamiliar that I simply stood there, frowning down at the spellbook until Ian came looking for me.

He seemed to notice the change in my mood and simply thanked me when I forced a smile and handed him the demon's phone.

As I accompanied him to the stairs, I couldn't help send my bedroom a worried glance. Not once had Grandma's spellbook failed to fill me with courage and the will to see my dreams come true. Had that been some kind of premonition?

"You will call me if something comes up?" Ian asked at the back door, the concern in his deep voice anchoring me in a way the spellbook had failed to do.

"Yes," I said, meaning it.

If there was something this whole adventure had taught me was that independence was overrated and whatever came my way, I would not have to face it alone.

The thought didn't help ease my worry one bit. Neither did returning upstairs after Ian was gone and holding the spellbook in my hands.

The strange feeling was gone, the familiar texture of the cover infusing me with hope once again.

But the memory remained.

If it had been anything else, I'd have considered it a moment of panic at the thought of dating Ian. But this was Grandma's spellbook, and that changed everything. I had been given a warning.

Now I just had to figure out why.

————

Thank you for reading! What's Grandma's spellbook warning Hope about? Find out in Fresh Old Bounties!

For a full list, please visit:

www.isa-medina.com

Good Bad Magic

Good Bad Witch

Right Wrong Shifter

Fresh Old Bounties

(ongoing)

Magical Artifacts Hunter

(Sequel to Magical Artifacts Institute)

Realms Unleashed: Red Angel

Mortal Secrets

Angelic Deals

Demonic Mayhem

Chaotic Souls

Magical Artifacts Institute:

Finding Fae Artifacts

Playing Fae Games

Breaking Fae Spells

Fixing Fae Problems

Extra Story:

Choosing Fae Gifts

———

Stand-alone Novelette:

Whispers of Ink

ABOUT THE AUTHOR

Isa Medina loves writing and reading Fantasy and Urban Fantasy books, playing MMORPGs, and scouring the Internet for pet pictures and beautiful art.

Her love for adventure Fantasy books was ingrained early in her childhood after getting her grubby little hands on the first Dragonlance trilogy, and it only grudgingly shared the spotlight when she discovered the wonderful worlds of Gothic novels and Romance in her early teens.

If it has Fae, ghosts, vampires, demons, mythical creatures, or magic in it, she's all in.

Find out more at www.isa-medina.com.